His eyes widened. "You were awake long before now. You've heard the speculation."

"I heard it all," she said bitterly. "It had always been my intention to wake up, but some fool called the physician. Another fool posted a guard on my door." To hide her mortification after the events of the day, Blythe had kept her eyes closed, her body still. A trick that she'd learned in childhood when she needed time to think.

Mr. Randall winced. "Leopold locked me in as well. Well, tried to. He thinks I'm a prisoner, too."

"Forgive me if I do not believe you." Blythe lifted her chin. "Since you have the ability to escape your confinement, I suggest you take yourself away."

His lips twisted into a smile that Blythe didn't trust. "But what happens if I am becalmed in your presence? A man like me has little opportunity to visit such an alluring lady's bedchamber."

HEATHER BOYD

BESTSELLING AUTHOR

FORSAKING THE PRIZE

Wild Randalls

2

The characters and events portrayed in this book are fictitious. Any similarity to real persons, living or dead, is purely coincidental and not intended by the author.

FORSAKING THE PRIZE © 2012 by Heather Boyd
Editing by Kelli Collins

All rights reserved. No part of this book may be reproduced in any form by any electronic or mechanical means—except in the case of brief quotations embodied in critical articles or reviews—without written permission of the author.

Dedication

For Mum.
Thank you for encouraging me to do better.
Any success I have is because of you.
You've always inspired me to aim high.

Chapter One

Once upon a time, Tobias Randall had expected a simple future—education, honest employment, and family. But the Duke of Romsey had stolen that bright future and discarded him to the whim of fate and the dangers of the sea.

Tobias glanced about him with a keen eye, surveying his current surroundings. Romsey Abbey wasn't the home he'd expected to return to. However, since his brother Leopold resided here, managing the estate for the Duchess of Romsey, he had little choice but to remain as a guest if he wanted to be close to his brother.

"Can I be of service, Mr. Randall?"

Tobias turned toward the voice and found Romsey's butler waiting at the doorway. "I'm well set up here, Wilcox."

"You may retire for the night." Leopold strode into the room and waved Wilcox away. "Come with me, Tobias."

Tobias glanced around as he followed along. "I thought you might be busy for a while with Her Grace."

"The duchess has retired for the night," Leopold said in a tone that allowed no discussion. "It's been an exhausting day for her."

Tobias swallowed, conscious that Leopold may still be very angry with him. "Wilcox is exactly as I remembered. How do you stand him?"

"Wilcox has been of great value to the duchess and to me." Leopold strode up the stairs quickly. "Unlike some I can name."

"Mama never trusted him, and I don't either," Tobias said quietly, gawking at the richness about him. He had learned the hard way when to trust his instincts. There was something wrong about the man, but he couldn't put his finger on what.

Leopold hurried him along a dim hall. As they rounded a corner, Tobias spotted a maid and a footman before a door somewhat farther along, whispering urgently to each other. They stopped speaking suddenly, and then the maid scurried away. What exactly was inside that room that could be so diverting?

And then it struck him.

The mad countess was likely housed in there.

Leopold stopped one door shy of that bedchamber and turned the knob. "Here you are."

Wonderful! Berthed next door to a mad woman. He hoped she didn't wail during the night and whisper evil through the walls.

Tobias crossed the threshold and whistled. If he'd thought downstairs was impressive, he'd been mistaken. This room could easily be part of a palace. Deep red velvet surrounding a wide bed, roaring fire burning in the hearth, and a set of large windows that he could easily escape through. Certainly not the worst sleeping place he'd been in.

He glanced over his shoulder at Leopold. "Bit small, isn't it? Have you anything grander?"

"Tobias," Leopold growled in warning. "Do not push my patience."

"Sorry. The change is a lot to take in. After all, just a few weeks ago I was a seaman aboard a whaler. I never expected a warm welcome at Romsey."

Leopold slapped his shoulder. "It does take some getting used to."

A knock sounded on the door, and Leopold bid them enter. Two footmen set a copper tub before the fire and two more carried pails of steaming water to fill it.

Tobias shook his head. He'd not had a servant for more than a decade. This would undoubtedly take some getting used to.

Another servant crossed the threshold, and when their eyes connected, Tobias scowled.

Eamon Murphy. They'd never gotten along when they were young, and the look in Murphy's eyes hinted he hadn't entirely forgotten the pranks Tobias had played on him when he was a boy. "What the hell are you doing here?"

Murphy's eyes narrowed to slits. "I really didn't miss you."

"The feeling is completely mutual."

"Your valet sent these for Tobias, Mr. Randall." Murphy laid a clean shirt and trousers on the bed. Then, to Tobias, "Your brother has engaged me as his assistant. He runs the estate, I do his leg work. Just like old times. My first duty is to see that you are fit to be seen."

Tobias scowled and crossed his arms over his chest. "Try it and you might lose your teeth."

"Oh, for God's sake," Leopold spluttered. "Have you two not outgrown this childish competition? Tobias, you will be made presentable and Murphy will assist."

Murphy shrugged. "Very well."

"Fine," Tobias groaned. "Can't have Murphy under the lash on his first dangerous assignment. As much as I would like to continue in this vein, how about we renew hostilities tomorrow? Do we have an accord?"

Murphy nodded. "We do."

Tobias smiled, glanced at his brother, and then began to laugh. "God, I missed this. Good to see some things haven't changed, brother. All right. All right. I give in willingly. I'll behave."

"See that you do," Leopold warned.

Tobias shrugged off his coat and waistcoat, ignoring how Murphy picked them up with two fingers and set them aside. He loosened his neckcloth and ripped the shirt over his head.

Behind him, Leopold gasped, and he remembered others might not care for the state of his back. He kept the view from Murphy as he kicked off his footwear, only to remember there were more scars circling his ankles.

"Murphy, leave us," Leopold murmured quietly. Murphy snatched up the clothing and fled, leaving an uncomfortable silence in his wake. "What happened, Toby?"

Tobias glanced up at the intricately molded ceilings and sighed. It had been too much to hope that Leopold would not ask. "I was unhappy. Dissenters are punished."

Leopold took a step forward and touched the scars on his back. "My God, have you even seen this?"

Tobias shrugged. "No. I have not had much opportunity to gaze at myself in mirrors. There's nothing you can do about it. Put it from your mind."

Leopold pushed him across the room until he stood between a set of mirrors. He could see himself from all angles. Every pain he'd suffered was before his eyes. White scars crisscrossed his back, flexing under his muscles in a way that even he found repulsive.

He turned from the view. "As expected."

"This is not what I expected," Leopold growled. "The duke said you were well cared for."

"The duke lied, or else has a different definition of care than most people."

"How can you not be furious?"

"The Duke of Romsey is dead. Cousin Edwin is dead, and the young duke doesn't look a bit like either of them. He's your son, right down to the perfect sweep of hair across his ears. He even has our mother's dimples. There is no one left to be angry with."

Leopold raked his hands through his hair. "Damn him! No wonder you wrote what you did."

"I didn't know our cousin was dead until I returned to England, or consider that the duchess might read my letters. Please believe me, I never meant to do her any harm."

Leopold embraced him. "You're my brother. My mischievous, troublesome brother. Of course I believe you."

When the embrace turned into a battle of wills, as it often had when he was a boy, Tobias quickly escaped. "Too slow, old man."

Leopold laughed, a sound Tobias would never grow tired of hearing. "It was easier when you were shorter."

"And considerably weaker. That is no longer the case."

A grin crossed Leopold's face. "I'll keep that in mind should I need to bring you back into line."

Tobias spied a crystal decanter across the room and poured himself and Leopold drinks, but his thoughts returned to the woman locked up next door. Her image flashed before his mind. Prim figure, tightly bound dark hair, pale green eyes wide with fright. "What will happen to Lady Venables now?"

Leopold perched on the edge of the large bed. "I don't know. You scared Blythe quite badly when you burst through the window to recover the Duke of Romsey but, according to Mercy, she hasn't been herself for a long time. Losing her husband and son at almost the same time took a toll. Let us hope the damage isn't permanent, and that she will recover."

Tobias swirled his whiskey around in the glass. He regretted his part in Lady Venables' current state. But he'd done what he had to do. He knew what they did when a ship—a grand lady of the sea—was destroyed beyond repair by battle, no matter how lovely her lines. They were scuttled and left to rot in some out-of-the-way port where no one cared. A mad countess would fare little better. "If she doesn't recover?"

"We will cross that bridge when we come to it."

Tobias moved to the windows and flung them wide. Night had fallen over Romsey Abbey and the grounds were bathed in moonlight. He felt the bite of cool night air whip across his chest. He had a pretty vantage point from his chamber. He could see for miles.

In the distance, he spotted the rooftops of his old family home, Harrowdale, just visible through the woods. A pang of longing shot through him. The old house was boarded up, kept exactly as his parents had left it before their deaths, and likely belonged to Leopold now. He'd stayed there since his return, and if Leopold allowed, he thought he'd like to live there. "You never went home."

"No. I couldn't face the empty house."

"It wasn't empty. I was haunting the place."

Leopold slapped his hand on his back. "How did you learn to climb so well?"

Tobias glanced at the grounds below. He was exactly the height from the mizzen mast to the deck of the Enid Wren, the American slaver he'd been traded to by the Williamstown's despicable captain. Back then, he'd scaled the heights willingly to escape the stench of those being transported. Leopold didn't need to know he'd served aboard a slaver. "Just a skill I picked up during my time at sea."

Leopold bumped against him. "I'd like to hear more."

A sound drifted to him on the wind, and he looked left and right, but couldn't discover the source. He thought he heard a woman sobbing. "Perhaps later. There is no rush, is there?"

"None at all. We have the rest of our lives to catch up on what we've missed."

When Leopold moved away, Tobias leaned farther out the window, peering at the windows closest to his bedchamber. Light flickered in the one containing Lady Venables, and the window was open a touch. Was she conscious at long last?

Leopold laughed. "Get cleaned up and I'll see you in the morning."

Tobias spun about. "Until then."

The door closed with a solid thump—and then a key turned in the lock.

Tobias stared at the door in shock.

Damn Leopold. He thought to make Tobias a prisoner, too.

Chapter Two

A woman was defined by her reputation. A lady, by the degree of respect others afforded her. She gained approval or censure by the way she conducted herself when in the public eye, by her charity to good works, by the strength of her family connections and the character of her circle of friends.

Blythe Walden, Lady Venables of Walden Hall, struggled to muffle her sobs so no one could hear her crying.

She was far beyond humiliation.

Her heart had been shattered by the events of today.

The servants guarding her were finally gone and she wiped at her eyes furiously, attempting to pull herself together. The footman and the maid had whispered, loudly, that she was evil incarnate. She could never slaughter small animals and leave them on her sister's bed. But that was exactly what everyone—including her sister, the Duchess of Romsey—assumed she'd done.

She didn't know how they could imagine her so cold and ruthless. Blythe couldn't even look at more than a drop of blood without feeling faint.

She had once thought she was wise in the ways of the world. She had thought she could navigate society's dangerous waters and remain untouched by scandal. Today, she had been proven a fool. Everything she had believed to be an incontrovertible truth was flawed.

She moved to the mirror and ran her fingers through her tangled hair, then squared her shoulders. There had to be a way to prove her innocence and restore her reputation. But right now, she couldn't decide how.

She lifted her gaze—and cried out in alarm.

Tobias Randall, the pirate who had terrorized Romsey Abbey for the past weeks, lounged on her bed.

"Quiet, luv," he said softly. "No need to bring the whole household running to gawk at you."

He may have attempted to improve his appearance with a bath, but his hair was still wet and he had several days' growth of beard on his chin. He wore only a loose unbuttoned shirt and breeches. If anyone discovered Tobias Randall in her bedchamber in this state, her remaining reputation would vanish.

"Get out of my bed this instant, you pirate," Blythe whispered urgently.

A slow smile twisted his lips. "Merely keeping it warm for you. You could always come back to bed and join me."

Blythe gasped. "Don't be absurd."

He laughed softly and stood beside the bed. It was like watching a great cat stalking prey…one ready to pounce if provoked. "Perhaps another time," he said.

Blythe rubbed her arms, gooseflesh rising over her skin as he drew near. He was a tall man, wide shouldered, and he made her feel decidedly uncertain. "How did you get in here?"

He pointed behind her with one long arm. "The window."

Her gaze caught on the bandage wrapped around his hand, hiding the injury that must have caused her to faint earlier in the day. She shuddered, spun around, and lifted the window pane high. "Then you can go out the same way you came in, you pirate. I have nothing to say to your kind."

"My kind?" He crossed his arms over his chest as if he didn't intend to move until she answered. Insufferable brute. Perhaps he lacked the wits to know he shouldn't be here. His brow rose. "You didn't complain when you were snug in my arms. I think I'll stay a while."

When he had burst through the window of a room twenty feet from the ground, he had shocked her sensibilities completely. He had been intent on reaching her nephew, and she'd tried to prevent him. Blood had dripped from his hand, a cut from the window glass, and she shuddered. "I don't remember any of that."

His face grew dark. "Why did you keep the boy from his mother?"

Blythe recalled the terror that had gripped her. "I had my reasons."

"Me?"

She stared at him. Right now, he seemed an ordinary man. But that afternoon, he had appeared completely murderous. She couldn't explain in ways he would understand. She barely understood herself.

She pressed her lips together. She had no need to explain anything to him.

"I could never hurt the boy. He is family."

The news that Leopold Randall was her nephew's father still didn't sit well with her. The young Duke of Romsey was Mr. Leopold Randall's offspring—the late duke's own cousin—and a product of blackmail rather than love. No matter that Mercy and Leopold Randall loved each other now and would marry as soon as it could be arranged. Such a situation would bring shame on the family, should the shocking details be discovered. "So I've learned."

He leaned against the bedpost. "You're understandably upset. But from what I hear, your sister and my brother had little say in the decision."

"I know that," she snapped. Really, she did not need to receive a lecture from a man who burst into ladies' bedchambers without invitation.

"Then why do you punish her with this ruse? You are scaring her."

Blythe clenched her hands together, fighting to control her temper. "Do you not think I have the right to feel overwhelmed at this moment? My sister has lied to me for years about Edwin. She has behaved without thought to her reputation, and you…you have taunted us all with your vulgar behavior! I love my nephew and wish to protect him, as I could not protect my own son. You were about to harm my sister! You could have killed Edwin. Can you not understand that a lady's delicate feelings may be provoked to do an irrational thing?"

He stared at her a long time. "Yes. I believe I do understand you. But you need to tell your sister this when you see her."

"I cannot. She thinks I'm mad."

His eyes widened. "You were awake long before now. You've heard the speculation."

"I heard it all," she said bitterly. "It had always been my intention to wake up, but some fool called the physician. Another fool posted a guard on my door." To hide her mortification after the events of the day, Blythe had kept her eyes closed, her body still. A trick that she'd learned in childhood when she needed time to think.

Mr. Randall winced. "Leopold locked me in as well. Well, tried to. He thinks I'm a prisoner, too."

"Forgive me if I do not believe you." Blythe lifted her chin. "Since you have the ability to escape your confinement, I suggest you take yourself away."

His lips twisted into a smile that Blythe didn't trust. "But what happens if I am becalmed in your presence? A man like me has little opportunity to visit such an alluring lady's bedchamber."

Blythe set her hands to her hips. "Let me make one thing clear to you, Mr. Randall. Your glib tongue won't work with me. I think you an utter scoundrel. A man not to be trusted, and if you were not so abnormally sized, and I a lady, I would have you thrown head first from the window."

"Abnormally sized? Lady Venables, have you been peeking at my rudder?" He gestured to his groin and chuckled.

When she simply stared at him, his expression turned serious.

He drew so close that Blythe could discern his shadowed eyes were brown, shot through with a bright shade of amber.

"What are you doing?"

"Fear not, my lady. I can assure you that the ladies have never complained about my size before. In fact, they quite often beg me to return to port."

Blythe amended her earlier description of Tobias Randall. He was a rude, vulgar-tongued pirate with a penchant for grandiose self-flattery. Given the unguarded way he spoke, he would bring disgrace upon Mercy and the Duke of Romsey within a day, if it hadn't happened already.

She glared now, determined to make her disgust plain. "Then the ladies were desperate women indeed. Were you the only man to choose from after years without? Now, get out of my chambers."

He blinked slowly. As he opened his eyes again, he shifted his body closer, until he stood inches from her chest. He radiated so much heat that her own skin grew warm with embarrassment. It had been a long time since a man had stood this close to her and caused such a reaction. The last to do so had been her late husband.

Although the action would suggest she feared him, she slid along the wall.

He tilted his head to the side and studied her. "Not mad," he whispered. "Just very, very unfriendly. Don't worry. I'm not drunk enough to bed you without causing myself considerable pain. My rudder would likely suffer injury should I dare to dock at your port. Splinters, you know."

Blythe gaped. How dare he say such a thing to a lady!

Before she could stop him, he brushed his finger beneath her chin. She snapped her mouth shut.

Then, to her shock, he vaulted out the window, one large hand locked on the window frame, and dangled there, twenty feet or so above ground. He poked his head back inside the room momentarily. "Try not to miss me too much, B."

The bounder. The cad! How dare he think to shorten her name to just an initial? She wouldn't stand for it a moment longer.

Blythe hurried to lock the window so he couldn't come back inside. She really didn't give a fig if he fell to his death.

Chapter Three

Tobias hung on to the side of Romsey Abbey outside Lady Venables' bedchamber, enjoying the wind ruffling his hair. The abbey was as stuffy as the conversation with the lady he'd just left. He much preferred the wildness out here than the frost building in there.

But he couldn't hang there forever. There were limits to his strength, and the stone walls were not as generous when it came to handholds as the rigging of a ship.

On a whim, he climbed the abbey walls until he reached the rooftop and swung himself over the lip. He set his hands to his hips and spun in a slow circle, surveying the horizon beyond the roofline. Storm clouds were rolling up from the south, obscuring the stars as they came. Wet, mucky old England. He grinned and sat himself down on the battlements to enjoy the approaching inclement weather.

The cool bite of the air stung his nose, but a sense of contentment flooded him. He'd spent years dreaming of white winters, huddled around the family hearth, and he would have his wish this year. After he'd paid penance enough for the distress he'd caused the duchess, he would go home to his parents' house to live. The old place might need a bit of work to make it livable, but after his years onboard ship, his standards were low. He had no illusions that he couldn't be perfectly happy there, even if it was falling down upon his head. He could finally come and go as he pleased and live his own life.

The problem Tobias had now was deciding what to do with that life.

He had no trade to speak of, besides the bit of carpentry skill required for ship repairs onboard a whaler. He wasn't a man of letters. Land management held no appeal. He had little money, except for what his brother might give him, if Tobias could bear to accept it.

Without purpose or independent wealth, he'd become miserable.

He scrunched up his nose. That outcome was unpalatable. He was a man of action, most happy when there was mischief afoot, a game to be won. He'd come up with something eventually, or else he'd have no choice but to leave in search of his own fortune.

Not yet though. Not yet.

He'd see how the game played out here before he moved on. He wouldn't mind getting to know his elder brother again, and he would like to find Oliver and Rose. Hopefully, Oliver would have fared as well or better than Tobias…but even as a young boy, he'd known Rosemary was bound for trouble.

He dug his fingers into the cold stone, imagining the worst that could have happened to his sister, his mind multiplying it tenfold.

Rose's last moments in his line of sight were imprinted on his memory. She'd been tossed onto a horse, over the thighs of one of the old duke's men, kicking and screaming her lungs out and threatening to bite the man if he didn't release her immediately. The duke's servant had called out to his companions but, maddeningly, Tobias couldn't recall exactly what he'd said to them before they rode away at a gallop.

He didn't like to think of his parents lying murdered in the carriage. He hadn't seen them to know for certain they were dead, but they had not made a sound when he'd called out to them.

His captors had left them where they'd lain.

On the trip to the harbor, the duke's men had assured him that Rosemary would be safe as long as Tobias caused them no further trouble. He'd complied. There were six of them, after all, all armed, and one of him—just a child still really, scared and alone. He'd gone along with them to the harbor and then…

No more England. No more family.

His captors had said Rosemary was to be returned to the old duke and held hostage to make certain Tobias behaved, but he'd later realized they'd lied. They hadn't known anything about Rose's fate once they'd parted company.

A window rattled below him, and he looked down between his

dangling feet. Lady Venables' head poked out into the night, looked left and right, and then a softly uttered "blasted pirate" filled the air.

He grinned. Even his conversation with Lady Venables hadn't impinged on his good humor. He enjoyed a good battle of wits with a worthy adversary. The beauty's outrage and mild insults amused him.

The window rattled closed.

He scratched his jaw. Lady Venables was not mad, as he had first thought. Not even close to that sorry state. She was angry with him, likely for having the indecency to make her faint. But she was also a very sad person. He'd listened to her muffled sobs as she'd covered her face so no one would hear. She'd been so caught up in her misery that she hadn't noticed him enter the room. He'd been quite ready to make nice and apologize once she'd stopped sniffling.

But then she'd spoken, and all the nice, long-discarded gentlemanly things he'd dredged from the corners of his mind had fled. Lady Venables could geld a man with that tongue of hers. Calling her prickly was the kindest description for the shrew. There was a thick layer of ice around her that he had not detected from a distance, a foil for the beauty to keep gents at bay.

That suited him fine. She was far too prim for his tastes anyway. It might be amusing to suggest otherwise just to rile her, but when the need arose, he'd find someone less inclined to frost to warm his bed at night. In the meantime, he'd verbally spar with Lady Venables when the mood struck, give some thought to his future…and consider who stalked the young Duke of Romsey. If Lady Venables wasn't the one leaving dead animals about the abbey, then someone else was intent on frightening the duchess away.

Someone who had escaped proper scrutiny so far.

Of course, it wasn't really any of his business, aside from the fact that finding the culprit would clear both his name and Lady Venables' once and for all. Leopold would undoubtedly find the truth in the end and ensure his son was safe. Not much stood in his brother's way for long once he'd made up his mind. But still, it wouldn't hurt to keep his eyes open.

A splat of cold liquid hit his cheek. His nose. His eye.

Perfect. Rain, not the snow he'd been hoping for, pattered down on his head. A bolt of lightning pierced the gloom, landing half a mile distant from the abbey grounds. Perhaps he should retreat to somewhere less exposed to the elements.

He climbed down the abbey walls, tapped on Lady Venables' window just to irritate the shrew a little more, and then slipped back into his bedchamber. He left his window open to better hear the rain while he stripped off his damp clothing.

Her window rattled. "Oh, would you just go away," she said.

Tobias leaned out the window. "Until tomorrow, B. Sweet dreams."

Another bolt of lightning pierced the gloom.

Her eyes widened. "Where is your clothing, sir? You'll catch your death."

"Damp." Tobias ran his hand over his bare chest. "But how nice that you are so concerned for my health, my lady. Such sweet consideration from your lips is music to my ears."

She scowled. "You are impossible. Go to bed."

"Was that an invitation to rejoin you, B?"

Maybe maneuvers with the lady wouldn't give his rudder frostbite. She had full breasts, a tiny waist, and he'd bet her long hair would feel like silk across his skin once released.

Her jaw clenched and she disappeared from view. The window slammed down quickly.

Tobias gripped the window sill tightly and released a deep belly laugh.

Gods, it was good to be on dry land again. Teasing Lady Venables was the most fun he'd had in years. He couldn't wait till morning. How would she behave if he patted her rear in the drawing room downstairs while her sister stood three feet away?

He'd have to try it one day.

Tobias closed the window, and then climbed into the obscenely large bed. He set his hands behind his head as lightning flashed through his window. He could become used to creature comforts such as this. Even nicer would be sharing the night with a woman's soft, silken limbs wrapped around him.

The idea appealed. Someone adventurous in bed, plump of pocket and biddable would make a very palatable arrangement. Marriage seemed a good way to obtain wealth easily. However, he had no intention of fathering children. Being born a Randall hadn't done him any good, and he'd never bring a child into the world to see him suffer.

Yes, tomorrow, after he'd made amends to Lady Venables, he'd investigate the possibilities of his new life and what might be done to improve it.

Blythe surveyed her maid's handiwork in the mirror, wondering what other people saw when they looked at her. To her mind, she appeared exactly as she always did. Not a hair out of place, the perfect model of propriety and decorum—a lady one should show respect to at all times.

However, all that had changed overnight. At least the maid's shaking hands hadn't made a mess of her hair. "You may go, Dobson," she said sadly.

Hillie Dobson, her maid since her marriage, bobbed a quick curtsy and then hurried from the room with unnecessary speed. Blythe turned to stare at the door as those waiting outside locked her in again. A prisoner still.

She clenched her jaw. This was impossible. She pressed her hands flat on the table and concentrated on controlling her temper.

A lady did not display her emotions, elated or otherwise. She would be calm and composed, and not shriek like a fishwife at the injustice she was currently suffering.

She stood and crossed to the wardrobe. She'd pack her own things, throw them and herself out the window if required, and leave this place today rather than suffer further slights.

The key turned in the lock behind her and the door slowly creaked open. "Blythe?" Mercy's voice whispered across the room, trembling with uncertainty. But then two sets of footsteps crossed the threshold—one heavy, one light.

Blythe kept her back to her gaolers. "I would appreciate it if you would call a carriage for me, Your Grace. As much as I enjoy the new level of attention I'm receiving from first the doctor and then the guards at the door, I am certain I should get out from underfoot so you can plan your wedding. Congratulations. I hope you both will be very happy together."

Mercy gasped. "You were awake."

"You forgot to tickle me to check." Blythe smiled tightly and added her hairbrush to the bag, holding back tears by sheer force of will. "There once was a time when we knew everything about each other. But it seems I don't know you at all, Your Grace." Blythe turned. "And you appear to know nothing about me, if you think you can treat me like this. Kindly get out of my way."

Both Mercy and Leopold Randall stood across the room, side by side. A wall. United against her. Blythe gritted her teeth as Mercy glanced at Leopold, looking to him as if for instructions on what to say to her request. If he suggested she remain as their guest, lady or not, she'd clobber him with the nearest vase.

Randall stepped forward. "Were you awake through everything last night?"

She nodded. Almost everything. There was a period of time missing from her memory. The exact period of time the pirate would have held her in his arms. She didn't miss remembering that event at all.

He frowned. "Then you heard what everyone else has said about your actions and suspected motives."

Blythe nodded again and picked up her bag. "I seem to be in need of a new maid. Would you be so good as to assist Dobson in finding a new position? I don't believe she will wish to remain in my employment any longer, thanks to the wild stories circulating about me. She could scarce carry out her duties today."

The door swung fully open. "You can't leave until your name is cleared," Tobias Randall added cheerfully as he stepped into her bedchamber without knocking.

Blythe glanced at him and then looked away, fighting to keep a blush from her cheeks. The younger Randall had come to add his tuppence worth to the discussion, but was only dressed in a sheet. How typical of his type of man. Of course he was free to come and go at will, and that increased Blythe's annoyance beyond an acceptable level. She backed away from them, holding on to her bag with all her might.

"For God's sake, get out of here," Leopold shouted at his brother. "You're indecent."

"If you do not like my current attire, then perhaps you'd be good enough to return my clothing." Tobias bowed to her. "Good morning, Lady Venables. Did you have a pleasant rest?"

She wasn't going to confess to Mercy or his brother that he'd kept her awake half the night with his antics. She wouldn't give him the satisfaction of proving just how big a nuisance he had been. "Fine, thank you."

He winked. "Wonderful. My brother has plans to show me around. Care to join us for a stroll about the abbey?"

Blythe stared at him. He didn't even have a pair of boots on his feet at the moment, and he thought she would be interested in remaining in his company a moment longer than she had to. He was the mad one. "Are you going like that?"

"For the moment, it seems very likely." He wiggled his toes.

Blythe quickly looked up at his face. "No, thank you. I'll be leaving today. Why, this very minute, if a bunch of rude and foolish Randalls will get out of my way."

Mercy gasped, but Blythe was so angry she did not care if she insulted her own family. The situation was intolerable, and she would leave.

Tobias merely laughed at her situation, and she scowled at him. What would it take to make him as uncomfortable as he made her?

"My God, that's a look to skewer your innards. Leopold, I think you should apologize this very minute for unjustly locking the lady's door. You do want your future wife's sister to be happy, don't you? Lady Venables appears the type to hold a grudge."

Leopold raised his hands. "Peace, my lady. You are not our prisoner, but we still do not wish for you to leave, and for the same reasons I mentioned two days ago. You are alone at Walden Hall, and the distance and isolation both worry me. Edwin and Mercy are still at risk, and you could be, too."

"But you believed me to be the culprit. To have done those evil things to frighten my own sister. A monster. They're all whispering that I tried to drive Mercy away so I could have the young duke for myself. I'll not stay here another moment and suffer further suspicion. And you can be sure I will never come here again."

Leopold Randall glanced at his brother, a scowl twisting his face. "I was led to believe that your behavior lately has been somewhat troubling. That you often go into the woods and lure rabbits to you with carrots and the like. The bulk of the so-called gifts left for the duchess have been slaughtered rabbits. We determined Tobias was behind the letters, but that still means someone else is involved. You can see where a man might wonder if there was a connection between your behavior and recent unpleasant events."

Blythe shook her head. "My son had a rabbit when he lived. I set it free but I still see it, and its offspring, about the grounds sometimes."

Leopold Randall frowned. "Near the woods?"

Blythe crossed her arms over her chest. "Near my son's favorite place. We made up silly stories. I go there often to remember them."

Her eyes filled with tears. She went there to pretend Adam was still alive, if only for a little while.

"Oh, Blythe," Mercy whispered softly. "I thought you'd stopped."

She stared at her sister. "You thought I'd stopped thinking of my son and the little time I had with him? How could you imagine, even for a moment, that I don't wish for him every day?"

Blythe continued to blink back tears as the silence stretched. Everything had changed, grown dim, when Adam had passed away. Time hadn't softened the loss.

Tobias Randall smacked his hands together loudly, and then made a show of rearranging his falling sheet. "Now that's cleared up, can something be done about my clothing situation? This sheet is damn drafty and my feet are cold."

Blythe bit her lower lip to rein in her emotions. Tobias Randall really was a ridiculous man, but he appeared very good at drawing attention toward himself. To think, she'd been afraid of him when they had first met.

Leopold nodded. "That does settle it. Forgive me, Lady Venables, for placing too much faith in gossip. I did not have all the facts at hand. I should never have suspected you would harm the boy." He turned and grabbed his brother's arm roughly. "You and I need to have a very long conversation about decorum, young man. Get back to your bedchamber this instant."

The sheet around Tobias Randall slipped as they gained the door, and Blythe saw more of his skin than a lady should. She also saw scars crisscrossing his upper back.

Blythe shuddered and glanced at her sister to see her reaction.

But it seemed Mercy hadn't noticed. Her sister crossed the room, eyes downcast as she tugged the bag from Blythe's fingers. "Forgive me," she said softly. "Edwin and I would be lost without you. I don't want you to go. Stay with us, Blythe. Please."

After considering, Blythe gave the bag up and her sister began pulling her possessions out again and putting them away. But sadness trickled through her. The damage to their relationship was done. They were family, and she did care that her sister and nephew were well, but she would never trust Mercy again.

Mercy returned and stopped before her. "I should apologize for Mr. Randall, but I fear I will be saying I'm sorry all day and wear out my tongue. It was he who put the idea in Leopold's brain about you going into the woods alone. I did not connect your actions with Adam, and I am so sorry for that. I should not have forgotten you used to make up stories of the woods." Mercy sighed. "I'm sure Leopold will do something painful to his brother for the misunderstanding, but this situation is as much my fault as Tobias'."

"I'm sure Mr. Randall will mete out the required punishment. However, I may never be easy here again, Mercy."

"I will restore your good name, I promise, and prove the whispers groundless." When Mercy embraced her, Blythe suffered through the hug for several moments before she shrugged out of it.

"That may never be possible." Blythe wiped her eyes as weariness tugged at her senses. She felt old…ancient and exhausted. However, she couldn't rest until the whispers about her sanity had ceased.

Mercy's fingers threaded through hers and squeezed. "Thank heavens we only had one brother. These Randall men are not above rough behavior. Quite different from our late husbands in so many ways. I thought they would kill each other yesterday."

Blythe had thought so, too, hence her decision to flee with the boy and spare him the horror of the fighting. "Leopold is very protective of you. A good trait for a future husband. Speaking of brothers, when is ours coming to Romsey Abbey to meet Mr. Randall? Have you written him?"

"Not yet. But I did receive a note this morning from him. Constantine has put me off again for the holidays, claiming he's busy. I'm sure once I tell him of Leopold, he will change his mind."

Blythe nodded. Their brother supplied a ready stream of excuses against travel, blaming his three daughters' delicate health most often for the delays. "He'll come as soon as he learns. When is the wedding?"

"We haven't set a date, but I'd like for Constantine to be here before the happy day. I'd like him to become acquainted with Leopold, and Tobias, too. He'll likely have a few things to say about me marrying again, but he will see I've made the right choice."

Constantine would rage when he found out Mercy was to remarry. While that was happening, Blythe planned to be elsewhere. "Are you going to tell him the truth about Edwin's father?"

"I will." Mercy's fingers curled over Blythe's arm and squeezed. "Do you mind very much? Neither of us had a say in the situation, but I would not change the past for all the world. I love Leopold so very dearly and, however unlikely it might seem, I have missed him these past years."

Blythe shrugged, trying to dispel just how hurt she still was by the news. It didn't change how she felt about Edwin, but it did make her feel on the outside of events. "Yesterday when we talked, Mr. Randall claimed to love you enough that he'd leave if it was in your best interests. However, if Tobias Randall isn't the criminal threatening you and Edwin, then he'd better remain. Marriage will dispel the hint of scandal at having a bachelor in your household. At least he may be able to control his brother for the duration of his stay, too."

"Tobias isn't so bad."

Blythe crossed her arms over her chest. "Really?"

Mercy had the grace to blush. "I concede Leopold's younger brother may have a few more rough edges than I'd imagined, or even believed possible, for that matter. However, I'm sure with the right prompting, he may be able to speak without sounding so shocking."

"You're hoping for a miracle."

Mercy chuckled softly and shook her head. "I know. Do you forgive me?"

Blythe sighed. What was the use of holding a grudge? She and Mercy had always been closest. "Fetch Dr. Heyburn to attend me again and we cease to be sisters. That man is incompetent not to have realized I was feigning unconsciousness."

Mercy leaped at Blythe and squeezed her in a tight hug. "You fooled me for certain that time, Blythe. Part of me was hoping you were tricking us, but part of me was afraid that Mr. Randall's entry through the window had been too much for your nerves. You haven't done that in years, and I don't care to be scared like that again."

Blythe untangled herself from Mercy's grip with as much dignity as she could muster and finished unpacking her things. "I'll say one thing about Mr. Randall, he does like to make a dramatic entrance."

A male voice cried out in outrage through the wall from the next room. The little bottles of perfume on her dresser shook.

"Don't. You. Dare!" Tobias Randall shouted.

"Just shut up and sit down," Leopold Randall barked in return. "You know this must be done."

Mercy looked at Blythe, a frown creasing her brow. "Sounds painful."

A warm glow filled Blythe's chest as she dragged in a deep breath then let it go. She smiled. "Sounds perfect to me."

Chapter Four

Tobias Randall had faced many dangers in his life; none compared with his current predicament. He would gladly face the enemy in battle, starvation, and the most godforsaken ship's captain ever to sail against England rather than make polite conversation.

But, as he'd been repeatedly warned in the last weeks, the proprieties must be observed if he wanted to remain in good society and have a chance of being acceptable to a well-to-do, marriageable woman. He was dressed now in the finest clothing he'd ever owned. Primped and polished until he shined like a newly minted penny. There seemed no end to the number of things that he could and could not do or say as brother to the future husband of the Duchess of Romsey.

He stood quietly on the edge of the Romsey drawing room, forgotten for the moment, as his brother and the duchess discussed plans for the future and the estate. A party here, a field plowed there, a trip to London and to Bath to visit with the duchess' relations and be introduced properly, raising the staff wages.

As his brother's future unfolded, mind-numbingly tedious by the sounds of it, Tobias tried to remain alert.

He was a man of action, and there was no action here. There was nothing he could do, nothing he could say, that would add any excitement to the morning.

Well, perhaps there was one.

He shifted his gaze across the room. He could, if he was feeling particularly adventurous, engage in conversation with Lady Venables. She was, and had always been, a rather prickly conversationalist. Was he willing to risk a verbal lashing to relieve his boredom? Maybe it wouldn't be too bad. Besides, he needed to practice for when he found a woman he wanted to wed.

He crossed the room to where she sat, her head bent over books, ignoring the activity around her. As always, she was dressed in somber tones, a dark priggish gown, gloves and delicate fichu covering up her skin. She appeared quite spinsterish today, rather than a widow of four and twenty years and long out of prescribed mourning.

He knew few other things about her life. He'd quizzed Leopold during the endless hours of fittings and instructions to pass the time. She'd been married to a man quite a few years her senior, widowed two years ago but still grieved for him. She'd also had a son who'd died of a fever. Aside from observing the proprieties without fault, she had no apparent interest in members of the opposite sex.

He'd never met with a woman like her before. Everything about her demeanor was designed to keep others at a distance.

Yet, he knew her to have a warmer heart than she let on. Those brief glimpses of merriment with the boy duke fascinated him.

Her face lifted as he drew closer, pale green eyes framed by thick lashes unblinking. Her expression changed to one of extreme distaste.

He forced a polite smile. "Good afternoon, Lady Venables. How are you enjoying your day?"

A very unladylike scowl crossed her face then quickly disappeared again. She marked her place in her book with her fingertip. "The same as I enjoyed it earlier this morning, Mr. Randall. And I am in perfect health, too, in case that was to be your next question. You seem extraordinarily interested in my health."

Her brow rose while he fumbled for something else polite to say.

Damn Leopold and his list of suggested conversational topics to engage in with proper ladies. He'd never been tongue tied before in his life, and he didn't like the feeling. He usually said the first thing that crossed his mind. Unfortunately, his previous conversations with Lady Venables had not made them the best of friends. Unlike the other women he'd known, suggesting they tumble into her bed and any other gentler teasing had not had a softening effect on her disposition. Quite the opposite, in fact.

At his continued silence, her gaze dropped to her book and she ignored him.

Being ignored wasn't going to alleviate his boredom. He sat beside her on the lounge. "What are you reading so studiously?"

Her lips twisted in a grimace. "I am attempting to unscramble the duke's journals, if you must know, in an attempt to discover the location of your siblings. However, I'm starting to regret taking on the task."

"Ah." Leopold had muttered something about them yesterday, but Tobias had been distracted by a wayward pin in his knee and hadn't remembered to ask for further particulars. "In what way are the journals difficult?"

"To start, they are not written in the King's English, they jump from place to place, as if they were pieced together long after the event." She rubbed her brow. "Quite honestly, I fear this may all be a waste of time and lead to nothing useful."

"May I see what you are looking at?"

She placed a small scrap of parchment between the pages and held out the book. The heavy, leather-bound tome's cover gave nothing away as to the contents.

"Do you have any inkling as to what the journal might be about?" he asked.

"At a guess, it's about a member of the Randall family—or someone else entirely. Just when I think I have the answer, there is something that does not ring true." She sat back in her chair, but she still had a rod of steel holding her to a stiff posture. Did she never unbend?

"About us? What on earth would he be writing about our family for?"

"A good question. The duke kept a detailed journal of your brother's affairs. When he traveled, what goods—silks and such—he sent to the abbey as part of their bargain."

"Bargain?"

Her brow creased again. "Did your brother not mention the duke's blackmail? I suppose it may not be a subject he cares to dwell on. You would need to ask him for the exact particulars." She sighed and tapped the book on his knee. "The persons referenced in the other journals are not easily identified. Have you done anything particularly noteworthy in your time, Mr. Randall, that may assist me in determining if one exists about your life?"

"Sailed the world, drank too much, and climbed into women's bedchamber windows. The usual thing a young man likes to do as often as he can arrange it," he said without thinking his response through properly.

Lady Venables sucked in a sharp breath, and when he didn't say anything else, she let it out slowly again. Was that all it took to put the wind up her sails?

She faced him. "I had been led to believe your brother had suggested you moderate your comments when in the presence of ladies. I see his instructions didn't take."

Tobias sat back, crossed one leg over the other and sat the book against his upraised knee. "Oh, I listened. I will, however, choose exactly when I need to be a gentleman," he met her gaze, "and when gentlemanly behavior would prevent me from acquiring my heart's desire."

It was tempting to try to loosen her up. She was much too pretty for the sour expression gracing her features now.

She turned away, back stretching farther, as straight as an arrow. Rigid to the core. "I doubt your heart will be involved, pirate," she said.

Tobias chuckled softly so Leopold wouldn't notice. "No disrespect intended. I was not referring to a wish to revisit your bedchamber, but I was actually referring to honest conversation, rather than the banal fripperies Leopold insists are proper for when conversing with unmarried ladies. How the devil can conversations about flowers be in any way a manly topic?"

She sniffed. "A man should learn to converse on subjects the ladies of his acquaintance hold an interest in. Our society would suffer without adherence to the proper forms of etiquette."

The pompous statement forced a groan from his lips. "Do you honestly care what I think of that flower arrangement over there?"

A small smile crossed her lips and disappeared just as quickly. "Well, maybe not that particular vase of flowers. I didn't do the arranging, so I have nothing to gain from any flattery on the subject."

Wretched wench. She'd been playing with flowers earlier. He scanned the chamber for another vase. "Is that one yours, then?"

Her head nodded a fraction.

Tobias pursed his lips as he assessed them. "They'll outlive the other ones by a day at least, maybe two."

Her brow rose. "You know a little of flowers? How extraordinary."

Tobias smiled. "My mother loved flowers. I'd been sent to pick many a bunch in my youth. Your flair for arranging is as good as hers."

Lady Venables pressed her lips together until the edges paled. After a pause, she relaxed again. "Was that your very first attempt at a compliment?"

"Second."

She nodded. "You might want to practice a bit more before the ball tomorrow night. Comparing a woman favorably to your mother, while kindly said, may lead to a premature expectation of romantic interest. Mercy is determined to introduce you to her acquaintances, and quite a number are unwed."

"Please don't remind me. It is all she has spoken of in days."

Lady Venables' spine sagged slightly before she sat up straight again and placed her hands flat on her knees. She cleared her throat. "I'm sure you will survive the event. Just try not to embarrass her by saying the first thing that crosses your mind. Are you even going to look at the journal? If not, I should like to return to reading."

He squinted at the squiggles and lines. "Dear God. I'd have tossed this nonsense into the fire long before this."

She held out her hand. "Yes, it does not surprise me that you are a man of limited patience."

He snuck a look at her again. Beautiful, but a harsh judge of character. Tobias could, in fact, be very patient when he wanted something badly enough. He'd waited for a chance to escape so he could return home, hadn't he? It might have taken him ten years, but Lady Venables' assertion that he lacked conviction tempted him to prove her wrong.

He kept the book, skimming over pages containing gibberish and the odd number.

Lady Venables' hand lowered as she sighed. "Please do not lose my place."

He spied his birth year, and his heartbeat increased. "I won't. How long have you been working on this journal?"

"A week or two. I juggle between them all. Trying to find a pattern to unlock the duke's codes."

He flipped forward a handful of pages. "All?"

Tobias opened the page containing the countess' place marker and tried to decipher the scrawl. Nothing else made sense. He closed the book as disappointment curled through him.

"Yes, there is a vast collection. Hasn't your brother shown you the duke's sanctuary yet?"

Tobias glanced over his shoulder, only to find his brother whispering in the duchess' ear. They kissed, and he turned back to Lady Venables. "Ah, no. He's had more than a few things on his mind of late."

Lady Venables glanced over her own shoulder, and a blush swept her skin. "Perhaps I should show you now."

She stood suddenly, crossing to the far side of the room with haste, leaving him to follow at his own pace. The sway and rustle of her dark gown mesmerized him momentarily, and he wrenched his gaze up to the back of her head. How damned inconvenient to admire the haughty wench's body. She was trim and lean. Two things he admired greatly in women.

She stopped at a wall, pressed her fingers to a carved rose set in the panel, and the wall clicked.

He cursed as a doorway opened. "Damn me, I never would have suspected."

"Mercy spotted the old duke slipping in here a few years before he died. The room needs to be kept secret from the servants, but for the moment, leave the door open, please." She moved ahead and stopped close to the wall so he might pass her.

Books and curios littered the bookshelves. "Did you find the journal here?"

"Yes, along with others. It seems the duke liked to keep an accounting of quite a few people in society, but never by any name I'm familiar with. I read an unknown lady's journal last week. She talks quiet scathingly of her husband's many scandals."

He snorted. Thoughts should not be committed to paper. It served no good in the end. "So, not a love match for them?"

Lady Venables' hands clenched at her waist. "Perhaps it was for her, in the beginning, but not by the end. I feel rather sorry for her, actually. She was utterly ignored, and despised by his family, if her ramblings are to be believed."

Sounded like a typical society marriage from all he'd heard of them, yet Lady Venables sounded disapproving. Marriage was for money and for position. His parents were an exception. They had loved each other openly until the very last moments.

He glanced at his companion. "I take it you married for love and not for your husband's title?"

Tobias immediately cursed his tongue. That subject, speaking of the late Lord Venables, was one Leopold had warned him to particularly avoid. His brother had not wanted her emotions stirred up again, and this topic of conversation was sure to do so.

"I did," she said quietly. Her gaze dropped to her clenched fingers. She didn't look up again.

Tobias scrounged for something appropriate to say in response. He'd made her sad, and he simply had to lift her spirits again before Leopold noticed his mistake. "Then he was the luckiest of men."

She tilted her head as she met his gaze. "I would have thought you held little store in the value of marrying for love."

He lifted his hand and slid his finger along her jaw gently. "I had parents, B. They were in each other's pockets from sunup till sundown, and what happened after sundown between them is not something I need to think about."

She stepped away from his touch. "Don't shorten my name."

"As you wish, Countess, but your title is quite a mouthful to say." He leaned close to her again. "No one will hear me do it. It'll be our secret. I promise."

"You? A promise?"

Tobias smiled tightly. She didn't know a thing about him. After the fright he'd given her, why shouldn't she be wary? But still, it irked him not to be believed. "I never break my promises, B. You should reconcile yourself to that. Life is too uncertain without burdening others with avoidable disappointments."

She twirled about and swept out of the room as if the devil chased her.

Frustrating woman! How the devil had he gotten stuck living in close quarters with a lady of her temperament? She'd drive him mad or to drink. If it wasn't too early in the day, as judged by Leopold's repeated warnings about imbibing before noon, Tobias would already have a glass in hand.

Life in Romsey was turning out to be a disappointing venture all round. Rules, rules, and more rules. He could not smoke in the house, maids were off-limits, as was gambling with Murphy, Leopold's new assistant, and seducing proper women like Lady Venables. Not an ounce of adventure to be found inside Romsey Abbey. This acting the gentleman business was no easy lark.

He considered the shelves before him. Trust the duke to have been up to his neck in muck and scandal. He plucked a thin journal from the shelf and tucked it under his arm. Maybe he should peruse the duke's papers and help find his missing siblings. It would give him something useful to do while he waited to find his heiress.

He strolled out the doorway and closed the duke's sanctuary. By the time he turned around, Lady Venables had resumed her study of her journal, sitting stiffly in her previous place.

Tobias hated being ignored. Their conversation had been the only bright point of his day. So, knowing full well that it wasn't the gentlemanly thing to do, Tobias stretched out on the opposite empty lounge, propped the book up on his chest and set one highly polished boot heel on the tip of the other to make himself comfortable to read.

Hopefully, something in the book would capture his interest before he did something rash. Seducing the countess to smile, or even engaging in something more scandalous, was terribly tempting.

Chapter Five

Good Lord, Tobias Randall had the habits of a cat. Blythe's gaze was drawn to him repeatedly as he shifted restlessly on the lounge, flicking pages of the book he'd brought with him, and then rearranging his limbs until he was comfortable again. The man's behavior was beyond belief. She was dreading the outing to Lady Dunwoody's soiree.

She'd do her best to shield her friends from Tobias Randall's blunt conversation if she could, but there was a great chance he would embarrass them if he continued to talk so boldly. He hadn't altered enough to be considered a gentleman. It was clear his brother's lessons hadn't taken.

Mr. Randall set the book down on his chest. Their eyes met, and warning bells rang through her mind before she wrenched her gaze away. Damn him. He always seemed to know just when she was looking at him. She kept her face free of expression and bowed her head to the frustrating page before her.

The problem was, she couldn't seem to focus on the journal easily today. Why couldn't the former Duke of Romsey have been a straightforward man? Must everything be a riddle to solve? He could have at least given clearer clues as to where Oliver and Rosemary Randall had been taken. But no, he had to act like he was a grand spymaster. Everything in code, everything jumbled.

Blythe closed the book and pinched the bridge of her nose. Confounded headache. She didn't need one today.

Tobias rose from his spot and passed by her left shoulder on his way to the drawing room door. Thank heavens he was going to take himself away. With him gone, she might have a chance to relax the way she used to. She might even be able to put her feet up on the footstool until her headache passed.

"A letter has arrived for you, Lady Venables."

Blythe jumped out of her skin, startled by Wilcox's sudden presence at her side. She hadn't realized he'd come into the room, and she hurried to close the journal to prevent him from reading the contents. She took the note and waited until he exited the room.

Once he was gone, she flipped over the letter. Venables' seal. What could her stepson possibly want with her now?"

She broke open the note and scanned it. The cold hand of dread washed over her skin.

Venables had heard she'd abandoned Walden Hall for the delights, as he put it, of Romsey Abbey. He insisted that she honor their agreement and return home, or he would consider their arrangement invalid.

Blythe bit her lip. He was within his rights to expel her from Walden Hall because there was little provision made in her late husband's will. Her stepson was not a gentleman in the true sense of the word. He gave her no choice but to leave Romsey Abbey.

She glanced at her sister. Mercy's brow creased into a frown, and she left Leopold to come to her side.

Rather than explain, Blythe handed her the note.

Her sister read it quickly. "Why, that horrible man. How could he?"

Blythe folded the note and stuffed it into her pocket. "He has every right, and you know it. We've been over this many times."

"Still, I had hopes for him being a little more like his father."

Blythe smiled tightly. "As had I."

Mercy covered her hands and squeezed. "Remember your promise to remain here, sister. If needs be, I'll speak to Venables, and if he will not heed my suggestions, I will make sure everyone in the district learns of his tight-fisted ways and broken promises. His father was well known for his generosity. He'd turn in his grave over these events."

"Don't. I can stay a few days more, and then I must return to Walden Hall. I cannot remain with you forever, and you know it."

"I don't see why not. Lady Dunwoody has a complete stranger residing with her at her country estate, and no one thinks twice about Mrs. Raglan. They will hardly bat an eye if I house a family member under my roof. Don't argue with me."

As Mercy rejoined Leopold across the room, Blythe shook her head. She couldn't remain with her sister indefinitely.

"A drink, B?" Tobias muttered softly. "You look like you could use one."

Blythe glanced at the hand hovering beside her face, holding a glass of sherry. The cut on his calloused thumb had healed to a red line, but nothing had softened his hands from the evidence of the hard life he'd endured before he'd returned to Romsey Abbey.

She took the glass. Her hardships were nothing to what he must have suffered. She would survive this setback. "Thank you."

"My pleasure." He rounded the lounge to sit beside her. "Don't worry yourself too greatly over the journals."

If only that were the whole of her problems. She sipped her drink. "Someone needs to read them. Who knows what might be found."

Tobias leaned back in the chair, stretched out his legs and crossed them at the ankle. "My father once said that the old duke preferred all eyes on him. It is not right for a beautiful woman to spend all of her time pondering the goings-on of a man long dead and unlamented. He shouldn't have that much importance, and surely not for you."

Blythe frowned. "Why not for me?"

"Well, as you've mentioned before, you are not a Randall. This is our burden, our problem, not yours. What do you normally do with your time, B?"

Blythe swallowed the hard lump forming in her throat. What did she do with her life? She visited with Mercy and Edwin until she felt she had to go home. But when she was home, she didn't feel comfortable there. It was unsettling to be a guest in the house you lived in, but that was where all her memories of her son came from. The house could never be hers. It was entailed, and as her stepson liked to remind her, he could take possession of it anytime he chose.

"What were you thinking of just then, B? I swear the expression in your eyes could break a heart."

Blythe sipped a mouthful of her drink before answering. "It's nothing."

"The letter?"

"Is none of your concern, either, sir."

"Well, you should talk to someone about these nothings one of these days. Problems are easier to bear when shared, and all that."

Since when did she need advice from a man? She sat up straighter. "Which is why I am helping with these journals."

Tobias Randall chuckled softly. "Clever, clever girl. You never actually answered me. Keep your secrets, my lady, and I'll hope they'll come to naught, whatever they are."

Had Tobias Randall been replaced by an imposter? He was actually being nice! There had to be some game afoot. She studied him. "What do you want?"

His lips pursed, and then a wicked grin twisted his mouth as his gaze dipped down her bodice and slid back up again. "Judging from your mode of dress, I don't think you'll let me have it, so I'll take a smile in place." He winked.

Blythe sucked in a shocked breath. The pirate was still there, beneath the properly tied cravat and neatly trimmed hair, and determined to make her uncomfortable. She'd been foolish to believe otherwise for even a moment.

A sharp rap on the door interrupted, and they both turned toward the sound and Tobias Randall moved closer. Unfortunately, that put her face within inches of his. She leaned away quickly as a hot flush stole over her cheeks and she listened to the butler.

"Lord Archibald and Miss Emma Trimble, Your Grace."

Emma had come. Oh, dear heavens.

Blythe met Tobias' gaze. "Please behave as a gentleman. Emma is a dear friend of mine, and I would not like to have her made uncomfortable by your forward behavior."

She clenched her hands together, hoping that for once Mr. Randall might be agreeable and not make a fuss about doing so. He was very fond of arguing over trivial matters with his brother, but good manners were essential around her friends.

His brow rose. "A very good friend, eh? Well, this could be interesting. I should like to know who is deemed worthy of your praise."

He stood and moved away to another chair. Blythe let out a relieved breath. Maybe he would not cause an uncomfortable scene.

"Do show them in, Wilcox," Mercy said, "and arrange for tea, please."

The butler tipped his head. "Very good, Your Grace."

Wilcox disappeared from sight for a moment then returned to show Emma and her cousin, Lord Archibald, into the drawing room. Both spoke warmly to Mercy and were introduced to Leopold and Tobias Randall.

When Lord Archibald appeared ready to engage Mercy and the men in exclusive conversation, Emma caught both of Blythe's hands and squeezed. "My dear, how are you?"

"I am very well, Emma. And you?"

"Oh, I am always well," she whispered. "But I would like to speak with you in private as soon as possible if I could. It is a very urgent matter."

Had Lord Archibald finally proposed to Emma? She dearly hoped so. "Of course you may." Blythe caught Mercy's eye and tilted her head to show they were going to ease away to speak privately. Mercy wouldn't mind. Blythe would relay the conversation later if it was truly important.

When Mercy inclined her head, Blythe caught Emma's arm and they strolled toward the windows, where their voices wouldn't carry too easily. "What is the urgent matter?"

"I was hoping you could tell me." Emma squeezed her hands tightly. "You have been staying here for months. That is not like you."

Blythe untangled their fingers. "I am helping Mercy solve a puzzle, and it is easier if I remain here than travel back and forth every day."

"What kind of puzzle?"

A matter that was of great importance, but possibly scandalous. She had to tread carefully. "Oh, Emma. I wish I could speak freely on the subject, but I cannot."

A bright blush stole over Emma's neck. "Is it about him?"

Blythe frowned. "Which him?"

"Mr. Tobias Randall, silly! He's watching you."

Blythe glanced across the room. Emma was correct, but at this distance, she couldn't determine exactly which one of them he had his eye on. Annoying man. He had better keep a distance from her friend. She pasted an unconcerned expression on her face. "Mr. Randall is not an issue. He is the duke's cousin, and he has returned to visit with him and the duchess."

Emma's gaze lingered on the pirate. "For how long?"

Now there was the question of the month. Just how long would Tobias Randall stay at Romsey? How long would she have to suffer his blunt invitations to share his bed? At least until the wedding, and for some time beyond, perhaps, unless he found something else to do with his time. Sadly, even a distraction couldn't be counted on. He was frequently underfoot. "For as long as he wants, I imagine. His brother proposed to Mercy, you know."

"Yes, I heard. Are you happy about it?"

"Of course I am. Despite the swiftness of the proposal, he has fallen completely in love with her. They are smitten."

Emma giggled. "I never expected her to marry again. I thought she would remain a widow, as you will."

Blythe pressed her lips together to cover her surprise. Did people think she would remain an eternal widow? Blythe hadn't given the matter much thought before. She was still heartbroken over the loss of Raphael and Adam. Losing your whole family was not an easy thing to recover from, but she'd never actually decided to live alone forever. She took a deep breath, pushing the matter from her mind, and offered Emma a wry smile. "I didn't expect Mercy to remarry either. But they make each other happy and that's all there is to it."

Emma sighed. "I suppose that I will just have to be blunt and come right out and ask you my question. They're saying that you remain close to the young duke because you fear Mr. Randall's influence, and that you're attempting to keep him at a distance. Why would people say such a thing if you like him?"

"Because society at large has the intelligence of a flea," Tobias grumbled as he joined them. "Lady Venables stays because she is fond of her family. Whoever is spreading such preposterous rumors?"

Emma's face changed to a bright shade of pink. "I... Ah," she stammered.

"Mr. Randall, there is no need for such impertinent questions," Blythe said quickly. "Rumors cannot hurt one when there is no hint of truth behind them."

And really, any rumors involving herself were none of his business, but she was thankful this particular rumor did not bring her sanity into question.

"Rumors have to start somewhere, my lady. I should like to

know where this one in particular began." His brow rose until he appeared as haughty as anyone she'd ever come across in society.

And…Blythe was curious about the rumor, too. "It is a good question though, Emma. Do you have any idea how it might have started?"

Emma fidgeted. "My maid mentioned something yesterday morning. I called at Walden Hall afterward, and again today, to ask you about it. When you were not at home, I had no choice but to come see you. It is a terrible thing they are suggesting. Surely Her Grace can be relied upon to determine the true character of the man she is going to marry."

"Of course she can. The duchess has no time for imbeciles," Tobias Randall added in a tone that brooked no argument. Blythe found his support for Mercy the nicest thing he'd ever done or said.

Wilcox arrived just then with the tea tray, and Emma quickly returned to a chair close to Mercy when she was summoned.

Tobias caught Blythe's sleeve to delay her from joining the others. "The servants are always the first to speculate," he whispered. "Which means Her Grace's staff are responsible for the talk about you."

She sighed as she pulled her sleeve from his grip. "At least they are not saying I'm mad."

"You might be relieved, but I don't like talk that sets you at odds with our family."

Blythe peered up at the pirate and scowled. "What would such talk matter to you?"

A look of chagrin crossed his features. "I frightened you, B. You might not expect it, or believe me, but that weighs quite heavily on my conscience. I would prefer to be on good terms with my brother's future family."

"Don't be absurd. I'm not afraid of you."

A sudden smile crossed his face. "So happy to hear that. Does that mean hostilities are at an end?"

"As long as you keep a distance."

His brow rose. "So, no more climbing through windows?"

"Absolutely not. My window will remain locked."

A sly grin crossed his face. "And if your window should slide open one evening, I shall imagine you wish to talk to me in private.

That's all it will take, B. Just open the window whenever you wish, and I'll be there."

Good grief, would he never stop the harassment?

Tobias left her and joined the others while Blythe fought the blush heating her cheeks. Insufferable, conceited man. Did he honestly believe she'd invite him to join her in bed? She wasn't that sort of woman. She wasn't so desperate to regain the pleasures of the marriage bed that she'd share hers with a brash scoundrel like him.

When Blythe resumed her seat, Lord Archibald smiled at her warmly.

A sudden wave of gooseflesh rose over her skin, and she shuddered.

"Are you all right, Lady Venables?" Lord Archibald asked, leaning closer as he did so.

Blythe forced a smile. "I'm perfectly well. It's nothing but a draft."

"Of course." Lord Archibald smiled again and sat back. "My cousin is forever chasing them down. According to my sisters, we boast the coziest parlor, thanks to her efforts."

Emma's skin colored with a blush.

"I quite understand her feelings on the subject," Blythe said. "Emma, dear, did you convince Lord Archibald to undertake the improvements to the drawing room you mentioned?"

Emma glanced at Lord Archibald, her blush increasing in color. "Not yet. He's been much too busy with the estate to worry about such matters at the moment."

Lord Archibald threw Emma a quelling glance, but then smiled once more at Blythe. "The estate takes up a good deal of my time."

Really, some men were entirely without good sense. Emma's vision for the room was breathtaking, and if it could be done before the winter ball, then Emma's brilliance would be seen by all and commented on. "Come now, my lord. I would have thought that keeping the three women housed under your roof happy would be paramount to your own harmony. Ladies like their creature comforts."

Lord Archibald's two younger sisters, Helena and Francesca, had little interest in the arrangement of a room until they were uncomfortable. They were nice girls, but Emma truly had the most sense of the three. Lord Archibald should have taken advantage of Emma's counsel long before this.

He leaned forward in his chair. "Do you approve of the alterations my cousin has suggested?"

Honestly, what would it take for the man to unbend and call Emma by her first name? At the rate their relationship was progressing, Emma would be an old maid before Lord Archibald did so.

Blythe wanted her friend to be as happy as she had been in her marriage. Working out how to bring Lord Archibald up to scratch for Emma vexed her. Emma was the perfect wife for him. "Emma has always had excellent taste. She would never suggest an unnecessary alteration to your property. I should be proud to sit in the drawing room once her improvements have been undertaken."

Lord Archibald sat back, a frown line between his brows. "Then I suppose the changes can go ahead, so that your future time with us is everything you could want it to be."

It was smoothly said, and although his agreement was a victory for Emma, a small trill of unease rippled through Blythe. Would she have to tell him whom to marry for that event to happen, too? Her friend had been trying to gain Lord Archibald's attention for years. She'd fallen in love quickly for the blind idiot and had never said a harsh word against his stubbornness to make changes. Blythe would hate to think she had more influence over him than her friend.

Emma's lips trembled as they stared at each other. She was upset by this turn of events, and Blythe had no idea what to do or say to make the situation better.

"Miss Trimble," Tobias Randall said suddenly. "I understand from Lady Venables that you are organizing a ball."

Emma faced Tobias. Her chest rose and fell as she took a deep breath. "Not a large ball, but an intimate party for Lord Archibald's closest acquaintances. We hope that you will still be here to join us as part of the duchess' party."

Tobias' gaze dipped quite shockingly to Emma's chest, and then rose slowly as a small smile played over his lips. "I am breathless with anticipation."

"Oh, he will be there," Mercy told Emma with a laugh. "I'll even make certain he dances with every unattached lady present so your party is an unequalled success."

Tobias glanced at Mercy sharply, as if he hadn't cared to dance so much, but then he turned back to Emma with an easy smile. "I would be most happy to dance with you at your ball. In the meantime, perhaps I might secure a set at Lady Dunwoody's soiree, if your card is not overfull."

A darker blush swept Emma's cheeks. "My card is not full, and I would be honored, sir."

Could Tobias Randall dance? It had never occurred to her to check. Blythe winced. Poor Emma. She may not feel very honored after three turns around the dance floor with her toes trampled and her ears burning. Could Tobias speak civilly, as a gentleman, for that length of time?

"Excellent. I shall look forward to our dance immensely." His grin broadened slowly, and Blythe clenched and unclenched her hands at the sight.

Don't flirt with my friend. Don't ruin things between Emma and Lord Archibald.

When Emma's skin had blushed to an alarming shade of red, Lord Archibald cleared his throat. "Well, we should be going, Your Grace. Miss Trimble." He stood suddenly and thrust his hand out to his cousin rather impatiently.

Emma appeared as startled by Lord Archibald's tone as everyone else seemed to be, too, but she set her hand in his. She stood slowly, her blush growing as she said goodbye. "Thank you for seeing us, Your Grace."

"It is always a pleasure to have you visit for however short a time," Mercy said, her gaze straying to where Lord Archibald stood. "Come tomorrow with Helena and Francesca and stay for lunch. We have much to catch up on before your party."

"I would like that very much."

Lord Archibald urged Emma to walk ahead of him and then held out his hand to Mercy. "Might I have a moment more of your time for a private conversation, your grace?"

Blythe stepped forward quickly and linked her arm through Emma's, pulling her away from the pair. "Come, I'll walk you out."

They made their way to the front entrance, but Emma cast furtive glances behind. "What just happened?"

"I'm sure it's nothing."

Behind them, Mercy had detained Lord Archibald, and his face had darkened to an intense hue of crimson as they spoke. "Perhaps he didn't like the way Mr. Randall smiled at you."

Emma stopped. "In what way was his smile wrong? I thought Mr. Randall was a very agreeable gentleman. Very handsome, too."

Blythe patted her friend's hand. "My dear, Tobias Randall appreciates a pretty woman as much as the next man. He just fails to hide how much. He was flirting with you in front of your cousin, and Lord Archibald did not care for it."

"With me? Oh. Oh!" Emma's smile grew until she beamed. "Oh, how unexpected and kind of him."

"There is no 'oh' about it," Blythe warned. "Trust me, Tobias Randall is definitely not the man for you."

"I know but…" Emma's hand rose to her cheeks. "He's not at all what I expected. He even asked to dance with me. Archie hasn't done as much, and he knows full well I enjoy dancing. I was in dread of being a wallflower at Lady Dunwoody's soiree, but now I cannot wait for the evening."

The object of their discussion, Tobias, stepped around the others. "It was a pleasure making your acquaintance, Miss Trimble. I look forward to seeing you often."

"And I you, sir."

Blythe's heart pounded. A man like Tobias would have no proper intentions toward a woman. His smile might make a woman's insides curl into knots, but he wasn't likely to have honorable plans unless there was something to gain.

With a sinking heart, Blythe remembered Emma had a substantial dowry. The lure of that wealth could be great for the penniless man.

She pulled Emma toward the waiting carriage and away from the brazen pirate before irreparable harm was done to her friend's eager heart.

Chapter Six

A thick cloud of dust rose up from the drive, partially obscuring Tobias' view of the feminine arm waving through the window. Nice lady. Insufferable prig of a lord, though. Blythe's friends were a mixed bag of personalities; Miss Emma so warm, Lord Archibald painfully stiff and proper. Would they all be like that? He had tomorrow night's soiree to suffer through without offending anyone important, and he was not looking forward to the event.

"A word, brother." Leopold caught his arm and led him down the front steps forcibly and across the gravel drive.

Tobias glanced over his shoulder as they reached the lawn and strolled out onto the grounds. Blythe stood beside Mercy, a worried expression marring her pretty features. Now what? "What the devil are you doing?"

"Getting to the bottom of a mystery," Leopold growled.

Tobias had not missed being pushed around by his elder brother for the past ten years. Leopold seemed entirely too happy to throw his weight and position as head of the family in Tobias' face. Up until now, Tobias had gone along to keep the peace, but there were limits to how much manhandling he would tolerate at four and twenty years of age. "Is there something else going on? Honestly, can't you just give up and leave Romsey behind? I swear you'd be a happier man without the responsibilities inherent with this place."

"Don't be ridiculous. I'll never leave Romsey Abbey. But this discussion is not about me. It's about you. What the devil do you think you are doing?"

Tobias shook off his brother's grip and tugged his coat sleeves back into place. "What now? Was I not gentlemanly enough today? Have I embarrassed you with my manners, or lack of?"

"The problem is that you were entirely too gentlemanly. Are you intending to pursue the lady for a wife? Because flirtations such as I've just witnessed usually lead to a marriage proposal."

Tobias stared at his brother in surprise. Blythe wouldn't marry again. She was still in love with her dead husband and disliked Tobias in the extreme. "Don't be ridiculous. I'm not interested in marriage, and I was not flirting with her as part of a seduction. She'd sooner cut me than marry me."

"Miss Emma Trimble is an unmarried young woman and well respected in the district. You have no cause to flirt with her again unless you're prepared to take a place before the alter and marry her."

Tobias laughed at his mistake. Devil take it, he'd thought Leopold was referring to his interactions with the prickly countess. He hadn't one iota of interest in Miss Trimble and had thought he'd acted the part of a gentleman. Apparently, he hadn't done well enough.

What would Leopold say if he learned of Tobias' nighttime visit to Blythe's bedchamber two weeks ago? While nothing at all had happened between them, it would be considered scandalous. More than likely, his brother would have a seizure over the harmless conversation. Tobias would have to be even more reserved when conversing with women. "Miss Trimble is lovely, and my intentions toward her are entirely proper, I assure you."

Leopold gave him a long assessing stare. "She has a dowry of four thousand pounds, and you have asked about marriageable young women recently. Have you set your sights on Miss Trimble already?"

If he was going to live comfortably, he did need funds. "Miss Trimble is attractive and has an easy manner about her. But there is just one small problem. She appears to already be in love." He shrugged. "She fancies Lord Archibald."

"Oh."

Tobias nodded. "Every word Miss Trimble spoke was followed by a swift peek at Lord Archibald to see how he reacted. Do you walk around with your eyes closed, old man? Her admiration is as plain as the nose on your face. Smitten—and that fool cannot see it or chooses to ignore it. Damn cruel, if the latter is the case."

Leopold crossed his arms over his chest, flexing his muscles so as to intimidate. "I'm not a fool. You were flirting with Miss Trimble."

Tobias held his hands up to ward off his brother. "All right. All right. A little—just to see if Lord Archibald would become protective of his cousin. Since he rushed to take his leave, dragging the startled woman away as quick as may be, my ploy worked perfectly. Men dislike competition, even if they don't yet realize they've staked a claim. However, if he can't be bothered offering for her, I could easily consider taking her off his hands."

Leopold checked the time on his pocket watch. "You play a dangerous game."

Tobias shrugged. "Life is meant to be a challenge. Although, by now, I'm sure Lady Venables has warned Miss Trimble against forming any attachment toward me. As you've repeatedly mentioned, people will listen to her opinions."

"You place great faith in Lady Venables' powers of persuasion. I would not have thought the two of you would get along as well as you have."

Tobias buckled over and laughed until his sides hurt. When he stood again, his brother's scowl could have cracked the earth. "Lady Venables tolerates my presence, Leopold. I'm sure she would rather not have met me at all." At Leopold's frown, Tobias swung his arm about his shoulders and led him farther from the house. "Tell me what's happening with you. I've barely seen you the past few days."

"I'm getting married. Isn't that explanation enough?"

Tobias squeezed his brother and then let him go. "Sounds positively dreadful."

"Not dreadful, but complicated. Mercy wishes to give up her title, and I disagree with her decision. I am sure when her brother arrives, he will add weight to my arguments against doing so."

"That is, if he agrees to the match at all. He sounds like another pompous arse."

Leopold laughed. "From what Mercy's told me, a debauched arse would be a better description. Mercy swears his daughters are suffering from a lack of mothering, shut away at Stanton Harold Hall as they are while he's off doing God knows what."

"Hmm, I like the sound of him. An unattached man has so many more vices and a willingness for good company. We could get along well."

"That is my hope for all of us," Leopold muttered fervently.

A prickle of heat swept over Tobias' neck, and he quickly glanced over his shoulder to see what had caused the sensation.

Mercy hurried across the lawn at a near run, Blythe following with the young duke in her arms.

"Leopold, we have company." Tobias peered at Blythe's white face. "And by the look of it, unhappy company, at that."

Mercy threw herself into Leopold's arms. "It's happened again! I'd thought it had all stopped. Why now?" She sobbed hysterically against his brother's chest.

"Calm down, my love. Shh," Leopold said as he cuddled her close.

Tobias turned as Blythe reached them.

"Another rabbit on her bed," she mouthed so the boy couldn't hear.

"Here, let me take him," Tobias said. "He must be heavy for you."

"I don't really mind. Soon he'll be too big for me to carry." She didn't make a move to hand him over, but pressed a kiss to the boy's dark hair before meeting his gaze. "Wilcox will deal with the matter, as he has all others, but it is exactly the same as the other instances."

"The timing, again, is interesting. Coinciding with visitors to the abbey, so we have doubts about who was where," Leopold said aloud.

Tobias rubbed his jaw. "We were in the drawing room all morning. Together, in fact."

Leopold's brow rose. "And before that?"

"I woke and went immediately down to breakfast," Blythe said quickly, "then went to the drawing room. I've been reading the old duke's journals all day."

A frown crossed Leopold's face, and Tobias guessed his brother doubted her story. Although Leopold still had concerns that Blythe could be involved, Tobias simply couldn't fathom how. He didn't believe the woman had it in her to be so cold. Bad tempered, perhaps, especially with him, but not cruel. Despite the frost, she loved her sister and nephew dearly. She wouldn't hurt them.

Tobias cleared his throat. "I woke to find Murphy in my room."

Blythe scowled at him. "Is that why you started the day shouting?"

Tobias grinned. "Wouldn't you shout out in horror to find Murphy shaking you awake?"

Blythe rocked the young duke from side to side as if she held a baby. "I imagine I'd act with a lot more decorum, and Mr. Murphy would have better sense than to enter a lady's bedchamber without her permission."

Before Tobias could form a suitably bland reply, the young duke lifted his face and rubbed the tip of his nose across Blythe's. She chuckled suddenly and hugged him to her. Her merry laugh, so at odds with the situation, caused a warm glow in the vicinity of his chest. The woman was so changeable, but always sweet with the boy. Anyone could see the truth of her heart just by observing her with her nephew.

Leopold stepped forward, hands held out for the young duke. "Are you two always so aware of what the other is doing?"

Lady Venables gave Leopold a quelling glare as she passed over the boy. "Some walls inside the abbey are thinner than others. I would prefer not to know what your brother is doing with his mornings. However, he has a propensity to shout at Mr. Murphy, so I cannot avoid hearing the cursing."

Damn it. Leopold would have a seizure before the day was out. Tobias smiled awkwardly. "He's really an annoying servant. I am unused to such mothering."

"He has better manners than some," Blythe muttered just loud enough to be heard.

"Good Lord, you two can bicker." Leopold juggled the boy and slung his arm around Mercy's waist, pulling her into motion. "We'll return to the abbey and investigate this latest occurrence. The two of you can butt heads later. We have bigger problems, it seems."

As they hurried back to the entrance of Romsey Abbey, Tobias fell into step beside Blythe. "Are you all right, B?"

A sad frown crossed her face. "Your brother still doesn't believe I have nothing to do with these troubling events. It was a foolish wish, but I suppose he shall never be entirely comfortable with me, nor I with him. I am unused to being doubted."

"Well, I believe you had nothing to do with this morning's event. I followed you down to breakfast, and then into the drawing room. We've spent the whole day together."

"Good lord, have we? How unexpected."

"Well, since the pair of us will always be first to arouse suspicion then, in my opinion, it is a good thing. You heard me shouting at Murphy to keep his paws off my trousers because I can bloody well dress myself, and I heard you pass by my doorway on your way down to breakfast. I caught sight of you at the head of the stairs, and again when I reached the morning room for breakfast. We've barely been out of sight of each other for a few minutes since you left your bedchamber. The only way to have a stronger alibi is if we were sleeping in the same bed."

"Sleeping together? You must be mad."

Tobias grinned. "Well, you are right about the sleeping. Too much excitement to be had if we shared a bed." He'd make sure she didn't sleep a wink if they shared a bed. They'd probably fight and make love all night long.

He frowned. It was a great pity that the idea of bedding Blythe kept recurring. He'd have to find a lover soon to take the edge off, because she'd never welcome the idea.

She shook her head. "You really do have a high opinion of yourself, don't you?"

Tobias laughed. "Well, someone has to think well of me. If I were a weaker man, I'd be shivering in terror from half the looks you've bestowed on me these last weeks."

They reached the bottom of the stairs, and Tobias cupped her elbow to steady her ascent. Her heat warmed and enticed. Her breath caught as he moved his thumb.

"Given half the comments you've made to me," she hissed, "I'm clearly not doing a good enough job of putting you in your place."

"My place? Where exactly might that be, B? Under your thumb or under your skirts?"

"Don't say such things to me." She wrenched her arm free of his grip. "Will you ever get tired of this?"

"Never. I've always enjoyed making a pretty woman blush. Besides, if Leopold has his way and turns me into the dull and proper gentleman society expects, then you may well be the one person to ever know who and what I truly am. I've never lied to you to spare your tender feelings, and from what I've gathered, you have no concerns for mine. Take my arm again so I may be a gentleman.

A man should not desert a lady halfway up the stairs, or so I'm told."

Blythe merely glared at him. "Am I to be grateful for having my senses shocked every time you open your mouth to speak?"

"Would you rather have false flattery? I dislike insincerity above all else, my lady. My brother insists I become a gentleman—forget the past so that I can belong here again. I thought you, at least, valued honesty. However, if my brand of honesty offends you so greatly, I will, of course, act as Leopold expects…but I wouldn't believe one word that comes out of my mouth. Trust me, I won't mean any of it."

Tobias strode up the stairs without her, but waited at the door so she could precede him inside. Stubborn wench. If she would rather boring conversation, then so be it. Tomorrow night, he would play the part of a proper gentleman. He would flatter and simper around the ladies, act gruff with the men, and bore himself and everyone he met to tears. He hoped he could pull it off without running screaming into the night.

Leopold waited for them just inside the doors. "Will you stay below with Mercy and Edwin, Tobias, while I take a look into this latest occurrence?"

Tobias rubbed his jaw. "I was actually hoping to see the carnage this time with my own eyes."

Leopold's gaze shifted to Blythe and back. "Perhaps we should all go together, then. We'll do our best to shield Edwin from the mess."

They ascended the stairs and hurried to the family wing, Mercy and Blythe striding along with arms linked together. When they reached a room, Leopold passed Edwin to his mother and gestured Tobias forward. "Exactly the same as all the other times."

Tobias blinked at the carnage on Mercy's bed. Blood-soaked linen, mangled rabbit corpse. Whoever was trying to scare Mercy away was a determined fellow. "So we can assume the same culprit is at work again."

"It looks that way," Leopold said darkly.

Tobias picked up the rabbit by the ears, watching the way the body dangled by the remaining thin cord of flesh and skin. The poor creature had almost been decapitated. A strong person had done this, someone without a shred of compassion in their being.

He dropped the rabbit. "I've seen enough. Let's take the boy outside to kick his pigskin ball around."

He met Blythe's gaze. She was pale, backed up against the bedchamber wall taking shallow breaths, but so far she hadn't fainted. He held out his arm and the beauty took it, a tremble of distress passing through to him as she clung. Poor creature, to be so affected by blood. These events must be quite unsettling for her. If not for his life at sea, he too might be feeling just as discomforted.

But there was little that could shock him after seeing a man cut in half before his eyes and hearing his futile pleas for help.

He shook off the memory.

After finding the child's toy, they walked outside to a patch of sunlit ground without a servant lingering nearby. Tobias led Blythe to a stone bench, saw her settled, and then moved away to think. He hunkered down against a low stone wall in the sun and closed his eyes to block out the distraction of his brother at play with the child.

There had been no further threats to Mercy or the young duke until today. There had been very few visitors at the abbey since he'd come home and frightened Mercy and Blythe out of their wits.

He pursed his lips. What gain was there to be had from tormenting the duchess? Revenge? But for what?

Approaching footfalls sliced through the grass. Tobias opened his eyes as Leopold stopped before him. "What are you thinking, brother?"

He looked for young Edwin, and saw that he'd tired of the ball and was digging in the earth at Blythe's feet with a short stick. Tobias squinted up at his brother. "Has it always been different visitors coming and going on the days of these atrocities?"

Leopold crouched down against the wall, too. "I believe so, yes."

"Is there anything to connect the visitors' servants to Romsey Abbey? A footman who has changed employers, perhaps—one who might want to seek revenge for a past wrong committed against them?"

"Not that I can tell. Wait—Mercy said the steward who managed the estate left suddenly after our cousin died. But that was, oh…two years ago now. I should discover where he went. Perhaps Wilcox will know. These acts only started a year ago, and it seems a long time for him to wait to seek revenge."

Tobias squinted at the cloudless sky. "It all started at the time Mercy came out of mourning?"

"Yes. About then, I suppose. I hadn't connected the timing of the two events."

Someone had wanted Mercy to leave Romsey Abbey as soon as her mourning was over. But why? "Is there a particular reason Her Grace did not return to London when her mourning finished, aside from the boy?"

Leopold ducked his head. "She said she was waiting…hoping I'd return."

Tobias laughed. Now that wasn't the response he'd expected, and it was particularly sweet to see his brother's discomfort.

He looked over at the duchess. Mercy was in no way a typical female, much less a stern aristocrat. It might have been an easy thing to do to frighten a widow from the country, if that woman hadn't been as stubborn as an ox and bent on remaining in wait for her lover.

She might parade around in feminine garb, but there was steel in the Duchess of Romsey's gaze. Fierce loyalty, too. Whoever was doing this had grossly underestimated her character. She'd leave when she decided to go and not a moment sooner.

The wind picked up, sending a chill through him. Whoever it was who'd committed these crimes may already be at the abbey, and they used the arrival of visitors to cast doubts about their identity. Add Lady Venables' odd behavior, fueled by grief, into the equation and the suspect might well have succeeded in driving Mercy from the abbey.

Oliver, if he lived, would solve this puzzle easily. He'd find the pattern in the chaos and offer up a perfectly logical explanation for the events that were unfolding. Without him, they'd have to muddle through as best they could and hope they didn't miss a clue.

He studied the women seated on the bench. Despite the troubles surrounding them, the sisters were still close. Family and the best of friends. Their recent problems had temporarily driven them apart, but now they appeared to have mended their fences completely. Tobias was glad for that. They needed each other.

He set his arm about his knees and leaned forward. "We must

read everything in the duke's sanctuary. Someone is trying to drive Mercy from the abbey. We need to work out why?"

"What do you think I've been doing?"

"Running the estate, arranging a wedding." He slapped his brother's leg and stood. "We'll get to the bottom of this together. I'll start today. Keep Mercy and the boy with you at all times. Lady Venables might not like it, but we are going to spend a lot of time together over the next few days. Can the duke's sanctuary be reopened from the inside if the door is closed completely?"

Leopold nodded.

"Good. As an added precaution, I'd like Mercy to refrain from using the drawing room as often as possible, so we can pull that room apart without worrying about someone snooping into things best kept within the family."

His brother stood, too. "I think Mercy will agree with that."

"Excellent. I'll go there directly and begin." He leaned close to Leopold. "Consider this: every time a visitor comes to Romsey, the servant hall would be scrambling around to provide tea and such. Someone could easily slip upstairs and lay out another grim offering without being seen and leave again the same way. Rather clever, really."

Leopold shook his head. "You do realize you are complimenting a villain, Tobias."

"Clever, but not smart enough. We must catch them at it."

"That could be dangerous."

"Leopold, do you think I could not defend myself against one man in an unfair fight? Or even two? I evaded the entire estate staff for days. Nothing bad will happen to me."

Leopold frowned. "Does nothing frighten you?"

Losing Rosie had terrified him. After that, everything else was easy. "I'm numb."

As Leopold strode back toward the duchess, another disturbing thought occurred to Tobias. Today was the first day that he had shown an interest in the contents of the duke's sanctuary.

What if the chamber held secrets the culprit didn't want to come to light? And in what manner could Tobias' interest influence events at Romsey Abbey?

Chapter Seven

Blythe attempted to control the fast pounding of her heart, but it wasn't working very well. She was still considered the enemy, still held under suspicion by Leopold Randall. Tobias Randall seemed to believe in her innocence. The irony of that astounded her.

She glanced across to where the men were speaking. For a change, Tobias appeared to be leading the discussion rather than bearing the brunt of another lecture. The tall man was as serious as she had ever seen him. He exuded confidence and tightly controlled anger. His whole frame was tense with it.

"What are we going to do? I thought this was all over." Mercy set her head on Blythe's shoulder. "I thought having more people staying at Romsey might convince this lunatic to go away, but I was wrong."

Blythe had hoped for that, too. "Whoever it is has likely been watching. Waiting for their next chance." Blythe set her head against her sister's, drawing comfort from the familiar gesture. "Your Leopold is a man of routine and order, as are we."

Mercy sat up suddenly. "That is true. I like my little routines with Edwin, and Leopold has fallen into mine quite easily. I need to be more erratic. I need to catch whoever it is!"

Blythe caught her sister's arms and gave her a little shake. "What you need to do is protect your son, not chase after shadows. We must gain the upper hand. If you promise to keep to your routines with Edwin, I can be the erratic one. A headache here and there, a forgotten shawl to be fetched from upstairs. Any excuse to catch this criminal before they can cause you more distress."

Mercy clutched at Blythe's fingers. "You could be hurt."

It already hurt to see Mercy so scared. Her sister had always been the strong one. "I'll be fine. If you are truly worried, you could ask Leopold if I may have his small pistol to keep about me. I may never be able to shoot anyone, but it does make a remarkable amount of noise. Perhaps I can scare them away."

"You truly are a terrible shot." Mercy shook her head. "I can't. This is my problem. My responsibility is to look after the best interests of the duchy."

"You also need to be here for Edwin until he reaches his majority. Stay close to him. This is the best way to ensure that happens."

"What are you two debating?" Leopold Randall asked, his scowl fierce.

Before Blythe could answer, Tobias joined them. "I imagine the countess is telling her sister to stay close to the boy while she investigates the matter herself. She's got that single-minded expression on her face again." Tobias' gaze fell on her and lingered. Blythe stared back.

Leopold shook his head. "It is far too dangerous. She could be hurt."

"I don't think mere words are going to change her mind," Tobias said. "Give her your small pistol then for protection, if you want to help."

"Not a chance of it," Leopold spluttered.

Blythe stood. "It is ill mannered to speak of someone when they are right before you—and to believe they have no say in what you decide. Excuse me."

She didn't really need a pistol for protection. She wasn't that confident of her ability to actually shoot at a man, but she'd keep her sewing scissors about her at all times. Who knew when such an innocent thing could be used to her advantage? But they were back in the drawing room. She'd have to fetch them now.

As she turned away, Tobias Randall called out to her to wait.

Blythe kept walking. These Randalls were bossy creatures. Go. Stay. Wait. Etcetera. Blythe had been looking out for Mercy's interests for more years than she could count. They were sisters in a world run by men. She didn't need a man to tell her what to do.

Tobias Randall fell into step beside her, his breath a rough pant from the exertion of running to catch up with her. "We should pair up."

Blythe stopped. "I beg your pardon?"

For a change, the pirate wasn't grinning. There was no sly twist to his lips to hint at another meaning.

"I think we should work together on the contents of the duke's sanctuary, to discover who is stalking Mercy," he said.

"The two are not connected."

"I'm not so sure. Someone wants your sister to flee. Gaining possession of the contents of the duke's sanctuary could be reason enough."

Blythe considered the idea. But there was no evidence she could see to connect the two together. The servants didn't even know about the existence of the chamber, as far as she could tell. Mercy had taken great pains to ensure that.

She looked up at Tobias, intent on asking him to explain his theories further.

"I fear the perpetrator of these acts is already at Romsey Abbey," he said. "Nothing happened until today. And today, both of us were in that chamber. Yes, it could be a coincidence, but it makes me suspicious.

Blythe snapped her mouth closed. Insufferable bounder. Couldn't he wait to let her ask her questions first before answering them?

She spun on her heel and hurried for the drawing room as a disturbing thought occurred to her—she'd left the journal she'd been reading out on a side table where anyone could find it.

She reached the terrace door and turned the handle. China rattled inside as the housekeeper swept from the room carrying the tea tray.

Blythe crossed the threshold as Wilcox turned back. "Do you require anything else, my lady?"

"No, thank you. That will be all."

He hurried out and pulled the doors closed behind him.

Blythe crossed the chamber, her eyes fixed on the side table. Had the book moved? She couldn't tell.

"Mine is still where I left it." Tobias gestured to the chair cushion he'd lifted, reading her mind again. His book had been better hidden than hers.

Blythe hefted the book and checked for the scrap of paper she'd used as a marker. When she found it still in place, she let out a relieved breath.

Tobias drew closer. "You know, I've never liked that Wilcox. Not even when I was a boy."

Blythe shook her head. "Mercy trusts him, as does your brother."

Tobias took the book from her hands and laid it atop his. "And I can see you don't."

Blythe scowled at his correct assumption. "He…seeks to rise above his position."

"Maybe it's him? He'd have ample opportunity."

"Mercy and your brother will not believe that. We'd have to catch him in the act to convince anyone."

Tobias stared past her to the closed door. "Exactly. We'll catch him—or whoever it is. Together." His smile returned suddenly as his gaze shifted to her face. "In the meantime, let's find out what's so damned important in that room."

Tobias might be preoccupied with the task at hand, but he was all too aware of Blythe. She was troubled, cautious, and rather prickly to begin with, but there was something about this chamber that added new levels of tension to her bearing. He'd noticed it before, but as the door swung shut with a soft click behind him, her shoulders seemed to lift.

Perhaps it was being in close confines with him that bothered her. He shrugged away the disappointment as he set their books aside. Sparring with Blythe could quickly become one of the highlights of his day. He found their conversations invigorating. Sadly, Blythe didn't appear to feel the same about their interactions.

He studied the shelves. "Which ones have you read?" He gestured to the wall of dusty volumes before them, keeping his voice low for fear of being overheard in the adjoining rooms.

"Not many," she replied softly. "I've been looking at the lower shelves, the ones within easy reach."

When she swallowed and curled her arms about herself, Tobias grew even more concerned. Something truly had upset her today. Perhaps it was the mess they'd viewed upstairs. But he'd thought, out on the lawn, that she was over the discomfort of that gruesome scene. She'd seemed full of glorious fire before, but now those brief sparks were gone.

"What's the matter, B?"

She shivered, eyes darting about the chamber—to the ceiling, the door, and back to him. Her skin had paled, her eyes widened. She stared at the door again. "I don't like this room. Mercy usually leaves the door open for me, so I can get out again."

Tobias winced. Fear of blood and confined spaces. Blythe's nerves were a mess. "I didn't know that. But the door can be reopened at any time." He slid his fingers around her upper arm and applied gentle pressure. "Would you like to step out again?"

She nodded quickly. "I'll get a book first, and then read it in the other room."

A ragged exhalation left her mouth as she perused the shelves beside them. Tobias kept hold of her arm and, when she picked up a book, he saw the tremble in her hands. He changed his grip, slid his arm about her waist and drew her against his chest. "You're safe with me. You're safe, B."

A deep shudder ran through her, and he took the book from her unresisting grip and guided her toward the door. She needed to get out, now. The poor woman should have told him of her fear of confined spaces earlier. He felt something similar for carriages. He'd rather walk ten miles with sore feet than step into one.

As he set his fingers to the lock, voices in the adjoining chamber stilled him. Damn and blast! Wilcox.

Tobias held Blythe tighter against him, away from the mechanism, and set his eye to the peep-hole.

Not just Wilcox, but the housekeeper and two footmen and maids were giving the chamber a thorough cleaning. Tobias cursed under his breath. Where were Leopold and the duchess? They were trapped in here until they returned and shooed the servants away.

He glanced down at Blythe. She still trembled with fear, her hand clutching at his arm about her waist. He leaned down so his lips were beside her ear. "Servants. We have to wait a bit."

She turned in his arms and gripped his waistcoat. A small moan escaped her lips and, worried that further sounds might be overheard, he shuffled them to the rear of the chamber. He had to calm Blythe down, and fast.

Tobias drew her tighter into his arms. She didn't protest. He thought she may not even be aware of his actions. Her breathing grew ragged, and she clutched him harder.

Very gently, Tobias lifted her chin and cupped her face with one hand. Her expression was usually so perfect and serene, but now her eyes were swimming with panic. They couldn't risk discovery. Desperate, he did the only thing he could think of.

He set his lips to hers and kissed her.

At first, she stilled, like that moment in battle just before cannonballs smashed the ship apart as if it were made of paper and not wood. He brushed his lips against hers lightly, fully aware that if she were in her right mind, she'd clobber him with whatever fell to hand for taking such liberties. Her lips were soft, cool against his. She didn't pull away or protest.

Emboldened, he teased her mouth open and sealed his lips over hers.

After a moment, her arms curled around his neck and she kissed him back, tongue sliding into his mouth in an intimate dance.

She'd forgotten to be scared. She'd forgotten to be proper. She'd forgotten everything except sensations—and damned if Tobias didn't revel in the change in her.

He smoothed his hands up her back and slid them down again. Devil take it, she felt good in his arms. Too good…as he'd suspected she would. Although tempted to take things further, he forced his hands to be still again.

She moaned a little against his mouth, and he tightened his grip at her waist. It might be the right thing to do, but Tobias didn't want to stop kissing Blythe. She responded to him with extraordinary passion. But he had to stop. He'd kissed Blythe to calm her, to distract her from the sensation of being trapped. If he'd succeeded, then he really should end this before it went too far.

Reluctantly, he drew away. Their eyes met, and a bright wash of color flooded her face. She backed up a step, and then more, until she leaned against the far wall of the chamber. Tobias remained still, uncertain what she would do next.

Her hand rose to cover her flushed lips as she stared at him. Her eyes widened impossibly and then squeezed shut.

He'd have to consider his distraction a success. Her gaze no longer darted about the chamber. Now, she couldn't bear to look at anything.

He picked a book at random from an upper shelf and settled against the edge of the table to read it. After a few moments of silence, Blythe followed suit, taking the chair beside him and flicking open to the first page. She didn't appear inclined to berate him about that kiss, but she did seem a great deal calmer.

He smiled. At least he could put his love of kissing to good use for a worthy cause. He'd be more than happy to kiss her again if the ideal situation arose.

Chapter Eight

If the world ended tomorrow, it couldn't come soon enough. Blythe could not believe that she had just been kissed by Tobias Randall—and that she'd actually enjoyed the exchange.

She pressed her knees together, fighting her arousal. Where had her mind been?

She stole a glance at the man beside her. Tobias appeared relaxed enough to lean against the table, flipping idly through his book. There was no trace of lust about him; he ignored her presence as if he hadn't had his tongue in her mouth or his hands all over her body just moments before. Did he go around kissing women as if such an act meant nothing to him at all?

To Blythe, it was the ultimate betrayal of her wedding vows. The very first time she had wanted another man to keep kissing her, instead of wishing for her husband, Raphael. She longed to run from what she'd just done, but the servants were still rattling around outside the doorway in the drawing room, and she was trapped with Tobias Randall.

Yet the sense of terror this room usually provoked had fled. And all because the pirate had kissed her witless. His warmth had filled her chilled soul until she'd forgotten everything except the feel of him against her body, his hands cradling her against his broad chest.

She shook her head. What a mistake to have made.

Tobias leaned toward her. "I'll check and see if they are done."

His words were whispered close against her ear, and gooseflesh raced across her skin. A bad sign. A very bad condition to be in for a proper lady.

With Tobias across the chamber peering through the peep-hole, she relaxed marginally and dropped her head into her hands. Stupid, ridiculous thing to have done. Tobias Randall wasn't the kind of man who she should be affected by at all.

She jumped as his hand settled on the back of her neck. Warmth radiated from his fingers as he brushed them over her nape, turning up the flames of her embarrassment. She was well aware that she had not once tried to end the kiss.

His fingers kneaded her skin for a few moments, and that was all it took for longing to return in full force. She fought to remain still and show no sign of her discomfort.

His lips skimmed her ear. "Unfortunately, they are being very thorough with their duties today. I wonder what's come over them."

She leaned into his touch, but then straightened her spine. What was she doing, encouraging him to continue? She should be putting him in his place and maintaining a proper distance between them.

Tobias crouched beside the chair. Their eyes met and held. His appeared to glow in the half light. "When we get you out of here, I will stand still for any punishments you'd care to inflict," he whispered. "But until then, don't brush aside the comfort you need to remain calm in this place."

His fingertips brushed over her cheek; his gaze fell to her lips. Blythe pressed them together lest she ask him to kiss her again. The corner of his mouth lifted as if he understood what her action meant. The pad of his thumb skimmed forward, touching her with brazen purpose. She parted her lips as need, unfamiliar and unwanted, flooded her again. She closed her eyes to block out the image of him sitting at her feet in wait of an invitation to another kiss.

He was certainly willing. His breath roughened to a pant; his hand settled on her leg, but did not wander any higher. He was poised for more if she gave him one word of encouragement.

Blythe kept herself rigidly in place.

He was nothing like her late husband. Thinking of the life she'd shared with Raphael, the tenderness of the marriage bed, the symmetry of their thoughts, doused Blythe's impossible attraction to Tobias Randall.

She was Raphael's widow.

That was enough.

Tobias withdrew his hands from her body and heaved a heavy sigh. When he stood without saying a word, Blythe missed his warmth immediately. But it was for the best. She shouldn't encourage him when there was no possibility for more between them. She was not a loose woman and would never take a casual lover.

She focused on the page before her, but her mind lingered on the comfort he'd given her. She must truly be mad to want Tobias Randall to touch her again. He was everything Raphael was not. Rude, unrefined, bold in expressing his desires for pleasure.

After this, he would certainly expect more than kisses if they were alone. She'd have to keep her door locked and avoid him at all costs.

Sadness filled her. She missed Raphael fiercely, but she was also angry with him for dying so soon. The best life had to offer had already passed her by. She hadn't known what she'd had until he was gone…and Tobias Randall had reminded her with one simple kiss.

Tobias withdrew his eye from the peep-hole. Leopold and Mercy had returned; the servants were finally gone. He faced Blythe. She still refused to look at him and guilt trickled through him. She acted as if she'd never been kissed before, but that couldn't be possible. No man married to her could resist those lips. Had she truly remained untouched since her husband's death?

He moved across the room slowly and crouched down beside her chair. "The servants are gone. Mercy and Leopold are seated in the drawing room."

A bright blush crossed her cheeks.

He set his hand to the arm of the chair. "Find me later tonight. I'll leave my door unlocked."

She jerked at his words. Her eyes were wide, her lips parted.

Devil take it! He wanted to kiss her again, but all he would get tonight was a slap across the face for his behavior.

Or would he? She had kissed him back quite enthusiastically.

Her gaze dipped to his lips. He wet them, and Blythe swallowed. Was she uncomfortable with his proximity or tempted by it? There was one certain way to tell.

But, as he moved closer to kiss her again, Blythe jumped to her feet and hurried for the door. She manipulated the lock and pushed the door open. Bright light filled the room and blinded him as Blythe disappeared.

Tobias hauled himself to his feet and picked up his book. No point following too closely on her heels. Blythe's reaction confirmed what he should have known—he should stay away from proper ladies. They wanted wealthy lords, not penniless lovers.

When he returned to the drawing room, Leopold sat alone, reading a newssheet. ""Find anything new?"

"No, nothing," Tobias said quickly. Nothing except a completely impossible desire to be exceptionally badly behaved around Blythe.

Leopold grunted and dropped the paper. "The old bastard must be laughing at us as we scratch around for clues."

Tobias shook his head. "I doubt it. He didn't know how to laugh."

The corners of Leopold's lips lifted in an evil smile. "Very true."

Perhaps now would be a good time to speak to Leopold about the future. Tobias took the seat opposite. "What do you intend to do about Harrowdale?"

His brother's expression grew wary at the mention of their childhood home. "Nothing, why?" The small estate was Leopold's legal property, but Tobias had come to the conclusion that his brother would never live there.

"I've given the matter considerable thought, and I'd like to live at Harrowdale."

Leopold stirred himself to sit at the edge of his chair. "I had hoped you would stay here a lot longer before you made any decisions about this sort of thing."

Tobias looked about him. "I don't belong here amid all this finery. I want to go home."

"When?"

"Not yet, not with Romsey still plagued by troubles, but I want the matter settled between us now, before the wedding business raises its head and distracts you. It's not so far away that we won't see each other often."

Leopold cleared his throat. "I'd just gotten used to seeing you over breakfast."

Tobias smiled. "You'll be a married man soon. I doubt you'll regret missing me at breakfast if you can have your wife instead. Newlyweds will want privacy."

Leopold's wry chuckle eased Tobias' concerns. He'd picked the perfect time to ask.

"Oh, all right. The house is yours to live in until you tire of living there alone. Then I want you to come back. I've not quite gotten enough of your company, but I do understand. We'll work something out about the servants later." His gaze grew sly. "Or is it you who needs the privacy. I know you said you had no interest in Miss Emma Trimble, but has another caught your eye?"

"No. There is no one." The only woman to tempt him was living under this roof. Leaving would spare him the frustration of wanting, and Blythe the embarrassment of being chased.

"A family of your own is just the thing for you," Leopold said suddenly.

Tobias shrugged. "Being born a Randall hasn't done me any good. I'm not keen to inflict suffering on an offspring."

"Things are different now."

Tobias set his hands to his hips and glared at his brother. "Really. So there is no danger to be found here? None at all?"

Leopold scowled. "You know full well what I mean. The old duke is gone, and our side of the family will be safe once we find them."

"How can you be so sure?"

"I am sure of it." Leopold picked up his paper. "Oh, and by the way, I just heard Lady Venables intends to leave us today. Despite her promises to Mercy, she must have had the same need to get away from the wedding plans as you."

"What?" Devil take it! He hadn't meant to scare her away. "Why? What did you say to her?"

Leopold shook out the paper. "I said nothing. She had a letter just now, she said, and is returning to Walden Hall immediately."

Damn it. Leopold might not be worried about the situation, but Tobias was. Letter or not, he was likely to blame for Blythe's hasty decision to leave Romsey Abbey. "What was the letter about?"

Leopold's shoulders lifted as he shrugged. "I have no idea. Lady Venables does not share the contents of her correspondence with me.

She simply said she had to go, and rushed out. She may have told Mercy."

Damn. Tobias hoped Blythe did not confide the details of that kiss to Mercy. Mercy would inform Leopold, and then Tobias' life expectancy would take a downward turn again. He should be used to that feeling, but after weeks at home, he'd become somewhat optimistic about his future. He was now certain he had a life worth hanging on to.

He shoved his book under the cushion of the nearest chair and strode out into the entrance hall. Voices carried to him from the front stairs, and he wrenched the door open just as an enclosed carriage drew to a halt.

Blythe embraced her sister without a word, and then climbed inside.

Mercy leaned close to the carriage window to speak, but Tobias still heard, "Blythe, it may not be as bad as you fear. I'll make him apologize if necessary."

Damn and blast, he had driven her away.

"No, it will be worse. Walden Hall," Blythe called to the driver. The carriage moved off, and within moments, Blythe was gone without a backward glance.

Mercy trudged up the stairs, her brows drawn together. "Foolishness," she muttered. When she saw him, her frown grew.

Tobias swallowed nervously. Maybe he could smooth the situation over before Leopold ever learned of his indiscretion and changed his mind about letting him live at Harrowdale. "Is there a problem?"

"Yes, but it is nothing any of us can help with." She smiled. "Were you looking for me?"

Blythe hadn't told her.

"Ah, yes," Tobias stuttered as he scrambled for something to account for his presence on the front steps. He'd come to speak with Blythe and reassure her that he wouldn't impose on her, but he'd been too late to prevent her leaving. "I was curious about supper tonight. What time are we dining?"

"Eight, as always. Why?"

Eight would give him ample time to fix things with Blythe

without Leopold being any the wiser. "Wonderful. I, ah, thought I might take a walk in the woods. Stretch my legs, that sort of thing."

Mercy tilted her head to the side. "I had a feeling that you were still uneasy about living here. Are we simply boring you instead, Tobias?"

He laughed. Tobias did like her direct approach. "Having the freedom to come and go appeals to me. I am not a man to sit still for long. I need to expend some energy in the outdoors." He leaned toward her. "And besides, Leopold may have a heart seizure if he catches me scaling the walls of the abbey again, so I had better do something else instead. Walking the estate seemed an appropriately harmless exercise."

"He's not alone in being terrified of your fearlessness," Mercy grumbled. "It is a dangerous thing you do, even if you say it is fun."

"I wouldn't climb if I had any doubts I could get back down safely again."

Mercy poked her fingertip into his chest. "I will hold you to that, Tobias Randall. Where are you going to be strolling to? Leopold will want to know."

Tobias ducked back out of her reach and waved his arm in the direction of Harrowdale. "That way, I think."

"To your former home?"

He nodded again. That wasn't really where he was going to go right now, and he hoped she didn't suggest Leopold join him.

Thankfully, she only patted his arm. "Enjoy your walk. Don't be too late to return or Leopold will worry unnecessarily."

Mercy stepped back into the abbey and, after a long, assessing stare from Wilcox, the main door closed. Again, the butler's behavior gave Tobias a bad feeling. For a moment, he was tempted not to go at all. However, he could not leave things as they were with Blythe and be easy.

Tobias rocked on the spot, letting the sun warm his face, and then set out in the direction of his former home to fool everyone at the Abbey into thinking that was his destination.

The gardens closest to the abbey were deserted at this time of day, and he enjoyed the solitude of his walk through the neatly clipped lawn. But, once he was out of sight of the abbey, and in a wilder part of the estate, he changed direction and increased his pace until he was running.

He was going to follow Blythe home and convince her to return to the abbey. He'd even get down on his knees to apologize all over again if it was required.

Chapter Nine

So much to do and so little time. Blythe whirled into her son's bedchamber at Walden Hall and grabbed up everything that had been dear to him. Why couldn't she be left in peace with her memories?

Her stepson, Aubrey, was coming to Walden Hall. He would be here for the entire winter season soon. She was to prepare the house for his arrival, and the arrival of a number of his friends. Unsavory friends, more than likely.

Blythe cursed under her breath at the inconvenience. She could bear her stepson sleeping in her husband's bed and not bat an eye. It was his right to do so, she knew. But she didn't want his wild friends breaking the few things that Adam had loved most in his short life and carousing until all hours. There was always some to-do between them, fueled by over-imbibing, and the inevitable rumpus disturbed her.

She set her hands to the bedpost and held on. As stepmother, she'd not been warmly received by her husband's firstborn son. Her husband's efforts to extract a promise from Aubrey to care for her, on his death bed no less, had been grudgingly given. Aubrey, a handful of years younger than Blythe, had made it plain he resented the burden of supporting his father's second wife.

Thank goodness her housekeeper, Mrs. Finch, had the wits to forward the delayed note to Romsey Abbey immediately. Blythe did not like surprise visitors.

She pulled the counterpane she'd stitched from the bed and folded it carefully.

Mrs. Finch took it from her. "I'll take that for you, my lady. Just place everything you want packed away on the end of the bed and I'll store them neatly. There's still plenty of time."

Blythe glanced about her with dismay. "I shouldn't keep doing this, should I?"

"You may do this as many times as you wish, my lady. We all miss him, and none of us want to see his things misused." The housekeeper's words reassured her that at least one person in the household understood her love for her son had never eased with his last breath.

Blythe nodded, grateful that her obsession did not concern her staff. She just couldn't bear to pack everything away forever as if he'd never existed.

"If I may ask a question, my lady. The last time his lordship was here, he was peeking into the storerooms and attic and took what he pleased home with him. What should I do with young Master Adam's things this time?"

"There is always my bedchamber." Blythe shook her head immediately as she remembered she would move to the rear of the house, to a lesser chamber—one above the kitchens, to keep his guests' noises from disturbing her rest at night.

The housekeeper set down her bundle. "There's not going to be much room."

Blythe fretted. What other option was there? If she removed Adam's possessions to Romsey, her sister would discover just how difficult her stepson was becoming. Mercy had troubles enough without Blythe alerting her to more.

There truly was too much to hide, but she especially wanted the rocking horse hidden. She moved to it and gave it a little push. Adam had loved rocking on the wooden beast, calling "faster, Mama, faster," over his whoops of joy. Her eyes filled with tears and she brushed them aside. She couldn't fall into a blue mood now. Time was of the essence.

She glanced out the window to judge the time of day. She still had hours till nightfall, but tomorrow Venables would be here and would undoubtedly make her life difficult.

Her gaze sharpened as she detected movement in the neat orchard beside the house.

Tobias Randall pushed off from a tree and set his hands to his hips as he stared up at her.

At her side, the housekeeper gasped. "Goodness, who could that be?"

Blythe scowled. "That, unfortunately, is Mr. Tobias Randall, of Romsey Abbey. I'd better go see what he wants and send him on his way again." What was he doing here now, of all times? She didn't have the time or the inclination to deal with him.

The housekeeper leaned closer to the glass pane. "That's not a man most women would give their marching orders to. I don't blame you for lingering at Romsey Abbey these weeks now. If I were a few years younger, I'd make a fool of myself over him, that's for sure."

Blythe glanced at the housekeeper. "Please don't let him hear you say that. He's conceited enough without receiving additional flattery."

"I bet he is." The housekeeper sighed. "I bet he's broken more than a few hearts in his time." The housekeeper lifted her hands to her hair and smoothed the loose gray wisps against her head.

Good grief, this was impossible. "I'll return directly." Blythe hurried down the stairs and stepped out through a side door closest to the orchard. Tobias was waiting, dressed exactly as she'd last seen him. Did he not possess a hat to cover his head or gloves for when he made calls?

"You left in a hurry," he said without preamble.

"I have much to do here."

His brows drew together. "About kissing you. You do know I didn't mean any disrespect, don't you? I just wanted to distract you from your location and calm your nerves. You didn't need to leave. If anything, I should be the one to do that. I apologize if I have given offense with my actions."

Blythe shook her head. "I haven't given the matter another thought. As I said, I have much to do here and cannot spend the time conversing with you about an inconsequential matter."

A loud crash rang out from the house, and she winced.

Tobias stepped closer. "What's going on, B?"

She sighed. If she explained properly, maybe he'd go away quicker. "Oh, you are a truly interruptive man. Very well. My stepson is coming to Walden Hall. He's also invited some of his unsavory friends this time, but his note was delayed in the mail. They arrive tomorrow, and I must have everything ready in time."

His face lifted toward the house as another thud reached them. "What exactly are your servants doing in there?"

Oh, botheration. "Why can't you just go away?" She didn't want anyone to know that she hid her possessions. It was humiliating.

A wicked grin spread across his face. "Because I find puzzles interesting, and you do puzzle me."

Blythe threw her hands in the air and stormed off. "Can you ever be serious? Good day, Mr. Randall."

"Wait, B. I'm sorry. I shouldn't have teased." He ran ahead of her and blocked her retreat. "Could you use some help to prepare for your visitors? I have nothing else to do today."

She stopped to think. He was a strong man, and he seemed to be somewhat eager to make amends for the kiss. Perhaps he could be put to use by her housekeeper and groom to take the rocking horse to safety without mentioning the incident to Mercy. Perhaps one of the outbuildings could be used, if the rocking horse was hidden well. "All right, but your being here must be kept a secret. I do not want any gossip."

"I have no intention of causing you distress, B, but I do feel like I just won at cards." His slow grin and the warmth burning in his eyes caused her stomach to tremble.

Perhaps asking for his help wasn't such a good idea after all. She couldn't worry about what he might do next and still get everything done in half a day. She assumed her haughtiest expression. "Don't feel too happy. I have a task that requires heavy lifting."

"Well, whatever I can do to make up for this morning, I'll do it gladly."

How funny that Tobias appeared contrite. Finally. He was the last person she'd expected to receive assistance from.

Although she had her reservations, she led him into the house, introduced him to her fluttering and blushing housekeeper, and showed him upstairs to Adam's room. She waved her hand at the rocking horse. "This and a few of the larger things need to be moved to a place they cannot be discovered and accidentally broken."

Instead of approaching the rocking horse, Tobias turned in a slow circle and looked about him. When his circuit ended, they faced each other. "This was your son's room."

Blythe swallowed. "Yes."

His gaze switched to the tall screen in the corner. Murals covered every inch: wild woods, calm seas, and towering castles. She'd had a great deal of fun decorating the piece for her son while he slept.

Tobias cleared his throat suddenly. "I think I mentioned that your husband had been a lucky man, but I think Adam lucky, too. This must have taken quite a while."

Blythe touched the edge of the screen, and then traced the path through the painted woods with her fingertips. "I had the time."

He stepped up behind her. He put his hands on her arms, causing gooseflesh to rise on her skin. "You did this yourself? I had no idea you were so talented."

Heat swept over Blythe's cheeks as she blushed at the compliment. "My stepson will wish this room prepared for one of his friends. I've learned the hard way that they have little respect for anything when deep in their cups, including me." She added the last part quietly before she thought better of her confession.

He turned her about until she faced him. A thunderous scowl on his features. "You stay here and are imposed upon?"

She shrugged. "It gets a little worse each time. So far, I have been fortunate to possess a stout door and lock."

Tobias nudged her chin so she had to look at him. "You haven't mentioned any of this to your sister, have you?"

"Aubrey has every right to come here. What could Mercy do?"

"I can think of a few things," Tobias muttered coldly. "Come on, I know the perfect place. However, it is far from here. Do you possess a wagon?"

Blythe nodded.

"Good." He moved past her, juggling the heavy rocking chair under his arm as if it weighed nothing.

"Be careful," she warned.

"Never fear. I've never dropped precious cargo before. I don't intend to start now."

Tobias wiped the sweat from his brow and then tested the ropes one last time. Everything Blythe wished protected was lashed to the wagon and ready for transportation. He just couldn't quite decide why he was freely offering her possessions sanctuary. Perhaps it was the things she would not say against her stepson that had caused him to act as he did.

A beautiful woman, a widow, should not be so anxious about her family coming to visit.

He came about, wondering where she was. He hadn't lain eyes on Blythe for some time. He hoped she wasn't hiding from him now that everything was settled for the temporary move.

The housekeeper bustled out with one last wrapped package and slipped it into a narrow gap between the legs of a child's chair. "That's everything."

Tobias nodded. "Good. We'll return with the wagon shortly."

"Oh, no, no, no. I'm not going to be left here, wondering where you're taking her ladyship's belongings. I'm coming with you to see them properly installed. Besides," her lips curved into a warm smile, "my mistress requires a chaperone if she's to go anywhere with a man like you."

Tobias' mouth dropped open. "I'm not... She's perfectly safe."

"Balderdash. A good-looking man like you, she'd be putty in your hands. No, I'm going with her. And that, sir, is final."

Tobias raked his fingers through his hair. While protecting Blythe's reputation was certainly a good idea, being saddled with the inquisitive housekeeper was not. She'd been peppering him with questions all afternoon, and he'd begun to feel a little hunted.

"Where might I find Lady Venables?"

The happy smile on the housekeepers face faded. "I'm sure she'll return shortly."

Tobias glanced about again. The gardens were deserted. "Where did she go?"

"I don't like to disturb her." The housekeeper and groom exchanged a long look. "You may as well know...she's gone to see her boy again."

Tobias should have anticipated that. And luckily, he did know exactly where Adam was laid to rest—on the far side of the house, hidden from sight. Since Blythe insisted on seeing where her possessions were to be stored, he strode off, skirting the house and heading into the woods. The burial plot wasn't far, and he caught sight of the headstones long before he saw Blythe. She crouched at the foot of a grave. He could just hear her talking.

Tobias scuffed his boot on the ground to let her know he was nearby, but waited at the boundary of the plots. This was how he'd seen her the first time, dressed in black and weeping over the two bodies buried here. Her husband and her son. He folded his arms across his chest while he waited.

After a time, she rose to her feet and moved to join him, wiping tears from her eyes. "You must think me foolish."

"No, I really don't." He shuffled uncomfortably. "Most people still living don't receive the love you so clearly show, even after all this time."

Her gaze flew to his. "Sometimes, I forget they are gone," she whispered.

He didn't quite know how to respond to her, so he placed his hand upon her shoulder and squeezed. "The wagon is ready."

She nodded, her eyes drifting to the crypt behind her.

Tobias gently slid his arm behind her back and urged her to come with him. After a few steps, she drew in a shuddering breath and drew herself upright again. Tobias dropped his arm and walked along at her side, puzzled by the compassion she stirred in him. If she wanted to mourn for her past, that was her prerogative, but he didn't think it healthy.

He glanced down at her.

She did puzzle him.

She annoyed him.

Yet her behavior stirred something in him that he was completely unused to experiencing around women. Protectiveness.

Blythe tugged on his sleeve. "Is that my housekeeper sitting on the back of the wagon bed?"

"Ah, yes." Tobias drew in a deep breath. "She insisted on coming with the furnishings."

"Whatever for? Adam's things are only going to be stored."

"That is exactly what I told her, but she wants to do the job herself, and she thinks you need a chaperone." He muttered the last part quickly as they reached the carriage. Blythe heard, and her gaze flew to his. What could he say to reassure her that a chaperone wasn't necessary except for keeping up appearances? Likely nothing.

He shrugged, caught her about the waist, and lifted her to the bench seat next to the groom. The feel of her tiny waist between his hands shook him to his bones.

Perhaps they did need a chaperone after all.

"Drive on," he called, and when the wagon rumbled off, he began walking toward his old home. Carriages, even wagons, forced a cold sweat to break out over his skin. Walking was much better for his disposition. He was already dreading the drive to the soiree tomorrow night, as he would be expected to sit inside a closed carriage. He hoped he could tolerate the cramped quarters without revealing his distress.

After perhaps a mile, Blythe turned on the seat, her eyes wide as she peered at him through the rising dust. He raised his hand and continued to enjoy the pleasant amble along the lane. The house was not far now, just over the next rise after the creek crossing. Despite the situation, he was eager to get there. At least he was on home soil at Harrowdale. He belonged there better than anywhere he'd ever been.

The wagon rumbled to a stop and Blythe jumped down. She shook out her skirts and, by the time he reached the wagon, she'd ordered the groom to continue on without her.

"What the devil do you think you're doing?"

She fiddled with the ribbons on her bonnet and removed it. "The wagon was not comfortable, and I would rather walk than endure it."

He glanced at the wagon and was rewarded with the housekeeper waving to him. So much for the chaperone. "Must you be so diffi-cult about everything? The hard bench of the wagon will seem like nothing once you have a muddy hem slapping round your ankles. There's a stream to cross shortly before we reach the house."

Her brow scrunched as if she hadn't known about the crossing when she'd jumped down. "I'll be fine," she muttered.

If she wanted sore feet then, so be it, but at the crossing, he'd toss her back up on the wagon again. "A fastidious lady like you? Water and likely mud up to your ankles? Don't be ridiculous. You'll hate every moment."

"Hmm, well, you may be right about that." Her hands fluttered then clenched at her waist. "Are you sure your brother will not object to our arrangement?"

"I don't plan to tell him. Besides, we spoke this morning about Harrowdale." Tobias tucked his hands behind his back. "It will be my home soon."

Chapter Ten

Blythe stumbled as her foot landed in a pothole in the lane. However, before she could fall, Tobias caught her against his side and kept her steady. "Thank you," she said quickly. But she couldn't bury her astonishment enough to not want answers from Tobias about his future plans. "When did you decide to leave Romsey?"

Tobias stared ahead, his expression serious. "I spoke to my brother about the matter this morning, but I've been considering my future accommodations for some time."

He had? "But why?"

He looked at her as if she were mad to question the decision. "We both know I do not belong as part of the duchess' circle. Moving to Harrowdale keeps me close enough to see my brother often, but far enough away not to be a daily embarrassment. You, of all people, should be happy about that."

Well, she didn't know if happy was the correct word, but his presence at Romsey Abbey, and their recent interactions, had caused her some distress. "You will cause a stir if you cannot keep your every thought from tumbling from your mouth."

Tobias laughed at her observation. "Exactly. I have no wish to cause problems for anyone. I should like to live here again." His arm lifted to point ahead.

Blythe shifted her attention as the wagon rolled through the stream and started up the curve of a long hill. In the distance, she could see a chimney and spire of a tall building perched on the other side of the rise. There was an untamed beauty about the landscape that reminded her very much of the man walking beside her. Tobias Randall belonged here amid the lush woods, rather than stuck inside Romsey. Watching him prowl the abbey was akin to watching a trapped animal with no hope of escape.

"Devil take it," Tobias cursed suddenly.

Blythe jumped and looked about her. What had happened while she'd been daydreaming? "Whatever is the matter now?"

He scowled at her and gestured to the empty lane. "Your groom didn't stop at the crossing to wait for you."

"Oh, is that all?" She winced. "I did tell him I would walk the rest of the way."

Tobias shook his head. "Do you realize I'm going to have to carry you across the damn stream?"

Oh, heavens. That likelihood had not occurred to her. There was a shallow crossing she remembered belatedly. Last time she'd passed this way on horseback, it had been ankle deep and hadn't caused any concern for her mount. Surely, it should only take a moment to help her across? If anyone was nearby, they would understand he was merely being gallant. She glanced about nervously, but they were completely alone now. Only the distant song of a thrush kept them company.

Tobias stopped at the edge of the water, his hands on his hips. Blythe joined him with a sinking heart. The stream was running perhaps as high as her knees this time, but much more swiftly. She didn't care for the idea of walking the rest of the way to Harrowdale in damp shoes and heavy, wet skirts, so she may have no choice but to allow him to carry her across.

She knelt to test the temperature of the water with one hand. Cold. She flicked the water from her fingertips as she stood again. "I do hate to inconvenience you."

Tobias wrapped his hand around her upper arm and tugged. "Come here, B."

Blythe had just enough time to gasp as Tobias hoisted her over his shoulder like a sack of produce. "What are you doing? Put me down!"

"Keeping you dry. It's deeper than it looks." He slapped his hand over her thigh to hold her steady and waded across the stream while she seethed. Water churned around his legs, indeed higher than Blythe had anticipated. She clung to his back when he wobbled on a rock, but eventually they reached the other side without either of them being pitched into the cold stream.

When Tobias dumped her on her feet again, she reached for him, suddenly unsteady after being flung about so roughly. He caught her fast against his side while she caught her breath. She'd not like to travel in such a fashion ever again. She'd make sure to stay on the wagon for the return trip to Walden Hall.

"Your housekeeper makes for a lousy chaperone. You're in my arms again."

Blythe licked her lips, her pulse pounding in her ears at the huskiness of his voice. "I've not needed a chaperone since before I married."

His breath tickled her ear. "Have you never even been courted since your husband's death? I'd have thought the fellows in these parts would be a dozen deep in your drawing room."

She shook her head, astonished that Tobias thought she could incite such behavior. "The gentlemen of my acquaintance have kept a respectful distance. Venables was well liked. None would dare approach me while I'm in mourning."

"Fools. Has no one even tried to steal a kiss since he passed?"

His hand slid around her back, and she turned in his arms. "No, no one." She set her hands to his chest, holding him at bay even when she wasn't sure she could. No one treated her as Tobias Randall did, and her body was betraying her sense of self-preservation.

"Hmm." Tobias caressed her back in a slow brush. "I imagine the frost can be off-putting to a weaker-willed man. They will never know what they missed."

Blythe looked up just as Tobias stepped away. She rocked forward, stunned by the loss of his attention and touch. She'd been so sure he was about to kiss her. Her heart hammered, disappointment making her cheeks burn hot.

Tobias leaned against a tree and struggled to free himself of one boot. It landed with a wet slosh on the grass, and he tipped the water out and shook it. "Damn things will chafe and hobble me if I walk in them wet. Forgive me, B, I've no choice but to be ungentlemanly and take them off here and now. At least we're on Randall property, and no one but you and your servants should see my latest indiscretion."

Blythe struggled to catch her breath while he stripped himself of his remaining footwear. For a moment—a very long, tempting moment—she had wanted Tobias to kiss her as he had that morning. She fought to bury her feeling of disappointment. He was all wrong for her. Blunt, crude and filled to overflowing with lust.

She closed her eyes. Yet, he was the only man she'd wanted to kiss since her husband. That shocked her completely.

Perhaps she truly had lost her mind.

Tobias wriggled his toes, glad to be free of the confining boots. He still hadn't become used to the new footwear, and wearing them wet was worse than wearing nothing at all. He ran his hand over the rough scars on his right ankle and grimaced. Hopefully, Blythe and her housekeeper would not notice them and become distressed. He did not want pity for the life he'd previously suffered through. Leopold's anxiety over his treatment had been bad enough.

He picked up his footwear and shook the water from them. Murphy would not be pleased with their condition. He hoped the fine boots were not ruined.

Blythe turned when he cleared his throat, but she didn't meet his gaze. Likely he'd overstepped again by almost kissing her. But at least he hadn't acted on the impulse this time. "The house is this way," he said, gesturing up the drive.

Blythe nodded and hurried ahead. It was her way, he'd discovered, to run from awkward situations, at least at first. When she'd worked out how to react, he'd undoubtedly be subjected to a lecture. And he'd deserve it, too. He was still waiting for her tirade over this morning's kiss.

As he trudged after her, he marveled at his predicament. Despite Leopold's lectures on propriety and gentlemanly behavior, he was not having much luck in avoiding situations where he and Blythe were alone. He was honestly attempting to be a gentleman where she was concerned. He did not want to cause her further distress. From what he saw, she'd had more than enough sorrow to last her a lifetime. He had not intentionally sought her out aside from his first night as a guest at Romsey. How strange that the woman who should despise him turned out to be the one person he was unwittingly drawn to.

The drive up to the house was rutted in places, so he lengthened his stride to reach her. She'd lifted her skirts with both hands, showing her sturdy, sensible half boots and shapely calves concealed by thick stockings. So prim and off-putting. He couldn't help but be intrigued by her. Her kisses were passionate, her behavior quite the opposite. She was the most confusing woman he'd ever met.

He slipped his hand beneath her elbow to steady her on the uneven ground. When he glanced at her face, her lips were set in a firm line as if she was holding back from blistering his ears. Oh, well. A proper scolding was long overdue. He wished she would get it over and done with. He didn't like to wait for unpleasantness.

When they reached the top of the rise, he dropped his hand. "Here we are."

Harrowdale waited silently before them. Its windows shuttered, vines creeping up the walls to the uppermost floors, leaves lying in a thick carpet where they'd fallen around the footings. His home had never been so quiet in his youth. There had always been someone calling out, someone tending the gardens, someone waiting to welcome him back. The emptiness made him uneasy.

"Oh," Blythe whispered. "It's lovely!"

He shrugged. "It is home. I'll go assist your groom with the unloading."

He left her and headed for the wagon waiting at the rear. When he neared, he tossed his boots into a patch of sunlit gravel in the courtyard. They'd dry eventually, but he could count on Murphy having a few words to say about the additional work. Another matter, another scolding, that couldn't be helped.

As he untied the ropes holding the rocking horse in place, he scanned the rear of the building. The house appeared exactly as he'd left it several weeks ago; neglected and overgrown. In time, he'd make the place the way he remembered. He'd be happy to have something useful to do with his days instead of snooping through the Duke of Romsey's papers in search of clues. But he did want to find Rosemary and Oliver before he established his own household here. He still had plenty of time.

The housekeeper approached, smiling as if she'd just been given an extra holiday. "If you'll be so good to give me the key, Mr. Randall, I'll open the house."

"No key. But I'll open the house momentarily." He lifted Blythe's precious rocking horse down carefully and gave it a little push. The horse rocked to and fro smoothly. Any child would have adored it.

He laid his hand on the rocking horse's head, halting its progress as Blythe approached. Her gaze was clouded and sad again, and he cursed his foolishness. Grief was never far from her mind. He shouldn't do anything to remind her of her loss.

He stretched out his hand as he passed her. Their fingers brushed, sending a jolt of awareness through him.

He wanted her. Foolish as that wish might be, he wanted her in his bed. He wanted to see her happy.

Another foolish wish. He was always doing something to upset her. He should leave well enough alone.

He stretched to reach the first handhold high up the eastern wall of Harrowdale.

Blythe tugged on his coat, preventing his ascent. "What are you doing, Tobias?"

He looked over his shoulder in surprise. She'd not used his given name before. He'd expected she never would. However, there was no friendliness in her expression. Her brows had drawn together. Was she afraid for him? He eased her grip from his coattails. "Don't worry, my lady. I've managed this feat many a time."

"But you were a boy then?"

He shook his head. "There's no danger. I've done this since my return. Where do you think I lived before we met in the flesh? I lived here, not in the woods like a wild beast."

"I never implied any such thing."

"No, you didn't have to. Step back now."

When she retreated a few steps, he set his toe to the first depression in the stone wall and climbed up to the second floor window, much more easily than he'd done as a boy. He hooked his fingers into the small gap under the sash window and hoisted it up. Cold air covered his skin as he threw his leg over the sill and squeezed himself through the narrow opening. He might be getting a touch too big for that particular window, but it was the only one with a faulty latch.

He glanced down. Blythe had covered her mouth with her hands, eyes wide with fear. He waved to show he was fine, and then padded through the silent house, down the creaking staircase, and through to the rear kitchen door, where she waited. He jiggled the door until the bolt slid free of its casing and opened it wide.

Blythe's expression was severe. "I think that is enough climbing, Mr. Randall." She set her hands to her hips. "I should not like to see you do that again as long as I live, so please do use a key next time."

"My heart's beating ever so fast," the housekeeper gushed. "'Tis too dangerous!"

He grinned at their fears. "Nonsense. I find the activity exhilarating." If they had seen him hanging from the rigging of the whaler in a frigid gale, then they'd have something to be terrified of.

"Well, I think it's the stupidest thing," the groom muttered. He lifted his hand, twirled a key between his fingers, and then handed it over.

"Well, I'll be damned. Where was that?"

He pointed to a garden bed where a rock had been overturned before doffing his hat and returning to the wagon to begin the unloading without him.

"Well, that's a happy surprise. No more climbing." Tobias swept his hand toward the interior. "Ladies, welcome to Harrowdale. Mind the dust doesn't make you sneeze. Unfortunately, there's a lot of it."

The housekeeper stepped over the threshold, plucked the key from his fingers, and peered about. She sniffed the air, and then sneezed. "The place needs a woman's touch and a good airing," she said as she wiped her eyes.

"It does," he agreed. "If you'll follow me, I'll show you to the empty chamber you can use."

Without waiting, Tobias hurried up the narrow staircase and gestured down the hall. He directed the housekeeper toward the old empty chamber, once Harrowdale's nursery, and left her there.

When he returned downstairs, Blythe was peeking into the rooms on the lower floor. She stopped next to one of the chairs he'd uncovered. The rose pink tapestry had faded with time and the light from the adjacent window, but the design was still clear enough to be pretty. Uncovering his mother's favorite chair had been a particularly hard task, and even now his throat worked to choke him.

Blythe set her hand to the material, eyebrow raised in query.

"My mother used to watch for our return from that spot. I should help your man with the unloading. Excuse me." Tobias hurried away before he blubbered like the boy he had been on his first night away from home and family. He hadn't time now for embarrassing sentimentality.

Together, he and the groom unloaded the wagon, carting Blythe's possessions upstairs, but he rarely caught sight of her again. He didn't mind her exploring his home or avoiding him. If she satisfied her curiosity without asking him questions, he would feel all the better for it.

When the last of the bundles were deposited upstairs, the housekeeper waved him out of the overflowing chamber. "I brought a bite to eat. Would you care for it inside or out, sir?"

Tobias frowned. "Out, I think, to avoid the dust."

She nodded and handed him a blanket. "I'll come and find you when it's done. Can you send the groom to me? I'll need some help with the fire and such to get the tea ready."

"Surely tea is unnecessary. Shouldn't Lady Venables be getting back to Walden Hall to complete her preparations?"

"Oh, no, no, no. Everything is done now for his lordship's arrival. It was just Master Adam's things to take care of. Now that is all done, she'll be wanting a nice cup of tea to relax with. These visits of his do put her in a queer mood. Not that I blame her."

Tobias leaned against the wall, intrigued by the housekeeper's remark. "Is Lord Venables really so difficult?"

The housekeeper nodded. "He's particularly bossy, nothing like his father. He's always asking her to account for her spending, and any time she visits with her sister or away from Walden Hall." Her lips pressed together guiltily at her gossiping, and then she bustled past him and disappeared into the kitchen.

Well, at least that confirmed why Blythe had rushed off today. She'd want to have her affairs in order and be as prepared as possible before such a man arrived. He couldn't imagine a woman of her caliber enjoying an interrogation of how she lived her life. Perhaps she wasn't too mad about the kiss after all. Maybe she hadn't given the matter another thought, as indeed she'd claimed.

His chest tightened. A pity. He couldn't get their kiss out of his mind. Could he have kissed her at the stream without her protesting?

He grinned; maybe fate would give him another chance to find out.

He wandered from the house, sent the groom inside to the kitchen then crossed the courtyard to check on his boots. Far too wet to wear yet, and his stockings were still damp. He spread them out again and headed for a protected spot to spread the blanket.

Seeing servants at Harrowdale made his heart race as memories of his childhood rose restlessly. There had been a gardener then, too. An old man, deeply attached to Harrowdale's fruit trees and flower beds. Three maids, a butler, and two stable hands for their two horses and the old gray pony he'd learned to ride on.

His father had been fortunate to have had ample means to support the property and his family, but they hadn't been wealthy by any stretch of the imagination.

Tobias set his arms on the top of his raised knees. He'd been happy then, and painfully ignorant of the dangerous undercurrent of hostility emanating from the Duke of Romsey. He knew now how fortunate he'd been back then. At least then, someone had cared where he was, what he'd eaten that day, and whether he'd slept well that night. Those small reminders that he'd once been loved unconditionally rose to choke him. He lowered his head to his arms and fought the urge to weep over his lost innocence.

Light footsteps approached, but he didn't raise his head. He couldn't. Not until he was in control of his emotions better. The long skirts of Blythe's dark blue gown brushed across his bare feet as she adjusted the blanket. When she sat, she was close enough for him to see her hand where it lay in her lap.

"You have a wonderful home. So peaceful."

He didn't answer her. His home had once been a noisy affair. The silence unnerved him.

Blythe sighed. "Thank you for allowing me to use your home, Tobias. You are a very generous man."

He lifted his head. Blythe stared at the house, her expression relaxed but weary. He much preferred her smiling. He lifted his hand to brush his fingers across her cheek. "Please don't let that information be passed around, or else I'll be overrun by ladies with questionable relatives."

She leaned into his touch. "Being known for generosity is an accomplishment for a gentleman," she sighed, and sat up straight once more. "Unfortunately, I cannot tell anyone of the service you've rendered me today. The gossip would be quite awful and it could reach Venables' ears. He would demand Adam's things returned to his questionable keeping."

Tobias dropped his hand. "He can try."

She twisted to face him, knees drawing up beneath her skirts. "He would be within his rights. But at least Mercy is spared any involvement in my problems."

He shook his head. This woman was always trying to avoid creating a fuss. "But it isn't a decent thing to do to you. I'll bear the brunt, should it become known. Being accused of theft shouldn't surprise anyone."

"It would surprise anyone who knows you."

Tobias chuckled. "Careful, B. You're encouraging me again without meaning to."

She dropped her gaze to the grass between them. Devil take it! When she didn't contradict his observation, he was very encouraged.

Her hand lifted from the ground, and then she touched his ankle, right where the worst of his scars were.

Tobias quickly tucked his unsightly scars under his other thigh, out of sight again, his pulse racing.

"You suffered greatly at the duke's hands, didn't you?"

More than he cared to let on. Life aboard the East India Company ship the old duke had sent him to, the Williamstown, hadn't been easy. The short-lived capture by the French a brief reprieve. But service on the Williamstown paled in comparison to the horror of service aboard the slaver, Enid Wren. The slaver captain had been a truly vicious man and had demanded immediate obedience from his crew. At first, Tobias hadn't been quick enough.

He shrugged to shake off his sudden unease. "'Tis not a discussion for a lady to hear, B. I won't distress you by relating the tale."

Blythe didn't need to know the truth of the matter. He'd healed and, if given enough time, he may even begin to forget the painful bite of leather beating across his bare skin and shackles around his ankles. The duke was gone, and he was the only one Tobias could have taken revenge on. The time for seeking retribution was over. He had to put the past behind him. He would when Rosemary and Oliver were found. If they were ever recovered.

Blythe's fingers clenched together. "How did you get the scars on your back?"

He tensed in shock. He'd no idea how she'd learned of them, or why she would bring them up. "I trusted the wrong person and paid the price."

"Do they hurt at all?"

Tobias ground his jaw. He didn't want to discuss them, least of all with Blythe. He stood. "Excuse me. I should go and see what is keeping your housekeeper."

Chapter Eleven

"Wait, Toby." Blythe grabbed his ankle to stop him leaving. She should not have brought up what must be a painful matter for him. She couldn't understand why she'd asked. But the rough, imperfect skin beneath her fingers caused her heart to skip a beat. He'd endured so much that she was embarrassed by her behavior. Who was she to lecture him about how to live his life when he'd been lucky to survive to have one? "I'm sorry for prying. Please sit down. Look, the tea is coming, and Finch has gone to so much trouble today that I would hate to disappoint her by quarrelling with you."

He hesitated, and then wrenched his ankle from her grip. Blythe rubbed her hands together, but she could still feel the uneven bumps and roughness as if she was still touching him. When he sat cross-legged, he positioned himself a little farther away on the grass than he had previously been, his brows drawn together.

Finch set a tray between them with Tobias' help. "Such lovely amenities in the house," Finch gushed. "So sad to think everything has been boarded up for so long. It'll be nice to have everything used again."

Tobias gave her a wary smile, and when Finch hurried back to the house, he stared after her. "She does know that this arrangement to store your possessions here is temporary, doesn't she?"

"Of course she does. Finch is an excellent housekeeper. She'd never leave Walden Hall. In fact, I am certain that should my stepson attempt to replace her, then Finch would do something drastic to retain her position. She is very loyal to the Venables."

Blythe picked up a teacup and admired the pattern. The pretty design was unknown to her, so Finch must have investigated the contents of the house. She'd lifted the corners of enough sheets to know Harrowdale held many items of obviously fine quality to agree with Finch. It was a shame that no one had lived here recently to enjoy them. To see them hidden beneath covers was a sad waste. She hoped Tobias did not mind her servant's curiosity too greatly. Or hers.

When she peeked at Tobias, his gaze was fixed on the house; his expression remote and uninviting of further conversation. Rather than interrupt his musing, she prepared the tea, sweetening his with three spoonfuls of sugar, as she had noticed he liked it, and held out the cup and saucer for him to take. After a pause, he took the cup and left Blythe holding the saucer. "I should return to Romsey Abbey," he said suddenly.

She set his saucer on the blanket close to him, and picked up her own cup and saucer. "I know. Thank you for helping me yet again."

He drained his cup and set it down on the saucer with a loud clatter. "You should return to the abbey, too." He picked up a piece of Finch's fruit cake and bit into it. He appeared to relish the taste. When he picked up a second slice and ate it with the same gusto, Blythe bit back a smile. It was not hard to determine this man's moods in most situations. He was often transparent when he liked something.

"My place is at Walden Hall. My stepson will expect me to be in residence to greet his guests."

The groom hurried from the house and into an outbuilding, his arms full of white cloths. "Mercy needs you," Tobias said.

No one needed her. Not really. Blythe sighed as the truth of the situation struck her painfully. "She has Leopold, and he has taken over the place completely. He'll be her husband soon and will take care of her very well."

"Then come back for the young duke's sake. He enjoys the time and devotion that you bestow on him."

As much as she loved Edwin, he couldn't replace her son in her affections. It was better to remain his favorite aunt than an annoying fusspot who had to be endured. "My nephew is not the reason to return. He has a mother to love him, and soon a father to teach him to be a good man."

Tobias, having finished eating for the moment, stretched out on his side and faced her. "What about the attempts to drive your sister from the abbey? Do you not wonder who is behind it all?"

"Of course I wonder. Having been a suspect myself, I feel very annoyed by the situation." Blythe snorted. "But you've seen how helpful I've been on that score. I cannot even look at what was done without breaking out into a discomforting flush. As you said, the problems facing Mercy do not directly involve me. No. I'm just in the way at Romsey."

"You're not in my way."

Blythe blinked as his words caught her unprepared. She'd have thought, aside from losing a woman to torment, he'd be indifferent to what she did with her time.

"Come back to Romsey tonight," he pleaded. "I need you."

Her breath stuck in the back of her throat. Was he about to suggest something scandalous? She shifted, moving slightly away from him on the blanket and regarding him warily. "For what exactly do you need me?"

He traced the pattern on the blanket with his fingertip. He didn't look up. "You're clever. Cleverer by far than I could ever hope to be."

She frowned. "I am clever enough not to fall for your flattery. Why else should I return?

His shoulder lifted as he shrugged without looking at her. "My education ended when I was taken from my family and put onboard ship. I can bargain on the docks and fix a headsail to catch the best wind, but the finer nuances of society and family connections escape me. I believe you understand the old duke better than anyone. I need you to catch the things I miss. Two heads are better than one, and all that."

A flush of warmth swept up Blythe's neck to her cheeks. It was incredibly flattering to hear a grown man ask for assistance from a woman he barely knew. To have Tobias Randall insist she return to Romsey Abbey to help with the search for his family caused her pulse to race. "What about Leopold? He is head of your family, and very clever."

"Forgive me if I don't share your observation with him. He's opinionated enough now. I'd rather not add to his ego." Tobias kept his eyes focused on the ground. "The company I kept did not care that my cravat was perfectly tied, so I never learned about the niceties. He forgets that I didn't have his advantages in life."

Impulsively, Blythe leaned across the empty space between them and placed her hand over his. When he didn't pull away, she squeezed. "Brothers can be impatient. My own is equally annoying at times, and I find it best to humor him when such moods afflict him."

Tobias turned his hand, shifting his until they were palm to palm. "I'm unused to my brother after so long away." His long fingers curled around hers in a light grip. "It is difficult to confide in him."

After a moment, Blythe withdrew her hand. She didn't know what had come over her around Tobias, but she knew she had to stop her foolishness. He made her forget who she was—a countess, a widow, and a proper lady. She sat up as primly as she could on the grass and set her hands in her lap. "I cannot imagine how difficult it must be for you to be here again, but your brother is unwaveringly proud of you. I see evidence of his affection every time you walk into a room."

Tobias didn't respond, and Blythe didn't dare peek. It was incredibly touching how Leopold hung on every word his brother uttered, even the incautiously uttered ones that scorched her ears with their vulgarity. Despite the long separation, they were close siblings. It should be natural for them to work together on the problem.

Tobias cleared his throat roughly. "Don't think I'll allow you to change the subject so easily. Come back to the abbey?"

"I'll just be in the way."

"Wouldn't you rather keep your distance from your stepson and his questionable company?"

Blythe stared at him. "Your brother does not trust me."

She fought back the hot, angry tears her confession brought on. It was humiliating to be so distrusted. She'd never been in this sort of situation before. She'd always had her family's unwavering support. Leopold Randall wasn't family yet. But he would be one day when the vows were spoken, binding him to Mercy. Would her sister come to regard her with the same unease if the threats continued?

Tobias grabbed her hand. He threaded their fingers together. "Did I say my brother was a wise man? I did no such thing. But he is overwhelmed with the estate and hasn't spared the time to get to know your character better. He will, though, but not if you leave before he has a chance to see the good in you."

Blythe peered into Tobias' face. His amber eyes held hers steadily, his lips lifted in a warm smile. Her heart beat erratically as he drew their joined hands against his chest. "Come back to Romsey and clear your name by helping me locate Oliver and Rose. I hope and pray they are still alive."

Blythe's breath caught. "Surely you don't think…"

His expression darkened. "After what the duke put me through, no, I don't hold out much hope. I had to find my own way home from half a world away, and if Oliver and Rosemary haven't done the same by now then I fear they will not at all. The most I expect is to discover where they were sent."

His grip tightened, and she covered his fist with her free hand. She'd never suspected he'd held so little hope of their recovery before now. Was the reason they hadn't returned truly because they'd died far from home? How would Tobias bear the news that he might have been the lucky one?

As she beheld Tobias' hopeless expression, she made a decision. She'd be there to help search, and if the news turned grim, she'd offer what comfort she could. She knew how it felt to lose loved ones. Perhaps, if the worst came to pass, she could help him through his pain better than she'd done her own. "I'll come back tonight."

"Blythe!" Mercy called as she swept down the front stairs of Romsey Abbey to embrace her sister. "You came back."

Tobias stepped back into the shadows of the entrance hall and let out a relieved breath. For a while there, he hadn't been certain Blythe would keep her word and return to Romsey Abbey. As night came closer, he'd moved to the window with a clear view of the drive, hoping for a glimpse of movement. When a horse and smart open curricle had come into view with Blythe at the reins, he'd poured himself a drink.

A small celebratory drink.

"Everything is ready," Blythe said as she handed her hat, gloves and pelisse to Wilcox with a smile, and then chafed her hands together.

"Oh, you're chilled through," Mercy scolded. "Come, let's get you warm again."

As she moved away from the main door, Tobias stepped from the shadows to reveal his presence. "Good evening, Lady Venables."

She curtsied. "Good evening, sir."

Then she swept from sight on her sister's arm, leaving Tobias alone with his elation.

She'd come back. Oh, not come back for him, but she had come back to help with the hunt. She'd trusted his word that everything would take a turn for the better.

That surely had to be better than fretting over the arrival of her worthless stepson or the graves of her family.

He followed them into the drawing room where Blythe stood before the fire, getting warm again.

Mercy rubbed her hands. "Why ever did you drive the open curricle at this hour?"

Blythe smiled slowly. "I was thinking of Raphael today, and how I never drive the last present he gave me. The curricle is very smart and perfect for short jaunts about the countryside if the weather permits. I'll not have to engage one of your servants for the task if I wish to visit friends."

Her gaze flittered to Tobias, and then darted away again. That one glance clarified two points. Blythe valued her independence, and second, she did nothing without giving the matter due consideration first. Having her own curricle at Romsey allowed her to come and go as she pleased.

"I've always admired that carriage," Mercy admitted, "but there is only room for two."

"Well, it's perfect for me nowadays. Am I too late?"

Tobias listened to Blythe as the two women chatted. She sounded almost happy to be back, and he was pleased she had listened to him. He honestly did need her help.

"No, we are to dine in an hour so you will have ample time to change," Mercy advised. "Are you very tired from your visit home? I could have dinner brought forward if you'd like. I'm sure Cook won't mind."

"No, that won't be necessary, but I would like to change. It's been a very busy day. I feel slightly gritty. I'll rejoin you all shortly."

Any grittiness would have come from her time in Harrowdale, but that was their secret. He had no intention of betraying her trust. Tobias nodded to her as she excused herself. The silence left in her wake deafened.

"I thought you said she was gone for good," Leopold said as he strolled in and kissed Mercy's cheek.

"Well, that is what she said to me earlier today." Mercy caught Leopold's hand and pulled him toward the love seat. "Something must have changed. She never usually reverses herself so quickly."

"Well, whatever the reason, I'm glad she's returned. At least now you can stop fretting over her."

Leopold pressed a lingering kiss to her knuckles, and Tobias looked away. They'd forgotten he was in the room. Again. Did all soon-to-be-wed couples behave in such a way? Tobias didn't think they did. Maybe he could ask Blythe for advice to fill the gap in his understanding. If he ever proposed to a woman, he should know how to behave and what was allowed. It was as good an excuse as any to follow her upstairs.

He grinned. Maybe he could catch her in the middle of changing.

He tugged on a button of his waistcoat that he'd noticed earlier was loose. It gave slightly after a few determined tugs, and he left it dangling in place.

He cleared his throat to gain the lovestruck pair's attention. "I've lost a button. Excuse me. I'll go find Murphy and change before dinner."

"Fine. Fine. Don't take too long," Leopold replied, without taking his gaze from his future wife.

Tobias strode out of the room and pulled the doors closed behind him. As he straightened, he clearly heard Mercy. "He is as handsome as his elder brother. I'm sure tomorrow night will be a success."

"I'll agree with you if we can get through the evening unscathed," his brother replied. "Are you still determined to try your hand at matchmaking? I warn you, he may not thank you for it."

"Oh, Leopold, you worry too much. I am sure Tobias will be very well received, just as you will be once everyone meets you. Blythe will be on hand, too, and will help smooth any ruffled feathers an incautious remark might cause. I'm sure some young lady will catch his eye. I should like to see him happier."

"If Blythe can be persuaded to support him, then I'm sure that is the best I can hope for. But it's clear she is uncomfortable around my brother," Leopold sighed. "Do not push for the other. If he wishes to wed it will be by his choice alone. Let him be. It is enough for me to have him here."

Whatever else might have been said was spoken in too low a tone for Tobias to hear clearly. He moved away from the door, but uncertainty gripped him. It was important that tomorrow night's outing go off without a hitch, for Leopold's sake especially. He hoped he didn't embarrass his brother, but he would avoid Mercy's traps and snares. If he married, he'd choose his own wife.

He climbed the stairs as a morose sense of inevitability gripped him. He was out of practice with polite conversation, if he'd ever indulged in the feat at all. Out of his depth. He needed help from someone without malice or a hidden agenda. He could ask Blythe to help him tonight. She surely wouldn't want her sister made uncomfortable by his mistakes.

His boots made no noise as he strode along the corridor leading to his bedchamber. The carpets were so thick in this part of the house that he didn't need to make the effort to be silent at all. And that was why he was able to approach the unmoving figure ahead of him, the one lingering outside Blythe's doorway, without being detected.

He set his hand to Wilcox's shoulder. "Lost, are you?"

Wilcox jumped out of his skin, setting one hand to his chest as he gasped. "Don't do that ever again, young man. You frightened me to death!"

Tobias raised a brow. He'd shocked Wilcox completely for him to speak so out of character. Or was he behaving in character at last?

He crossed his arms over his chest. "What are you doing, lingering outside the countess' bedchamber?"

The butler's expression grew sly. "Her Grace asked me to determine how clearly sound traveled from the guest chamber you occupy to the hallway, and to the rooms on either side."

Tobias glanced at his doorway. No light shone beneath his door. "But no one should be in there, so there is nothing to hear."

"I know that now. But since the countess has returned so unexpectedly, I was using her presence as a test."

"And what were your findings?"

Wilcox scowled. "I could not hear her, or she speaks very softly."

"Good, because from where I'm standing, you, sir, are spying on a lady in a most disturbing way. Do it again, and I'll speak to Her Grace about the matter."

Wilcox spluttered. "I did no such thing. I heard nothing."

"Be that as it may, you should not be here. Go about your usual duties."

Wilcox's skin darkened to a deep red. After a long pause, he stormed off.

Tobias tapped on Blythe's door. "May I have a word, Lady Venables?"

The door creaked open and light steamed out into the hall. When his eyes adjusted to the greater illumination, he caught a glimpse of Blythe's face through the gap.

"What do you want now, Mr. Randall?"

"We need to speak privately. Tonight. I've just caught Wilcox listening at your door."

Blythe struck her head farther out into the hall, and he caught a glimpse of what she was wearing. Color. No black or dark shade, but a pretty blue gown he'd never seen on her before tonight. Instead of the usual buttoned-up attire, Blythe was dressed for a ball.

Was this what she'd be wearing tomorrow night?

She frowned. "What exactly was he doing?"

He moved toward her door, drinking in the beauty of her pale throat and the brief glimpse of creamy, smooth curve of breast above the cut of the fabric. Mercy was right to be concerned about Blythe's sudden change of heart…but what a change it was. "Come to my room tonight, and I'll explain everything."

Her expression grew wary. "We can talk now."

"There is another matter I also wish to discuss. I don't wish to be overheard."

After a time, she nodded slowly. "Very well."

Then she ducked back inside and locked the door.

Tobias' pulse raced. If she wore a gown like that tonight, he would have a hard time keeping his eyes, and hands, still. He could remember every detail of their previous encounters. Her quick breath across his cheek, her body pressed against his. The taste of her lips.

He glanced down at the unfortunate tenting of his breeches. That had to go before he could return below. He shook his head. Miss Trimble was the better choice of the pair for a wife, with her four thousand and sweeter temperament.

He stepped into his bedchamber and flung his wardrobe doors wide. He wished the task of choosing a replacement waistcoat could be a better distraction from the temptation that glimpse of Blythe's skin offered. He'd need all the help he could muster to get through the evening.

Chapter Twelve

The discomfort of being stared at by the most severe members of the ton was nothing compared to the scrutiny in the casual sideways glances bestowed by Tobias Randall. Blythe shifted in her seat yet again. She was tired from her long day and found no enjoyment from the constant questioning looks he sent her way. Had he glimpsed her in a colored gown earlier? She'd brought a few of her older gowns from Walden Hall with her tonight, just to try out the idea of wearing them again. Yet she wasn't sure she could.

"I trust all is well at Walden Hall," Mercy said.

Blythe set her fork down and gave her sister her full attention. "Yes. Everything is done and Venables can have no cause for complaint. Finch will manage everything in my absence."

Mercy patted her lips with her napkin and pushed her dessert away uneaten. "I feared you would stay on to welcome him."

Blythe eyed the unfinished plate. Her sister usually had a steady appetite. It wasn't like Mercy to watch her figure. "Venables has no need of me."

Mercy stretched to pat her hand. "I wish he was a nicer person. I dreaded his coming until you came back. At least now I'm spared the need to call at Walden Hall just to see you."

"I am, too. I shan't need to go back until he quits the district, I imagine."

Mercy beamed. "I am so glad you will stay with us."

Tobias bumped her foot under the table, as if to remind her that he'd told her Mercy would want her here. Annoying man. Up until now, she was feeling charitable toward him. She ignored him and continued to eat her dessert, keeping up her end of the conversation when required. When the meal ended, she would slip away and leave them alone. Yet her heart raced that she'd promised to go to Tobias' room later tonight. She hoped he didn't have the wrong idea of why she would be there.

"Gentlemen," Mercy said warmly when Blythe set down her silver. "We shall await you in the billiard room. I know how you both enjoy your games."

Leopold laughed. "He thinks to best me tonight."

"Who's to say I haven't been letting you win," Tobias retorted with a quick grin. "Age before beauty and all that."

Blythe pressed her lips together to hide her amusement at their competitiveness. Tobias was quite fond of teasing his elder brother, and Leopold never failed to rise and take the bait.

She followed Mercy out, listening to the brothers bicker with half an ear, and strolled along to the billiard room. When the door shut behind them, Mercy suddenly sagged against the wall.

Startled, Blythe returned to her. "What is it?"

Mercy waved her hand before her face. "I suddenly feel overcome."

Blythe slipped an arm around her back and led Mercy to a nearby chair. "How long have you felt this way?"

She swallowed and made a face. "Just now, at dinner."

Blythe counted back swiftly. Leopold Randall had been at Romsey Abbey for over a month. Long enough, perhaps, to make a fast marriage absolutely necessary. "What if…?"

"It cannot be what you're thinking," Mercy murmured as she reclined on a lounge at Blythe's prompting. "My courses have not altered."

Blythe withdrew her handkerchief from her pocket and mopped Mercy's face.

"I'll be all right when I catch my breath. Don't fret."

"It isn't like you to be ill, Mercy. How can I not be worried?"

Mercy smiled. "You always worry about everyone else, but I am sure it will amount to nothing. The discomfort has already passed."

Blythe regarded her sister. The spark had gone from her eyes. She captured her wrist, searching for Mercy's pulse, and found it beating strongly. "Perhaps you should retire early."

Mercy shook her head. "I cannot disappoint Tobias and miss their game. He intends to win and wants an audience for his triumph. Leopold is much caught up by the estate business, and I fear he has neglected his brother because of me. The pair need every chance to become brothers again and for us all to become a family." A brief glimmer of excitement lit Mercy's face, but it soon drained away. She pressed her hand to her stomach as if she might be ill.

Blythe looked about desperately. She grabbed a blanket to capture any indiscretion Mercy might make. As she laid it over Mercy's lap, the door opened behind her.

"Here we are," Leopold said. "Now—what the devil are you doing?"

"She feels ill, Leo," Blythe warned him.

Leopold rushed forward, clasped Mercy's hands, and pressed them to his lips. "My love?"

"I'm sure it's nothing," Mercy assured him. "I just suddenly felt a little ill."

Blythe moved back as Leopold fussed, shifting the blanket, fetching a glass of water for her to sip. He really did care. Raphael had reacted exactly the same when Blythe had felt unwell during their marriage. But Mercy insisted she couldn't be with child, so there had to be some other explanation.

Tobias joined her. "What can I do?"

"Nothing, I imagine, except to keep your brother calm."

"Easier said than done," he muttered as he stepped forward. "Would she be more comfortable upstairs?"

"No." Mercy grabbed Leopold's arm. "I'm well enough to watch you play your game."

Leopold glanced at his brother, a plea in his gaze.

Beside her, Tobias sighed. "The game isn't as important as her health. Take her up to bed, brother. We can play against each other another night."

Mercy shifted. "Thank you, Tobias. Perhaps I should have an early night. I am sorry, but you must entertain each other this evening."

A blush heated Blythe's cheeks at how Tobias might like to be entertained, but she managed to murmur her agreement.

"Thank you." Leopold quickly scooped Mercy up into his arms and hurried out of the room, shouting orders as he went.

After a moment, Tobias smirked. "He should have had a title."

Blythe settled against the billiard table. "He does excel at giving orders. He would have made a good duke," she conceded.

"He's always been that way. Father was often busy elsewhere, and he relied on Leopold to keep us in line. At times, I swear Leopold forgets I'm fully grown."

She smiled. "Your behavior does seem to prey heavily on his mind."

"Hmm, if only he knew the worst of it." Tobias laughed, his eyes lighting up with amusement.

Their eyes met and held. Was he thinking of their kiss, and the near kiss by the stream? She swallowed nervously. They were alone once more. "You said you wanted to speak with me tonight? Perhaps now would be a good time."

A brief look of disappointment flashed in his eyes. But then he shrugged. "I am concerned about tomorrow night's soiree."

"We may not attend if Mercy remains indisposed."

He glanced toward the door, brow creasing. "You don't think she's with child already, do you?"

"Mercy is certain she couldn't be increasing." However, it may only be a matter of time since the pair already shared her sister's bedchamber. "Not yet, in any case."

Tobias set his hands to the billiard table. "About the soiree, then. Assuming we go, I wonder if you might offer me some advice."

"On what?"

He grinned. "On how to behave?"

Ah, the proprieties must baffle him after so long away. "Just do what your brother has suggested. Talk of pleasantries. Keep your hands from straying while dancing. Although your brother and my sister are terribly familiar here at Romsey, they will behave very differently in public. Or at least I hope so." Blythe chuckled. "Kissing is a private matter, and to do so in public will incite the most vulgar sort of gossip. Not even a married man may kiss his wife without society going up in flames."

"And dancing. Must I dance every dance?"

Blythe frowned. "You did secure a dance with Miss Trimble."

"I know that. However, I believe your sister is planning to try her hand at matchmaking me. I'm not keen to comply with her wishes. Who knows what sort of woman she'd throw at me."

Goodness. Mercy had not shared that tidbit. Who could Mercy possibly have in mind? She doubted many young women would be ready for a man of Tobias' substance. "No man is at first, but my sister does have a way of getting what she wants eventually, so be warned. Dance with a few ladies to appease her, but I'm sure you can avoid dancing every dance. Most gentlemen find a way into the card room to avoid demands on their time."

"Will you dance with me?"

Blythe shook her head. "I haven't danced in years."

"That makes two of us."

"Oh dear. That could be a problem. Did you dance much before you left England?"

"Frequently, but never in public. I was forced into the worst sort of torture as my sister's dance partner. You've heard of Rose's nature. Can you imagine a worse fate?"

Blythe chuckled at the image his words evoked. "You poor fellow."

Tobias slapped the tabletop. "At last, a little sympathy for my lot in life. Leopold never had to dance with her. He always managed to be busy elsewhere when a partner was called for."

Blythe laughed at the idea of a young Leopold dancing with a little sister. Rosemary was sounding more and more like a woman she wanted to get to know. She hoped they met one day. Her smile faltered. "There is no reason you'd need to dance with everybody. Just smile and be civil, fetch punch if the opportunity arises, and try not to offend ladies with delicate sensibilities."

"I'll do my best to curb my tongue."

Their eyes met, and a little thrill of excitement swept her skin. He was standing close enough for her to see the widening of his eyes, and then the slow shift of his attention to her lips and back again. It was disconcerting to be attracted to him. They were poles apart in circumstance and nature. He was everything she shouldn't desire but oddly did.

She licked her lips nervously. "I'm sure you will. Was that the whole of your questions?"

"No, but to voice any further queries would be indelicate. I have no wish to make you uncomfortable. I'll ask the rest another night."

He moved his hand until it rested against her side. Slowly,

painfully slowly, he shifted it until he held her arm. Blythe's breath caught, and she couldn't seem to catch it again as he slid his hand down over her glove to capture her fingers in his.

His grip firmed. "Breathe."

Blythe dragged in a large breath, appalled by the effect his nearness had on her.

He shifted, and his breath skimmed her ear. When she turned her head, his lips bumped her skin. Blythe lifted her chin…

Tobias' lips crashed against hers, smothering the small whimper that escaped her control.

But she wasn't protesting his kiss, only her response to it. She was mad to kiss him back, but she opened her mouth willingly and let his tongue invade. While they kissed, she was aware that he held her lightly. One hand held hers, the other rested against the small of her back, gently stroking her body. She could step away at any moment. He hadn't trapped her, but she was powerless to move.

Blythe lifted her hand to his chest. So warm and vital. So different from her late husband.

She had no doubts about what Tobias wanted from her, but she didn't think she could go through with it. He might think her a tease, but she pushed against him.

The kiss softened, and then stopped altogether. His lips hovered above hers, an inch apart, his breath harsh across her tender skin. He didn't protest the end of their kiss; he didn't rush to apologize, either.

Blythe lifted her lids slowly. Tobias studied her, his amber eyes bright with excitement, his lips parted as he breathed. She bit her lower lip, suddenly ashamed of herself. She'd never been a tease, but there was no future with him.

"Play billiards with me," he whispered.

"Ladies do not." Blythe swallowed. Ladies also did not allow gentlemen to kiss them witless, either. She glanced toward the door. It had been left wide open after Leopold had carried Mercy out. Any one of the servants could have seen her in Tobias' arms.

"Just one game. I'm sure if your husband had had any sense, then he would have indulged you." His grip tightened, reminding her they were still holding hands. If he lowered his head again, he could kiss her in an instant.

Her heart raced. "Not often."

"Then play against me. I promise to play fairly. I won't let you win just because you're a lady."

Blythe frowned. "I think he did let me win unfairly once or twice."

Tobias' lips brushed her skin again in a soft caress that added to her confusion. "A fair game?"

She looked up. "A fair game."

Tobias grinned, and then swung away to collect cues and arrange the billiard balls on the table while she hunted for her scattered wits. What had come over her to behave in such a way? She pressed her hands to her cheeks.

When he returned, his expression held no hint of wickedness, just his usual impertinent smile. He held up a penny. "Heads or tails?"

"Tails."

Tobias flicked the coin into the air, caught it and then slapped it onto the back of his hand. When he uncovered it, tails was visible. She'd won the toss.

Tobias moved back from the table with an exaggerated bow.

In the heat of battle, no matter how certain the outcome, a man must keep his wits about him. Tobias had no need to let Blythe win at billiards because he would surely lose. Billiards was not his game, not yet at any rate. He was still learning the art under his brother's tuition.

But in matters of desire, he was not prepared to accept defeat as easily. The game he played with Blythe was not one to rush, no matter how good she tasted.

Blythe lined up to take her shot, leaning over the table slightly. The position did nothing to dampen his arousal. His gaze caught on her rear, more defined because she'd stretched over the table and stayed.

Damn but she was a tempting wench.

She took her shot, balls cracked against one another, and he quickly looked at the table. She'd sunk a ball with her first shot, and had another to take. His breath caught as she lined up for her next.

She faced him, teeth clamped over her lower lip, focused on her goal and oblivious to everything.

Those pale green eyes of hers fascinated him. They showed everything she felt at any given moment. She desired him. She enjoyed kissing him. How much more he could experience would depend on her and his patience. Every desire uncovered was swiftly followed by guilt lit large across her face. Did she feel she'd been unfaithful? Tobias assumed she did, and that was why he could break away so easily.

Thanks to his past, he knew nothing good ever came easily. He had the distinct feeling that having Blythe in his bed would certainly be worth the wait.

When she sank another, her face broke out into the widest grin he'd ever seen cross her face without the young duke being present. She was lovely when she smiled. Beautiful and true. A faithful, exciting woman.

She missed the next shot, and her smile dimmed.

Tobias stepped up to the table at her side. "Bad luck, my lady. You were doing so well, too."

Her smile returned. "That's the best run I've ever had."

He nodded rather than answer. He didn't want her pleasure in the game to disappear too quickly once she'd realized she was feeling happy. When he took aim, his shot went wide. Damn. Her good mood must be the distraction. He was usually a little better than this, or he wouldn't have suggested a game in the first place.

She took her shot, sank two balls easily, but when it was his turn, she stopped him. "You're not holding the cue stick properly."

"Oh?" Tobias said as he straightened. He'd thought he'd copied Leopold's grip perfectly. "What am I doing wrong?"

She touched his hand, the one at a distance from the tip, and wriggled her fingers beneath his. "You look awkward. Your arms are long. You should hold the cue farther down so your strike will be true and strong."

He shifted his hand to the end. "Like this?"

Her hand slid over the back of his as she nodded. "Now try."

He would if she would let him go. Eventually, she snatched her hand back, granting Tobias his freedom. He approached the table again, getting used to the different grip. As he stretched out over the table, he did notice the difference. His shoulders were more relaxed with this posture. He lined up to take the shot and for a change, landed a solid hit.

Satisfaction flooded him as a colored ball wobbled on the threshold and then fell into a pocket.

"Well done."

He looked back over his shoulder. Blythe grinned at his success. He straightened and moved toward her. Her eyes widened, her cheeks reddened, her lips parted. Although tempted to kiss her again, he merely stroked his fingertip over her cheek. "Thank you, B."

"You have another shot to take," she said suddenly, backing away.

Two steps forward, one step back. The game to bed the countess would not be won by rushing.

He'd be patient, especially when the prize was so great.

They finished without further incident and, true to his word, Blythe did win the game fairly.

Chapter Thirteen

"Thank you." Blythe heaved a heavy sigh as the last pin secured her hair. "You may return to the duchess."

The maid, her most recent replacement attendant since the "incident," scurried for the door and the implied safety of being as far away from Blythe as possible. None of the Romsey servants bothered to hide their nervousness in her presence. The footmen merely stared. But even that scrutiny set her teeth on edge.

She gave her appearance another quick glance and stepped out into the hall. A servant standing down the hall hurried away and disappeared into the servants' staircase. Annoyed, Blythe clenched her fists. She wished she could return to the comfort of Walden Hall and her own servants. However, Venables would arrive sometime today, and any peace the place might offer would vanish as if it had never been.

Before she had taken too many steps, Tobias' door opened and he joined her. Her heart skipped a beat at the way he smiled.

He bowed. "Good morning, Lady Venables. How are you this fine day?"

She glanced at him. "It is drizzling rain outside, Mr. Randall."

His lips quirked. "So, no jaunts in your little carriage today?"

"Not today. I do hope the weather eases before the soiree tonight. I do want the evening to be a success for Lady Dunwoody."

"You had to remind me?"

Blythe pressed her lips together to hide her amusement. It was a soiree, not a public hanging. The evening should be extremely pleasant, and she was looking forward to catching up with friends. While she loved her sister dearly, Romsey Abbey and the goings on here made her anxious.

As they reached the head of the stairs, Tobias slipped his hand under her elbow. "You didn't answer me yesterday, about the dancing. Will you dance with me tonight? I should like that very much."

Blythe swallowed as his grip firmed, conveying his determination to make her answer. "It is not necessary, but if you insist, then yes, I will dance with you. But not the first or second set. You must dance with Mercy before you dance with me."

His eyes lit up with mischief. "So I've been told. How about the dance before supper?"

Blythe nodded, even as she feared her actions would spark even more rumors. After the dance ended, Tobias would escort her into supper, wait on her, and then sit at her side while they ate. People would remark upon their interactions, and they might speculate. What had she agreed to?

She looked ahead resolutely as they gained the lower floor and headed toward the breakfast room. A young boy, unfamiliar to Blythe, sat alone on a wooden bench placed in the hall. He glanced at them, and then quickly looked down at his feet.

Tobias squeezed her elbow, but she shrugged. She didn't have the faintest clue who he was.

Another few paces along, Wilcox materialized before them. "Excuse me, Lady Venables, but Mr. Randall requests you join him in the study."

Blythe nodded, but then she realized Tobias still held her. She couldn't shake him off without Wilcox noticing. "I'll be there directly."

Wilcox bowed and then disappeared back the way he'd come.

"King Leopold calls," Tobias muttered softly.

Blythe thought the nickname quite apt. "I've no idea what he can want with me at this hour, but I'd better get any unpleasantness out of the way."

As she moved away, her skin tingled from the loss of contact. She strove to shake off those feelings as she knocked on the heavy wooden door.

"Come," Leopold Randall called.

Blythe let herself in, at once annoyed by the command in Leopold's voice and curious by the summons. A pretty blonde woman sat before his desk.

"You wanted to see me?"

"Yes, thank you for coming so promptly. I'd like to introduce you to Mrs. Turner, an old acquaintance of mine."

The woman stood up, her hands clenched together. Blythe knew of the widow by reputation, but they had not met prior to this occasion. There was no need. They were not of the same circles. Blythe nodded. "Mrs. Turner."

The woman bobbed a surprisingly elegant curtsy. "My lady."

"Mrs. Turner was married to my old friend, but he's since passed on. She has a boy to care for. I imagine you passed him in the hall."

Ah, that explained the boy, but not the reason for this meeting. "I did. How can I help you, Mr. Randall?"

Leopold set his hands to an unoccupied chair set before the desk. "Will you join us?"

She sat and waited for Leopold to seat himself. He leaned forward, hands clenched. "I was wondering, Lady Venables, if you might be able to help me make this woman see reason. As I mentioned, her husband was an old friend, and I want to ensure that his widow and son are properly provided for."

"And the problem is?"

"She refuses to take my money."

Blythe faced the woman and raised a brow.

Mrs. Turner scowled. "We are not Mr. Randall's responsibility. I came because Eamon Murphy led me to believe there was an urgent matter Mr. Randall wished to discuss. I cannot take any more charity from him without causing the worst sort of gossip."

Blythe faced Leopold again. "What has been done so far?"

Leopold picked up a stack of papers and shuffled them restlessly. "The house is in good repair now, but I want to do more."

Beth Turner shook her head. "Mr. Randall, you should know that some forms of charity can leave a certain tarnish on a woman's reputation, no matter the good intentions it was offered under."

"She is correct about that," Blythe said quietly. Too much charity caused uncomfortable talk, especially when the woman was a pretty widow.

Leopold scowled at them both. "The boy needs a tutor in order to make something of himself." His jaw clenched stubbornly, giving Blythe the impression that it was something he'd already declared repeatedly prior to her arrival. Blythe's respect for Mrs. Turner rose a notch. It would be hard to turn down such a generous offer of financial assistance.

"Mr. Randall, please understand that I am grateful for all you have done, but our lives are set on a different path. You've done more than enough."

Leopold slammed the papers down. "I disagree. If Ollie was here, he'd tell you the odds are against you and the boy thriving as you are."

The mention of the missing brother surprised Blythe. What exactly was this woman to the Randall family that Oliver was mentioned so earnestly?

Mrs. Turner shook her head. "But he isn't here, and therefore cannot confuse me with his statistics," she said. "If he'd have anything to say in the matter, that is."

"He would want to see you happy."

"Living off your charity will not make me so," Mrs. Turner asserted.

They had reached an impasse, and Leopold Randall appeared infuriated by Mrs. Turner's stubborn refusal to take his aid. His jaw was set, his glare aimed squarely at Mrs. Turner.

Blythe wracked her brain, trying to think of a socially acceptable way for Leopold to do more, and for Mrs. Turner's reputation to be unaffected by the charity. Mrs. Turner could go into service at Romsey, but if the woman was as good a friend as she was coming to believe, then such a fall would be a hard choice for the woman to make.

Mrs. Turner's calm determination to refuse assistance added to Blythe's respect for her. Some women would have taken what was offered and endured the gossip. But what other options were there?

Blythe pressed her hands to her lap, noticing her glove had begun to tear at the seam of one finger. A proper maid would have noticed and not handed them to her. If she had a decent lady's maid, her mornings might start off on a better note.

She stilled. An ordinary servant role wouldn't do for the close friend of the Randalls…but would Mrs. Turner turn down the superior position of lady's maid or companion if one was offered? Blythe was not unnecessarily demanding, and the woman did not appear to be the flighty type. She might be poor, but her gown was well tended, her hair neatly pinned back, her voice refined. She could do very well as a companion.

Leopold tapped on the desk to draw her attention. "Have you thought of a solution, Lady Venables?"

She frowned. Leopold really did have all the makings of a lord. His impatience was irksome. "I may have, but it will depend on Mrs. Turner's skills. Can you sew well, Mrs. Turner?"

A frown crossed her face, but she nodded.

"Can you get along well with others and not listen to gossip?"

"Oh," Leopold said as he sat back in his chair. "I'd not thought of employing her as a maid."

Mrs. Turner's expression darkened.

Blythe lifted her hand to halt any protest before she finished explaining herself. "Not a common housemaid, Mr. Randall. No, that would never do. It is clear that Mrs. Turner is a cut above the average widow. I need someone who can dress my hair, organize my things as a lady's maid would, but perhaps a companion would be a more accurate term. As you have frequently pointed out, I live alone, and the extra company could benefit us both. There is also Her Grace's wedding to organize in the near future. She could help Mercy with aspects of that. Being a friend of the Randalls would ensure things are done properly."

And also that gossip about the family remained within the family.

"That is a perfect solution!" Leopold's lips curled into a smile as he faced Mrs. Turner. "You would have a worthy occupation as Lady Venables' companion and all the necessities in life. I would have the satisfaction of knowing you are well cared for, and your son can be educated here at Romsey when an appropriate tutor can be employed."

Mrs. Turner blinked furiously, and then turned her face away. After a time, when she didn't turn back, Blythe cleared her throat.

"The offer stands, Mrs. Turner, should you need time to consider. I dislike discussing such matters, but the terms would be sixteen pounds a year, and eventually I will return to Walden Hall to live. There is ample room for your son. We can consider the first month here as a trial period, with pay, of course." Blythe stood. "Shall I leave you to convince her, Mr. Randall?"

"Thank you, Blythe," he said quietly. "I will certainly do my best in that regard."

Blythe let herself out, bemused by the morning. She assessed Mrs. Turner's son as she passed. He didn't appear wild or sickly. He seemed to possess a great deal of patience as he waited, and that was a rare thing in young boys. She nodded to him and then made her way to the morning room.

Tobias Randall pounced on her the minute she crossed the threshold. "What was that about? What did Leopold want?"

Blythe picked up a plate, grateful the servants were absent, and helped herself to the dishes on the sideboard. "He wanted my advice on a delicate matter."

"How delicate?"

Blythe frowned at him as she took a seat. Tobias appeared out of sorts now. She set her hand to his clenched fist. "I understand that Mrs. Turner has refused Leopold's charity. I think I was summoned to convince her to accept more. But he's already done more than he should have, and has made her uncomfortable."

"Beth Turner is here?"

When she nodded, Tobias jumped to his feet, chair scrapping harshly across the parquetry in his rush to leave the room. This Beth must be a favorite.

A woman yelped, and Tobias laughed. Curious, Blythe carefully set her cutlery down and crept to the doorway. She peered along the hall.

The door to the study remained wide open, and Tobias was spinning with Mrs. Turner in his arms. They stopped, and he stared down at her a long time before he kissed her cheek.

Very good acquaintances.

Blythe hurried back to her seat as her stomach roiled. How could she have been taken in so completely about Mrs. Turner's character? There was more to the family friendship than had been let on. Was Mrs. Turner a past love of Tobias'?

She set her hand to her stomach as humiliation washed over her. She'd just offered the widow employment. Mrs. Turner would be free to continue any relationship with Tobias under this very roof.

But the offer of employment had already been voiced, and she couldn't go back on her word without good reason. Feeling the harsh bite of jealousy wasn't reason enough, and that wasn't a pleasant sensation or one she'd expected to feel. She'd remain vigilant over the first month, and if she detected any unbecoming flirting with Tobias then she would reconsider the situation. She couldn't allow a woman she employed to engage in an affair with a man she, herself, had kissed.

Blythe stared at her plate, but her appetite had fled. She picked at her meal as her sense of disquiet grew. She couldn't hear Tobias anymore. As she got up to pour herself another cup of tea, the door closed behind her back.

When it was locked, too, she spun about.

Tobias caught her in his arms. "Thank you! Leopold just told me the wonderful news. Beth accepted the post and will start today."

His mouth met hers in a hard kiss.

Blythe pushed against his chest until he gave way. "Don't you think you've had enough attention for one day?"

He frowned. "Not from you. Barely enough." He pursued her around the table as she backed away, and she put a chair between them to gain a little breathing room. He confused her with his behavior. Was he that happy that his past love would be so close at hand? Perhaps she had misjudged what his kisses meant?

He stopped.

Blythe steadied herself by holding on to the chair. "I will expect Mrs. Turner to behave with the appropriate reserve while in my service."

"Of course she will. Beth is a prime lass and full of fun. You two should be the best of friends in no time."

"That remains to be seen."

His head tilted to the side as he studied her. "My mother liked Beth immensely."

A crushing weight of disappointment filled her heart. "Is that so?"

He nodded slowly. "She was often at Harrowdale, and when she left to return home, my mother insisted she be escorted. I tagged along quite often."

"Oh."

Tobias skirted the chair and crowded Blythe against the table. "Now, where were we?" He drew in a deep breath. "God, you smell good enough to eat." His lips met Blythe's in a soft kiss and, despite her misgivings, she couldn't help but kiss him back. His hands settled on her hips and jerked her toward him. He tasted like toast and coffee. He tasted of warmth.

The locked door rattled behind him.

Tobias drew back, brushed his finger across her bottom lip, and then gestured for her to return to her chair. When she'd sat, he hurried to open the door. "So sorry. Must have stuck."

Wilcox glanced at him, distrust clear in his expression. "Is everything to your satisfaction, Lady Venables?"

Blythe hoped her cheeks were not as red as they felt. "Yes, thank you, Wilcox. Everything is perfect."

A quick grin crossed Tobias' face. Wilcox fussed at the sideboard and then withdrew.

Blythe picked up her silver. Would Tobias kiss her witless and carry on with another woman at the same time?

She peeked at him, and her pulse raced. He stood at the morning room window, staring out at the view of the east gardens. As there was nothing of particular interest in the east gardens, she was intrigued by what could capture his attention so thoroughly that he would keep his back to her for so long after such a kiss.

Chapter Fourteen

There were times when a man could have too many eyes upon him, especially when he was aroused to the point of pain. Being alone with Blythe, kissing her, and holding her against him eroded his control considerably.

Although he was pleased to see Beth usefully employed, her presence in the abbey would add another complication to his life. Beth was an observant woman, one of high morals like Blythe, which was why he was so happy she'd offered the position of companion rather than maid. They were very much alike.

Beth would take care of her exceedingly well. Well enough to likely get in the way of his goal of seducing Blythe.

He should be thinking of the future and his goal of finding a wealthy wife. However, he wasn't sure what he wanted more; Miss Trimble's money or Blythe panting after making love to him.

Sadly, the latter was in his thoughts more often than the first.

He glanced over his shoulder to see if Blythe had finished eating and caught her staring at him. He grinned as a blush stole over her cheeks. Damn, but she was a tempting wench. He'd have her over the table this very instant if he didn't think she'd hate herself the moment it was done. Not that he had any intentions of bedding her fast…or just once. There was an energy about her that drew him closer, even as he recognized he should be the last man on Earth to have her. Yet Blythe was a woman who couldn't be rushed, even though she returned his kisses with astonishing passion. "Shall we continue in the sanctuary today?"

She daintily pressed her napkin to her lips and stood, smoothing the folds of her skirts as she did so. "I believe that is a very good idea."

He allowed her to proceed him, but not from any gentlemanly inclination. He enjoyed watching her move. Dainty. Economical with her movements, but rigidly straight at all times. The exceptions were when she pressed herself against him while they kissed, and he'd begun to live for those moments.

As they traversed the short distance to the drawing room doors, Wilcox appeared before them and cleared his throat. "A servant has come from Walden Hall. It seems Lord Venables has arrived and is in something of an uproar."

Blythe stopped. "Whatever could he be upset about? Did the servant leave a letter?"

Wilcox grimaced. "No, my lady. I've put him in the library so he might pass along the message in person."

Blythe frowned. "Very well. I'll see him now." She hurried into the library, closing the doors behind her with a soft click.

Tobias scowled at Wilcox. "Do you know what that is about?"

Wilcox shrugged. "Lady Venables would not like me to be involved in issues that do not relate to Romsey Abbey. I didn't like to ask."

Tobias crossed his arms over his chest and scowled. "But the servant whispered it to you anyway. Out with it."

Wilcox glanced around a little guiltily. "He wanted to know if we had acquired any new servants. I thought it an oddly timed question, given Mrs. Turner has just joined the household."

"Very oddly timed. I wasn't aware that Mrs. Turner had any connection to Lady Venables before."

"I'm not aware of any," Wilcox supplied.

Tobias checked the hall to be sure he was unobserved, and then pressed his ear to the door, ignoring Wilcox's spluttered gasp. But inside, he could hear nothing of the conversation. He drew back. "She does speak very quietly, doesn't she?"

"Too quietly. Excuse me," Wilcox murmured.

Had Venables noticed the removal of Blythe's son's things already? He hoped it was about another matter altogether so she need not become distressed.

Rather than wait where he couldn't hear anything anyway, Tobias retreated to the drawing room. Blythe would join him when she could and he'd question her about the matter.

While he waited, he prowled the room. The former dukes of Romsey had a penchant for dramatic paintings throughout the house, but here they seemed to him to be a poorly chosen collection. The large portrait of the old duke, of course, drew the eye, but the smaller works were not cast in the same style or elegance. They lacked the presence Tobias thought necessary for such a formal chamber, as if they were hung here without thought to the effect.

The drawing room door clicked shut, and Tobias spun around. Blythe's face had creased into worry again and he hurried to her side, slipped an arm around her back and pulled her against him. "What is it?"

She pressed a hand to her cheek. "I am stunned. My servants have all handed in their notice and left Walden Hall this morning! Venables is livid."

"Surely not all of them?"

"I cannot believe it! Mrs. Finch packed up and left without a word, or offered an apology for the timing. Apparently, she's taken a place in another household. The rest of the servants—cook, gardener and groom—went with her, leaving Venables with only the servants he brought from London. Mrs. Finch said nothing of this yesterday!"

Tobias ran his hand up and down her back. "Looks like Venables will have to butter his own bread for a while."

Blythe shook her head. "What will I do without her? I depend on Finch."

Tobias wrapped her in his arms and squeezed. "It was a good thing you had her assistance yesterday with young Adam's things. Perhaps that was her farewell gift to you."

"I suppose." She pushed out of his arms. "She's been with me so long that I cannot imagine anyone else looking after my house." She offered a sad smile. "Or me."

"Well, then it is a very good thing you have Beth now to take care of you."

She nodded then suddenly shook her head. "I've sent a note to Venables, voicing my surprise. I don't know what else to do to rectify the situation."

Tobias could care less for Venables' outrage. However, Blythe was another matter. "There is nothing you can do. It is his house, and he is more than capable of acquiring replacement employees."

She stared at him as if he'd sprouted a second head. "But what if he hires the wrong sort? It is not he who has to live with them when he returns to Town."

Tobias eased onto the arm of a chair. "Why not live here with your sister instead of returning to Walden Hall? You've given me the impression that Venables is somewhat of a bore. Would it really be such a hardship to move away?"

If she lived here, it would be easy to continue his steady seduction. He'd have all the time in the world, up until he decided to take up residence at Harrowdale. He could put that off for some time if he had the right incentive. Having Blythe in his bed, or himself in hers, would be ample reason to remain at Romsey. But could she leave off her graveside vigils? That might be harder for her to do.

"Yes, it would. I have been mistress of my own house since I was sixteen years of age. It is very hard to do nothing with ones days, and that would certainly happen should I remain here."

He understood her problem very well. He didn't like to be idle either, hence his decision to make Harrowdale his home and repair the last ten years of neglect the property had suffered. He would have ample projects to occupy the rest of his life. Blythe wouldn't have that if she lived at Romsey. However, he was buoyed by the fact that Blythe made no mention of her long-dead son or husband. Perhaps she wasn't as tied to the place as he'd first thought.

However, there was no easy solution to her problems today. He approached her, put his arm lightly across her shoulders, and steered her toward the duke's sanctuary. "Well, lucky for us we have something we should be doing ourselves right now. Let Venables take care of Walden Hall. I need you now."

He opened the chamber door and Blythe slipped inside without comment. She stood before the shelves, gaze lifted to the tomes above her. "I cannot help feeling that this is a waste of time."

"I had the same thought this morning." He closed the door behind him with a soft click. "What prompted your misgivings?"

Blythe's shoulders lifted, tensed, at the closing of the door. "There is no sense to how the books are shelved, for one."

Tobias moved to stand behind her, set his hands to her waist and looked up. "There are a lot there."

"Yes, but I cannot figure out his system. There must be one. How could the old duke have found a journal, should he want a particular one? There is no catalogue to be found. Did he rely on memory alone?"

Tobias smoothed his hands up and down her sides. "I don't think so. You said the journal concerning Leopold was very detailed and was kept close to the desk. Perhaps the ones at a distance were unimportant to him by the end of his life."

"That is as good a theory as any." A ragged breath left Blythe's lips as she shuddered. "Please stop."

He glanced down at where his hands rested just below her breasts. He bent close to her ear. "You really don't wish for me to continue?"

Her breath left her in ragged pants as he pressed his lips to the column of her throat. Such smooth, unblemished skin deserved to be worshiped. He couldn't get enough of touching her.

He raised his hand to cover her breast.

She gasped…but didn't make any move to dislodge him.

While he firmed his grip over the orb, he pressed light kisses over her skin. Blythe tilted her head and sagged against him, pressing her bottom against his erection.

He groaned. Too damn tempting.

He slid his hand from her breast, and turned her face to his. Her lips parted as he covered them. He drew her tightly against him, closed his eyes, and plundered her mouth until he was wild for her.

If not for their location, and her strong sense of propriety, he'd back her against the wall and take her here and now. But he couldn't take Blythe as if she were a common whore with a dark corner for her lovers. She was a lady, and she deserved to be treated as such.

He opened his eyes as he drew back. Damp lips and pink skin, but not a hair out of place. He skimmed his hands over her body, rejoicing when she molded herself to him, clearly aroused and oblivious of her actions.

This passion between them would be quenched. But such a pleasure required time and her full participation. He wouldn't take her to his bed unless she was ready and aware.

He pressed a kiss to her cheek, stood straighter, and tucked her head beneath his chin. He inhaled deeply and fought to regain control before he begged for pleasure.

Yes, soon. Very soon. But not here and not now. Not in a musty room full of old books that stank of scandal and corruption. "Perhaps we should concentrate on the journals kept closest to Leopold's," he said eventually, cursing the rough huskiness of his voice.

Blythe pressed her face against his chest and rocked her head from side to side. Her hands tightened on his waist. "That is as good a theory as any."

He glanced down at her. Did she not want to end the exchange? Her eyes were closed, her lip caught between her teeth. He smiled at the sight, satisfied beyond measure. He'd aroused her. He was certain of it. If there was a bed nearby, he'd lay her upon it and feast on her perfect skin for the next few hours.

Eventually she drew away but wouldn't look at him. He faced the wall of journals and set his hand to her shoulders, rubbing his thumbs over her delicate neck. "Where did you say Leopold's journal was kept?"

Her arm lifted to point. "Here."

He slid his hand from her neck and along her outstretched arm slowly, covered her tiny one with his. He tapped their fingers against the spine of a plain leather-bound volume. "This one?"

She moved their joined hands farther along the shelf. "No. This one."

"Ah." He pulled a different journal off the shelf at random, relinquishing his grip on Blythe in the process. She pressed the hand he'd been holding against her belly and curled it into a fist. He gave her a quick reassuring smile and sat on the table edge. After a moment, Blythe relaxed.

He flicked open the book and studied the first page.

His date of birth was clearly written on the first line, along with other details of his birth. But he stared at the numbers scratched out beside it.

At the beginning, it had been a five, but that had been crossed out and amended to the number four, and then changed to number five again. He pointed at the numbers as recognition dawned. "This was my place in the succession at the time the old duke died. I'm third now, I suppose, until Oliver is found alive."

Blythe shifted closer to see, her cheek pressing against his shoulder. "Really?"

He pointed to the first number and tapped out the order of succession. "Cousin Edwin, my father, Leopold, Oliver and then myself." He shifted his finger. "It changed when my father was murdered. Then changed again when young Edwin was born. Oliver must have been alive until the end of the duke's lifetime."

"Goodness. That's the first time he'd been so obvious, and I've looked at these books for weeks." Blythe leaned over him and flicked to the end of the book. She pointed to an entry.

"Lady Margaret? Never heard of her." He frowned. "Not even a ship of that name. If it's of any use, I was taken to the Williamstown first, and later removed to another ship."

A frown creased Blythe's brow. She flicked pages until she was somewhere in the middle and ran her fingers over the page. "Here it is. 1803. The Williamstown."

He stared at the name as fury filled him. "Yes, that's the one."

His voice came out as a growl, and Blythe's gaze flew to his. "You were on that ship, but not the Lady Margaret?"

"That is correct."

She took the book from him and pointed to an earlier entry—June, 1799. "Where were you then?"

"I lived at Harrowdale with my family."

She stared at the book then returned to the last pages. She returned to the entry about the Williamstown, running the tip of her finger down the page. "Were you moored off Swansea in eighteen-six? Captain Fenwinch wrote His Grace that he was to take up duties on the Lady Margaret next. He mentions taking someone with him."

Tobias took the journal and stared at the entry. Captain Fenwinch had gleefully traded him to the slaver two years before in Charleston. He swallowed. "Not me. I was in service aboard a slaver, the Enid Wren, from eighteen-four to eighteen-eleven."

Blythe gasped. "A slaver? You've never mentioned anything about that before now."

Tobias smiled, but it was tight with strain. "It's not something suited to delicate ears, and I'd much rather not think about those days ever again."

Her head bowed back over the book, and she asked him more questions. Some he could answer, most he could not. Eventually, she set the journal aside on the table and covered his hands with hers. He couldn't hide the way they shook.

"I am so sorry, Tobias. So very sorry. It appears the old duke was lied to by Captain Fenwinch. The duke may never have known where you truly were, or that you suffered so much." She licked her lips. "He lost you."

Chapter Fifteen

"Discarded like rancid whale meat," Tobias said tonelessly.

Blythe set her hands on either side of Tobias' face and brought his gaze to hers. "The duke appears not to have known, and was convinced you were still aboard Fenwinch's ship. There are pages of entries after the first mention of the Williamstown, and he wrote to Romsey of his business in command of the Lady Margaret."

"I wrote to Romsey. None were answered."

Blythe sighed. "Perhaps any reply was sent to the Lady Margaret."

Tobias snorted and moved out of her grip. She curled her hands into fists, uncertain how to ease Tobias' anger over what must be a cruel betrayal. To be sent away was one thing. To be unknowingly lost was entirely worse.

It grieved her to see him in such pain. When they'd first met, she'd thought him largely unaffected by the past. He was always ready with a wicked grin, vulgar words, or searing invitation to join him in bed. How wrong had she been about him? His depths were as scarred as his skin.

She set her hand to his broad shoulder just as the mechanism to the door clicked. She snatched her hands back as the chamber was bathed in brighter light.

"I had an hour free," Leopold said as he stepped into the chamber.

Tobias drew himself to his full height. "Good. I'm sure you'll find out something about yourself here. I'm just a ghost."

He stepped around his brother and disappeared.

Leopold raised a brow. "What was that about?"

Blythe picked up the tome they had been looking at and opened it to the first mention of the Williamstown. "I've determined this book is about your brother. However, from this point to the end, it is a work of fiction. The duke unknowingly lied to you. He may not have had a clue where Tobias really was during his exile."

Leopold stared at the book then his lips curled back from his teeth in a snarl. "If that old bastard wasn't seven feet deep and covered in marble, I'd dig him up and scatter his bones to the bloody fishes!"

He spun about, calling out to his brother as he went.

Blythe sighed and returned the book to the shelf. Perhaps Leopold would be able to soothe him and restore his good humor.

There was another way that such a feat might be accomplished… but she wouldn't open her bedchamber window tonight and invite Tobias into her bed just to cheer him up.

Uncertain of what to do next, she chose another journal and stepped out, closing the sanctuary. But as she faced the room, she jumped out of her skin.

Wilcox stood just inside the drawing room, holding the door latch as if he'd intended to leave the next moment.

After a long, uncomfortable silence, Wilcox cleared his throat. "Is there anything I can fetch for you, Lady Venables?"

Blythe hugged the journal to her chest. "Nothing, thank you."

"Very good, my lady. Mrs. Turner has arrived to begin her duties." He bowed stiffly, glanced over her shoulder to the now hidden doorway before quickly departing.

Blythe's heart raced. The secret was out. She'd have to tell Mercy the butler knew about the duke's sanctuary.

She hurried along to Edwin's playroom, nodded to the footmen standing outside the doors, and waited impatiently for them to open. When they finally allowed her to pass, she rushed forward to whisper in her sister's ear, "Wilcox knows about the sanctuary."

Mercy reared back, eyes wide. "How did that happen?"

"I was careless. Tobias was upset, and Leopold went after him. The door was left open and when I went to leave, Wilcox was already in the drawing room, watching me close up the chamber."

Mercy rubbed her fingers across her brow. "This is terrible."

"I know." Blythe took up her sister's hand. "Mercy, I don't think Wilcox was surprised by the chamber being there. I feel sure he already knew."

Mercy shook her head. "He never hinted he knew anything

about the secret rooms in the abbey. I trusted him, but if he knew about the chamber all along, why didn't he say something in the first place?"

"I don't know, but Tobias doesn't trust him completely. Neither did his mother. I am aware that you and Leopold depend upon Wilcox, but he's a servant. He was in the old duke's employ long before you came here," Blythe said quietly. "He may have always known."

Mercy rubbed her hands over her arms. "I feel besieged again."

Blythe drew her sister into an embrace and squeezed. "We'll muddle through. We always have before."

Mercy chuckled. "You've become optimistic again. I desperately need that right now."

Blythe glanced at where her nephew played. "You must not let your spirits decline. You have Leopold and Tobias now. You have the family you craved."

"True. And I have you as well. Perhaps we should not attend the soiree. What do you think?"

Blythe thought it over. "Nothing has ever happened when you have been out making social calls before. These things only occur when you are entertaining friends here. Tobias feels the servants bear investigation."

"Tobias has had a lot to say to you lately, it seems." Mercy drew back, frowning. "What was he upset over?"

Mercy was silent while Blythe related the particulars of her discovery, leaving out his time aboard the slaver. Unwillingly involved or not, that sort of thing would not sway public opinion in his favor.

"It surprises me that someone could outsmart the old duke so thoroughly," Mercy mused.

"When Tobias' notes arrived at last, if they ever did, someone should have realized he was not where he was reported to be, but perhaps time and distance made seeking confirmation impossible. His Grace would have been furious had he known. He wasn't a man to take a betrayal calmly, and I imagine being the bearer of bad news would not have appealed." Blythe bit her lip. "Wilcox is always the first to see any correspondence that comes into the abbey."

Mercy stared. "How could he not have shown them to me?"

"I don't know, but I think you should not be alone with him when you ask." If he had withheld information, Wilcox's tenure as butler of Romsey Abbey was going to come to an end, unless he had a believable explanation. She'd never cared for Wilcox or his influence on Mercy. She wouldn't mind seeing him gone.

"I'll be sure to have Leopold with me." Mercy tapped her arm. "I hear you've engaged a new lady's maid."

"A companion. Mrs. Turner has just arrived, in fact."

"Excellent. I've been meaning to take another look at the woman."

A small kernel of uncertainty gripped Blythe. "Oh? Why is that?"

"You'll think me foolish, but for a short time, I suspected Mrs. Turner of having been Leopold's lover. I wasted a good deal of my temper over the matter."

Blythe's anxiety grew. "I was led to believe she's an old family friend. Was I misinformed?"

"No, no. She is a very good friend, given what Leopold has done for her. But you know me. I have a possessive temper, and I've discovered it is somewhat worse when it comes to Leopold. I did not like to think there might be another woman to tempt him away from me."

Blythe stared at Mercy in surprise. "That's utterly ridiculous."

Mercy shrugged. "When one is in love, and uncertain whether that love is returned in full measure, one does tend to imagine the worst. You were lucky with Raphael. He never looked at another woman but you. Come, I must meet the woman myself to see if she will be suitable for you. It will also be good to have another ally between us and the servants."

Mercy assigned Leopold's valet, Colby, to stay with Edwin, and then they hurried upstairs. Mrs. Turner was just being shown about by the housekeeper. They stopped in the hallway outside Blythe's bedchamber, and Mercy waved the older woman away with a request for a tea tray to be sent up. "Mrs. Turner, so nice to finally meet you."

Beth Turner sank into a deep, perfect curtsy. "Your Grace, Lady Venables."

Mercy smiled. Mrs. Turner smiled. And then both looked at

Blythe next. She smiled, too, and tried not to laugh. "Have you been shown the house and to your quarters?"

"Yes, my lady."

"Good. And your son is settled and occupied for the afternoon?"

"He is, thank you. Mr. Randall suggested he might spend some time in the stables. I believe the coachman has boys a little older than my George, and they will show him about the grounds and tell him where he might venture."

"Good. Good. Well, if you'll follow me, I can show you your duties."

Mrs. Turner followed Blythe about as she showed her where her things were kept. Unfortunately, when she opened her wardrobe doors, she revealed the colored gowns.

"Blythe? Is there something you forgot to tell me?" Mercy asked.

"No." Blythe shut the doors quickly. She'd changed her mind about coming out of mourning. She wouldn't need the gowns. Perhaps Mrs. Turner would appreciate them.

Mercy smiled. "There is nothing to be embarrassed about, Blythe. If you're finally ready to cast off your mourning, everyone will understand. In fact, I can assure you that I know of several gentlemen who will be very pleased."

"I'm not interested in other men." Blythe bit her tongue. That sounded very bad, even to her own ears. She couldn't help it if she thought of Tobias' torments more often than she should. She hoped Mercy would miss her slip and assume she referred to Raphael.

Mercy stepped around her and opened the wardrobe doors. "Were you going to wear one of these tonight?"

Blythe sighed. "I hadn't decided, but I don't think I will now. I brought them with me to see if I liked them still."

Her sister pulled out the blue silk, the one Blythe had quickly tried on last night. "I had a note from Miss Trimble that she and her cousins cannot come today, as arranged, so that gives me ample time to convince you to discard your somber tones and wear this instead. I've always admired you in blue."

A knock sounded on the door.

"Come," Blythe called.

The housekeeper swept through the door, tea tray poised in one hand. "Here we are, Your Grace."

"Thank you, Mrs. Callinan. Just set it over there."

The housekeeper's gaze passed over the room slowly, and then she left again.

Mercy sighed. "Mrs. Callinan is such a busybody, she'll have told everyone about the gowns by the time our tea is cold. Mrs. Turner, would you be good enough to pour? I fear my sister may need a refreshing cup or two before she is comfortable with my choice of gown for tonight."

"I will not wear any of the colors," Blythe protested. "I'll wear my favorite black brocade instead."

"That is where you are wrong, dear sister. I have been waiting for this day very impatiently. Black is much too severe a color on you. On any woman, for that matter." Mercy's hands settled on her shoulders and Blythe was steered toward a chair. "Let's have tea and discuss tonight. I think diamonds would look very well with that gown. What is your opinion, Mrs. Turner?"

Turner endured Mercy's stare, neither fidgeting nor automatically agreeing. That could only be for the best. Mrs. Turner was Blythe's employee, not Mercy's. She would be the one with the final decision on what stones to wear with the blue silk.

Turner passed over a tea cup with a steady hand. "I am unsure, Your Grace. It would depend on the style of the gown and the size of the stones. They should match the occasion."

"Exactly." Mercy clapped her hands together and leaned forward. "Now, about her hair…"

Chapter Sixteen

Devil take it. A closed carriage.

Tobias clenched his fist as the conveyance rumbled to a stop before the stairs of Romsey Abbey, horses tossing their heads impatiently. He was alone in the drawing room, waiting for the others to come down to get this torture over with.

The sight of the dark coach and four, similar to the one his parents had been murdered in, chilled his blood. So far, he'd managed to deflect Leopold's invitations to go anywhere in one. But he couldn't walk to tonight's entertainment. It was simply too far away, and he wouldn't arrive on time or in the expected pristine elegance of the gentleman he was to pretend to be.

Soft footfalls echoed in the hall and he looked up as Blythe stepped into the room, nervously gripping a cream shawl in her hands. She wore the blue silk he'd glimpsed on her last night and costly jewels at her throat, the rich colors reminding him of the clear waters of the Caribbean and the sunlight sparkling on the horizon at dawn.

Her throat moved as she swallowed, and then she smiled nervously. "I take it Her Grace is not ready?"

Thank God Mercy was not. If anyone else was here, he would not be at liberty to drink in the sight of her so completely. "So it would seem."

Blythe glanced over her shoulder. "Perhaps I should—"

"No, stay here and let me look at you."

She stilled, and he prowled closer. The color really did suit her complexion better, but the change of attire did suggest something else. She'd put aside her mourning. Had she done so because of his few kisses?

"You take my breath away."

She blushed and looked down, fiddling with her shawl. "Thank you."

Tobias caressed the skin beneath her chin until she lifted her face. Although tempted to kiss her again, he was hesitant to muss her up. She was perfect. Elegant, warm, and mouthwatering. "The gentlemen will be lined up to dance with you now. I have no doubts on that score. I may not deserve the honor, but I still claim the supper dance."

"Of course," she said. "I wouldn't go back on my word. Are you in better spirits now?"

He nodded slowly, surprised she asked. Her question went a long way to improving his mood. It seemed the revelation of his time aboard the slaver had not repulsed her.

"How did you get away from the slaver? I've heard such terrible things of them."

Tobias bit his lip. He hadn't intended to reveal the details of his past. Ladies certainly should not know. But Blythe had asked the question, and he'd promised to be honest with her. He couldn't very well lie outright after making such a point about his truthfulness. However, he could soften the details considerably. She'd most likely still be shocked. "The captain died suddenly two years ago, and we returned to port in Charleston soon after. In the confusion of the first night, I managed to slip away and swim to shore. I made my way on foot to Boston, where I hoped to find safe passage back."

Her eyes widened. "You've been to the Americas?"

He nodded. "I've been to many places. Most of which are not fit for your ears."

"It took you two years to return to England? How did you manage that feat?"

"I was hired on by Captain Arnold, a good man, and the owner of a whaler bound for England. I spent two years in the frigid waters of the North Atlantic hunting whales before the ship came home."

"That's dreadful," she whispered.

"That is my past."

Blythe was silent for a long while, head bowed. He stared down at the top of her head. She must be mortified now to have kissed a man with so little to recommend him.

Her hand rose to the corner of her eye and she sniffed. "I used to think well of the duke and his son. It seems I am an abominable judge of character."

He winced. "You judged me correctly."

"I have been surprised by your candor many times."

There wasn't much Tobias could say to answer that. He stepped away from what he couldn't have. Keeping to a good mood tonight while other men pawed at Blythe during the dancing was going to try his temper. He wanted Blythe, now, before any other gentleman could lay a finger to her pale skin, but now that she knew the truth of him, he'd never have a chance.

Heavy steps plodded down the central staircase and Leopold walked in, speaking as he came. "Mercy won't be much longer. She's saying good night to Edwin and seeing that Beth and George have everything they need…" His words died slowly to a whisper as he stared—rather stupidly, in Tobias' opinion—at Blythe.

Tobias stepped between them and waved his hand before his brother's face. "'Tis rude to stare at a lady."

Leopold coughed to cover his lapse, and then bowed. "Forgive me. You look lovely tonight, my lady."

Blythe acknowledged the compliment with a slight tilt of her head, but then she moved away, pacing the room while they waited for Mercy to join them. Devil take it. Was Blythe coming out of mourning that big a deal?

When Mercy arrived, she gave a little squeal at Blythe's attire, and then they hurried out to the carriage. Tobias trailed behind as panic threatened. Blythe had distracted him earlier with her beauty but the dark carriage, door open and waiting for him, sent a chill over his flesh.

He stopped before it.

"We haven't got all night, brother. Time is running from us."

Tobias closed his eyes at the familiar expression. Those had been his father's last words as they'd all left Romsey ten years ago.

A groom held the door, one brow raised.

Tobias couldn't make his legs work well enough to move forward. He couldn't climb inside. It would be like reliving history— the darkest day of his existence.

Blythe's face appeared in the carriage window, and she peered out at him. As she stared, he regained some of his courage. Her scrutiny challenged him to face his fear.

He took one step forward, then another, until he was at the door. One last step and he'd be inside with his memories to smother him.

Blythe smiled, and his panic eased. With a deep breath, he took his place beside her, facing the rear. Exactly where he'd sat on the day his parents had died.

The door shutting made him jump, and he glanced across the carriage to the opposite seat.

In the muted interior, Leopold reminded him even more of their father. Like his memory from the past, the two opposite were talking to each other and ignoring him. He gripped the bench seat beneath him, listening to the fine dark leather creak beneath his fingers, and closed his eyes.

Up until now, he'd managed to keep the memories at bay. He let them out rarely, and only when asked for specifics by Leopold. But as the carriage rolled away from Romsey Abbey, the memories overwhelmed him.

Rosemary had been angry, but that was nothing new. She'd not wanted to take the trip and had sulked on her side of the seat. As for him, he'd been dressed in his best clothes, scrubbed because they were to meet someone important, an old acquaintance of his mother's. Unfortunately, their identity escaped him, but the atmosphere in the carriage had not. His mother had been so sad that she hadn't been able to hide her sorrow. She'd clenched a handkerchief in her hand and repeatedly dabbed at her eyes. His father had done his best to comfort her, but he hadn't been very successful.

The carriage rattled over the estate bridge, and Tobias' eyes flew wide open as the sound stirred up another memory. His father might have told anyone who had asked that they were going to see an old friend in London—but they had changed direction as soon as they'd left Romsey.

They had not been overturned on the road to London, as he'd previously thought. They had traveled west instead.

His heart pounded. Why had their destination changed?

He shook his head, struggling to make the images clearer. Long stretches of silence, and the dark woods around them. Panic and anguish. His mother crying out in pain.

Blythe's gloved hand settled over his fist.

He grasped her hand quickly, desperate for the distraction she gave.

Blythe winced as Tobias crushed her hand in his. A violent tremble flowed up her arm from their joined hands, confirming her suspicions that Tobias was far from well. She twisted slightly on the bench, attempting to see his face better. His jaw was clenched, his lips pressed together, but his breathing was rushed as if he'd been sprinting. His hand was fire against hers, damp and warmer than it should be.

Although he had a strangling grip on her hand, she could move her thumb a little, and she strove to calm him by drawing small circles over his glove. She didn't know what had come over him, but he had to be well again before they reached the ball.

She glanced across the carriage, but her sister and Leopold were simply too caught up in their own conversation to notice Tobias' distress. However, she couldn't travel along holding Tobias' hand the whole way. She had to extract herself and find another solution.

With her free hand, she nudged her blanket to the floor, and then bent to retrieve it. As she did, Tobias released her.

However, his hand somehow ended up beneath her breast. Blythe sucked in a shocked breath as he took the opportunity to learn the shape of her breast again and caressed her nipple.

Heat swept over her cheeks, and she was grateful for the failing light. Blythe pulled the coach blanket higher up her chest to hide the fact that her nipples had hardened to embarrassing points.

Mercy glanced at her, smiled, and went back to her conversation with Leopold. Beside her, Tobias cleared his throat and then began to chuckle.

"Do share the joke, brother," Leopold demanded.

"I was, ah, just thinking about surprises. You never expect them."

Leopold scowled. "Well, of course. If you expected them, then you wouldn't truly be surprised."

"Quite right. Quite right," Tobias agreed.

He fell silent again, and his breathing returned to normal. At least her embarrassment had achieved something.

Tobias shifted on the seat, coming closer. Did he really find her presence a comfort, or had the mere thought of a dalliance wiped his mind of whatever distress ailed him?

The Dunwoody estate came into view, candlelight streaming through the windows, and she drew in a deep breath. If Mercy's, Leopold's, and Tobias' reactions were anything to go by, she would be subject to even more scrutiny because of her choice of gown. Mercy had been terribly persuasive, but Blythe was a touch anxious about how she would be received.

She raised her hand to her neck, feeling the comforting weight of her jewels against her skin. She was doing this by her own choice, even if Mercy had bullied her into it.

The carriage rolled to a stop and, after the stairs were lowered, Tobias bolted from the carriage, followed by his brother. Mercy reached across the space and patted her knee. "You look lovely, my dear. I'm sure you'll be much admired."

A small kernel of doubt rose up into her throat.

She reached for the gloved hand suspended in the doorway and the moment she grasped it, she knew it was Tobias'. His grip firmed, distracting her from her worries.

She wriggled her fingers loose once she was firmly on the ground and waited for Mercy to join them.

"Thank you, Leopold," Mercy whispered. "Lady Venables, shall we go in?"

Together they swept up the staircase, arm in arm, leaving the gentlemen to follow in their wake. She handed off her things to the waiting servants and then they were announced.

"Her Grace, the Duchess of Romsey, Lady Venables, Mr. Leopold Randall, and Mr. Tobias Randall."

The usual hush swept before them, and then the whispers started, fanning out to the far reaches of the room. Heads bobbed high over others to gawk. At them.

"This is as bad as a cattle sale," Leopold muttered.

"I was just thinking of a whaler's hold after a long voyage," Tobias replied dryly. "Stank just as bad, too."

Another ripple of conversation swirled from those standing closest, and Blythe held her head high. More comments like that, however accurate, might turn the tide firmly against Tobias. She really didn't want him to be on the outside of society from his first night. He might never recover to be well received anywhere.

Their hosts, who'd been absent from the door, rushed forward and fawned over Mercy. "My dear duchess, we feared you'd had a change of heart."

Mercy smiled. "Forgive me for our tardy arrival. I was distracted by the duke this evening. He wanted to speak of frogs, of all things. I do hope he doesn't wish to be a naturalist when he grows. He has far more important things to look forward to, after all."

The crowd around them twittered at her remark, and the mood changed to one of pleasure again.

After a time, Blythe's stepson, Venables, came forward. He acknowledged Blythe with a quick glance then turned his attention to Mercy. "Your Grace, such a pleasure to see you again."

"Lord Venables, it's always nice to be seen. It's been so long since you've visited the district that I considered you'd never return." Mercy's smile was as fraudulent as her words. "May I introduce you to the new additions to my party? May I present Mr. Leopold Randall and Mr. Tobias Randall, both newly returned to Romsey."

"More Randalls, heh?" He looked about him. "Soon we will be overrun."

"That is my hope, too. Life is much more lively with family underfoot. I do prefer it. Mr. Leopold Randall has asked me to marry him, and I have accepted gladly."

Another deafening rush of whispers rose around them. Mercy's statement had effectively put paid to any wild rumors about the match. Now they knew it for a fact.

Venables' skin changed to an unhealthy shade of gray. "Married?"

"Yes, married, or soon will be. I am quite looking forward to it. Would you excuse us? I simply must visit with Miss Emma Trimble."

Mercy smiled at Leopold, and he came forward to offer his arm. When she took it, another whisper swept the chamber and together they moved ahead.

Venables grabbed Blythe's arm and held her back. "Who is this fellow she's been convinced to wed?"

Blythe stared down at her stepson's hand until he released her. "Not that you hold much store in tender emotions, but he is the man who captured her heart. Isn't it a wonderful development that my sister has fallen in love again?"

"Of course, of course" he said quickly, but he didn't look at all pleased.

When Venables took his leave, claiming to see an old acquaintance across the room, Blythe was glad to see him go. He hadn't mentioned their lack of servants, and that was a blessing. He also hadn't remarked upon the absence of Adam's things and she didn't want to have a conversation about either topic in a crowded ballroom with every gossiping ear within hearing range.

Her gown moved as Tobias stepped up to her side. His face offered no clue as to what he was thinking. She snapped out her fan and waved it before her face. "Shall we rejoin the duchess?"

His gaze moved to the crowd where Venables stood. "Charming family you have there. Not even a polite greeting." His lips lifted in an easy smile. "I am at your service, my lady."

Two paces forward, their progress was halted by the bulk of Lord Archibald blocking the way. He reached for Blythe's hand without asking and pressed a lingering kiss to her knuckles. "A pleasure to see you again, my lady. You look," his gaze swept over her gown, "utterly breathtaking this evening."

His voice held an unfamiliar rasp and, disconcerted by his behavior, she reclaimed her hand quickly. "Lord Archibald." She gestured toward Tobias. "I am sure you remember Mr. Randall."

"Yes, I believe I do," Archibald said without warmth. The men shook hands, but it was the briefest of contact possible.

"Is Miss Trimble here? I cannot see her."

When Lord Archibald shrugged, Tobias gestured across the room. "She's dancing."

Blythe stretch up on her toes, but her view was blocked by a party of taller guests. "I cannot see who with."

Archibald stirred himself to check. "She's partnered by Lord Shaw at the present."

Blythe was stunned. If Lord Archibald had any real feelings for

Emma, he would never allow her to dance with Lord Shaw without watching over her like a hawk.

At her side, Tobias stirred restlessly. Rather than give Archibald a piece of her mind before witnesses, she smiled tightly. "I will catch up with Miss Trimble when she has a free moment. Excuse us."

She'd listen for the music to stop and catch her before Shaw could lead her astray.

"Lady Venables?" Lord Archibald asked suddenly. "May I have the pleasure of securing the supper dance on your card?"

Tobias cupped her elbow in a firm grip. That was his dance, of course, but Blythe was rather shocked by Archibald's request. She'd hoped he'd claim Emma for that set. "Forgive me, my lord, but that dance has already been claimed by another gentleman."

His gaze flittered around the room and when it settled on Tobias, his eyes narrowed. "Ah, then perhaps the one directly before the supper dance," he murmured.

Blythe agreed, but she was uneasy. Lord Archibald's behavior was just a little disconcerting. She couldn't shake off the sense that something had changed since last they'd met.

He bowed to her. "Do not forget our dance later, my lady. I am looking forward to our time together." His glance switched to Tobias, an unpleasant smile curling his lips.

She set her hand to Tobias' offered arm and moved away. What on earth had that last smile been about? Why would Lord Archibald behave so strangely with Tobias after just two short meetings?

When they reached Mercy, Tobias spoke with his brother, and then he moved to the rear of the group, out of the way and distant from any conversation. Blythe frowned. That was not the way to enter society and stake a place among the people here. His reticence would be remembered.

Someone tugged on her sleeve. She turned, startled to find that, while she'd been worrying about Tobias making a good impression, the music had stopped and Emma Trimble had found her first.

Emma grinned. "You look wonderful."

Blythe caught her friend's hands and squeezed. "As do you. Emma dear, do you remember Mr. Randall?"

Tobias came forward at her urging, an eager smile—one she immediately distrusted—on his face.

"Of course." Emma struck out her hand. "We have a dance later in the evening."

Tobias took up her hand and kissed the air above it. "After supper, correct?"

Emma's face creased into a delighted smile. "Thank you, sir. I shall look forward to it very much."

An awkward silence followed as Emma continued to stare. After a moment, Tobias excused himself and disappeared into the crowd. Emma's gaze followed him.

Blythe coughed. "When are you dancing with Lord Archibald?"

Emma's smile disappeared, replaced by a glum frown. "He's not asked. He's been distracted since I saw you last. We've barely spoken."

"Oh, Emma. I am so sorry." Blythe laid a hand to her throat. This wasn't going well at all.

"I dislike admitting this, but I do feel Mr. Randall's attention the other day was rather well timed. It seems I should resign myself to the fact that Archie sees me as a sister, even if we are third cousins."

"Don't give up so soon. I still believe you are the right woman for him."

"I'm no longer so sure he is the right man for me." Emma peered about. "Where do you think Mr. Randall has gone?"

Blythe wondered that, too, but only so he might stay away from Emma. He had made too big an impression on the young woman, and Blythe wouldn't like to have Emma's hopes dashed. Tobias wasn't the man for her, either.

She glanced over Emma's shoulder and spotted him, lingering beside the balcony doors, appearing ready to make an escape. His face was carved in grave lines; no trace of his usual smile. Since he wore a serious expression so rarely, Blythe fought the urge to roll her eyes. Actions of that nature were not ladylike, but so tempting when it came to him.

"Lady Venables."

Blythe turned to find herself surrounded by a dozen figures, men she knew ranging in ages from her own to far older. "Gentlemen," she greeted them nervously.

Lord Shaw stepped close. "Might I have the pleasure of the next dance, if you are not otherwise engaged?"

"Might I secure the supper dance from you tonight?" another asked.

"I'd like to request a set as well, my lady."

Blythe gasped. She'd not expected to have a full card tonight, and there were more gentlemen standing before her than were sets in the evening. She accepted those she could, but a few gentlemen left disappointed.

When she glanced at Emma, her friend's expression was bleak. "They all asked you to dance, but none asked me. Even the ones you disappointed."

Poor Emma. Blythe sympathize. "I cannot account for it, but I'm sure there is an explanation."

Emma's gaze dipped to Blythe's gown, her eyes narrowing. "There is an explanation. That dress and you're out of mourning at last. Excuse me. I should go join the wallflowers, where I belong." She broke away and disappeared into the crowd.

Blythe started after her, but Tobias stepped into her path. "It's not your fault," he said softly.

"No. Yet I do intend to say a few words when I dance with Lord Archibald later. He should have asked Miss Trimble to dance."

"The man should be shaking in his boots." Tobias smiled suddenly. "I'm still waiting for my punishment, and just thinking about it makes me unreasonably cold. Care to soothe me again?"

Rather than lecture him about his comment, Blythe returned her attention to the earlier event. "What happened in the carriage?"

He sighed heavily, amusement draining from his face. "Not now, B. I've almost found my sense of humor again. Let the matter rest."

She studied his face. He did look more like his usual self, but she could still remember the tremble in his hand. "For now I will, but you owe me an explanation as compensation for my crushed fingers."

"After supper." He nodded toward the crowd. "Right now, I believe you have another swain come to beg a dance of you. Try not to break too many hearts, my lady."

He stepped back with a laugh just as Lord Palmister joined her and promptly asked for a set, a slow one that suited his stiff knee, he joked. Blythe had to decline. Her card was full. It had been many years since she'd danced all night. She wasn't sure if she was up to it.

Chapter Seventeen

Leopold handed Tobias a drink. "You know, Mercy talks about Blythe as if she's a saint but by the looks of her tonight, her halo has been left behind. Watch over her, will you?"

Tobias sipped and discovered punch in his glass. Where was the whiskey when he needed it? "She's not our sister for me to have the right to watch over her."

"No. But she will be mine soon enough." He shook his head. "Why come out of mourning now? This is the worst possible time. We're going to be besieged with suitors at the abbey."

Tobias choked on his drink. "She might be out of mourning, but who said she's aiming for another husband?"

Leopold swallowed his drink and swapped it for another. "That dress does. If she was the type to take a casual lover, I wouldn't worry so much. But those men around her have determined expressions. Each is hoping she favors them. None, according to Mercy, would have honorable intentions. They're likely betting on who'll get into her bed first. I may have to break some heads."

Tobias clenched the glass in his hand. She'd be in his bed or none.

He quickly downed the glass. Where had that possessive thought come from? He lusted after Blythe, certainly. But anything else was impossible, unadvisable and definitely bad for Blythe's reputation. "I need a stronger drink."

"The card room has whiskey, I'm led to believe," Leopold murmured. "I'll take the first watch until supper. You can take over then."

Yes, definitely a stronger drink was required to get through the evening. "I have a dance with Blythe before supper."

Leopold slapped his shoulder. "Excellent. That makes things

even simpler. Just shadow her for the rest of the evening and keep the scoundrels at bay until we leave."

Easier said than done. He might just be the worst scoundrel in attendance tonight, for all the things he wanted to do with her. He took one last look at Blythe's surprisingly happy face and then edged out of the ballroom. He'd find the whiskey, and then maybe a nice quiet corner to get drunk in.

As he crossed the foyer, he heard a woman sniffling. Although he peered around, he could detect no trace of her. Mind you, if he was crying at a ball, he'd want to remain hidden, too.

He entered the card room, plucked a promising-looking glass from a footman and downed the contents. Ah, sweet whiskey. A balm for his bad mood.

Although he found cards interesting, he kept to the sidelines. Far too rich for his blood, and his pockets would never be deep enough for such play. He shook his head. Why gamble when you have nothing?

He listened to the conversation of the two gentlemen closest.

"Prime, if you ask me."

"Sensible," the other advised. "She won't demand a man stand on his head and hand over a fortune for her favors."

The two shared a long look and broke out into wide grins. "It's a bet."

They turned as one for the ballroom.

Tobias drained two more glasses as he told himself that both men could not have been referring to Blythe. Unfortunately, he couldn't entirely convince himself.

Too restless to remain still, he sauntered from the room in search of a new distraction. Again, soft sniffling reached him, but this time he stopped. A lady was truly distressed to still be crying like this. Despite his best interests being to ignore the sound, he couldn't. Perhaps he could be of help.

He took the stairs two at a time until he stood on the first landing. He scanned the shadowed alcove above. A glint of gem struck by moonlight. He climbed the rest of the way, and stopped a few yards from the weeping woman. Her head rose, and he discovered Miss Emma Trimble in tears. "Are you all right, Miss Trimble?"

She gasped and fell back in shock. "Where did you come from?"

"I heard crying and came to investigate." He edged a little closer. "Should I send Lady Venables to you?"

Miss Trimble sobbed. "You can't. She's dancing with Mr. Smedly Pierce now."

"Perhaps after she's done with him?"

Miss Trimble's bottom lip trembled. "Then she's to dance with Lord Parker."

Blythe's full dance card did pose a problem to engaging in conversation with her. He glanced down the staircase to check that they remained unobserved and moved closer to Miss Trimble. "Why are you sitting up here, crying on your own?"

Despite her tears, Miss Trimble scowled. "Well, I wouldn't cry in the middle of the ballroom, would I? People would gossip in the most horrendous fashion."

Tobias sighed. "I can see why you and the countess get along so well. You sound just like her when you are out of sorts. Why are you crying, girl?"

Miss Trimble sniffed some more. "I am crying because my dance card is empty of names for the rest of the evening, save yours. Even Lady Venables has more sets claimed."

"Ah," Tobias said softly. "Then I am the luckiest of men."

Miss Trimble stared at him, and smiled.

Engaging in conversation alone with Miss Trimble could give rise to a scandal if they were discovered. That could be one way to shortcut the courtship, except, then he would be winning a wife without any effort on his part. That thought didn't settle well with him.

He took a pace toward the top step. "I must return to the ballroom before we are noticed, but I have a question for you before I go that may lighten your mood. When was the last time Lady Venables danced?"

Miss Trimble wiped her hands over her cheeks. "Oh, not since she was widowed. Oh…" the girl whispered as realization dawned.

Blythe had been a spectator on the sidelines for years, and in Tobias' opinion, it was about time she had a little harmless fun. "Exactly. She is finally enjoying herself as she hasn't since her husband died. Try to be a little understanding and happy for her. Imagine what standing on the sidelines for a few years might feel like, and then decide if you should be crying over her success. Until our dance, Miss Trimble."

He moved down a few steps.

"Sir, wait."

He paused. "Yes, Miss Trimble?"

"Thank you. You've made me feel so much better about tonight."

Tobias nodded, and then returned to the ballroom, his gaze drawn to Blythe as she twirled about the dance floor. He did like to see her happy. He craved her smiles. But as he looked around, he spied those two gentlemen—and he used the term loosely—watching Blythe with predatory smiles.

As Blythe was led from the dance floor, flushed and smiling, he smoothly rejoined their party to keep the wolves at bay. Blythe shifted to stand at his side.

He glanced down at her as she fanned herself. Her breasts rose and fell beneath her gown in the most beguiling way. Her other gowns had much higher necklines and he'd been deprived the excellent view until now. He hoped he could survive the set without gawking and embarrassing them both.

A footman came closer, and Tobias secured a glass of punch for Blythe before the wolves descended to do the same.

Her gaze rose to meet his. "Thank you, sir."

"You're welcome, B."

Blythe leaned closer. "You haven't asked anyone to dance yet," she whispered. "I strongly recommend you do. There are many young ladies of good family who will be happy to accept you as a partner."

Tobias wrenched his gaze from the smooth curve of her right breast. "Lady Venables, do you perhaps remember our conversation of last night? I don't need you to make a match for me, too."

"Of course I remember. I said dance, not propose marriage to them." Her fan fluttered faster while she looked over the crowd around them. On the surface, Blythe appeared remote, serene even. He just happened to know she kissed like a bad man's fantasy.

"Well, I'm not keen on having anyone but you in my arms, so leave it be," he murmured.

Her eyes widened, kissable lips parted in surprise. Did she really think other women were more alluring? He wanted to kiss her here and now and damn the consequences. The only thing that stopped him was his determination not to make an arse of himself or embarrass her.

A new dance partner appeared and swept Blythe off for another dance.

Mercy moved to his side and clutched his arm. "Isn't it a wonderful evening, Mr. Randall?"

He offered her a fraudulent smile. "It is, Your Grace."

Mercy sighed happily as she clapped in time with the music. "I'm so glad for Blythe. She deserves a bit of fun after all she's been through. One day, the right man will turn her head and she'll be the happiest woman in England. Well, after me, of course."

She turned back to converse with Leopold with a laugh, and Tobias cursed under his breath. Three sets seemed an eternity before he could have Blythe in his arms. Letting her go again, he feared, would be problematic.

She was to dance with Lord Archibald before his set, and Tobias had the distinct feeling that the earl had something else besides dancing with Blythe on his mind. Some lucky, wealthy bastard would win her.

He headed for the card room so he didn't have to witness the start of a proper courtship.

It may not seem that way to others, but Blythe was fairly certain that Tobias was well on his way to being foxed. He was polite to everyone he met, but his eyes had a glazed look about them. She executed a turn, linked hands with Lord Archibald, and then continued on. She'd never danced so much in one evening, and she was looking forward to her set with Tobias and a quiet supper with him.

He had some explaining to do, too.

She clapped as the dance ended and walked from the floor at Lord Archibald's side. His behavior while they danced had increased her anxiety. "You dance like an angel," he said.

Blythe hoped it was a terrible misunderstanding on her part, but he gave her every indication that he was flirting with her. "Thank you," she murmured.

Archibald had spoken of his estate, of how pleased he was that she got along with his sisters; he spoke of the future, hinting at how happy he would be then. At no time had he mentioned Emma in his plans. It was as if she didn't exist to him.

The next set was announced, a waltz, and she looked for Tobias. He was watching her, a frown turning down the corners of his mouth. Oh dear. Did he not know the steps? She hadn't thought to inquire about that particular dance before she accepted his request.

After a moment's hesitation, he crossed to her side and led her out onto the floor. He pulled her into his arms as people craned to see who danced together. His touch took her breath away, and she tightened her grip on his hand as panic assailed her. She didn't want him to fail at this. "Can you waltz, Tobias?"

His smile was brief. "We're about to find out, aren't we?"

That didn't sound terribly promising. When they moved off, Blythe held her breath.

Tobias' movements were not the smooth steps she'd grown accustomed to from her partners, but he wasn't terrible. As she let her tension drain away, their movements fell into a beautiful symmetry. They could dance together. She just needed to relax and trust him.

She spun in his arms, content and stirred by the music.

"Careful, B. You'll have everyone whispering."

She looked up. "Why?"

"Because you are smiling."

"I'm enjoying my evening, Mr. Randall."

He drew her closer; still respectable, but near enough to make her heart skip a beat. "You didn't smile so brightly for your other swains."

She frowned. "I don't have swains."

"Would you prefer it if I said suitors?"

Blythe glanced about her nervously. "You've come to the wrong conclusion. Regardless of my attire this evening, I'm not interested in marrying again. I love my husband."

Tobias laughed bitterly. "I am well aware of that. The late Lord Venables must have been quite a man. However, it appears that every gentleman you've spoken to tonight considers himself in the running to win you. One way or the other."

That didn't sound so good. "What do you mean by one way or the other?"

"Honorably…or dishonorably."

Blythe blanched. A bitter taste filled her mouth. "How much did you wager on having me?"

"Nothing. It isn't a fair bet."

She scowled at his answer. He sounded sure of himself. "Do you think you've already won?"

The dance came to an end, and they stopped. Tobias raised her hand to his lips and then merely bowed over her hand. "I'm certain, given the exalted gentlemen after you, that I'd lose." He smiled suddenly. "But that isn't the whole reason. I may have been polished till I shine as bright as a new penny, but we both know what kind of man lies beneath the finery. Shall we go in to supper, my lady? You appear done in."

Chapter Eighteen

Tobias had not lied when he'd told Blythe he'd lose any wager made about getting her into bed. As the evening progressed, he'd observed the fellows Blythe danced with. Most were landed peers, wealthy and influential. She'd be a fool to fall into his bed if she had a chance to snare one of them for a husband.

However, Blythe's mention of her abiding love for her husband had soothed him somewhat. The dashing, late Lord Venables was much admired and talked of, and Blythe loved him still. Any man worthy of her hand had to convince her to set that love aside and start afresh.

That man wouldn't be him.

He held her chair as she sat, and then fetched a plate of supper and a cup of tea. When he returned to the table, Blythe pounced on him. "What happened in the carriage?"

His heart, previously slow and steady in its beating, lurched. Damn her for bringing up his anxiety now. He shook his head.

Blythe leaned forward. "Tell me now, quickly," she whispered. Her foot touched his and tapped against the leather of his boot under the table.

"I learned the hard way to dislike carriages," he managed to growl out.

"But why?" Her eyes suddenly widened. "Oh. Oh dear…I'm so sorry for bringing it up again tonight. I never thought."

She covered her mouth with her hand. Her foot pressed harder against his boot.

Mercy and Leopold joined them, giving Tobias the chance to escape. He stood. "I find I'm not hungry after all, Lady Venables. Do you forgive me if I abandon you? I need some air."

He didn't wait for her answer. He had to get as far away from the memories as he could. He threaded his way through the crowd and reached the relative safety of the terrace. A few people had gathered at the head of the staircase leading to the gardens, but they were far enough away not to bother him. He leaned his hip against the balustrade and folded his arms across his chest.

He shouldn't have deserted Blythe like that, but she should not have asked for the cause of his panic when she did. He'd just started to forget the unpleasant beginning of his evening.

He raked his fingers through his hair, striving to think of something better.

Blythe. Damned if he could forget the sweet taste of her lips. He wanted more, and he couldn't have more. She was destined for someone else.

Frustrated by his fixation on her, he reentered the ballroom by the side door, and a woman standing on the edge of the crowd caught his eye. Smooth auburn hair, smoky-dark bedroom eyes. She fluttered her fan restlessly, inviting him for more than just conversation. She wasn't anything like Blythe, and he was sorely tempted by her.

He circled the room, picked up a glass of punch from a footman and approached the woman. Her lips lifted in a merry smile, but then she turned her back on him and left the ballroom at a leisurely pace. Tobias followed, curious about her antics. Proper women did not encourage improper attention so brazenly unless they were eager for a lover.

Leopold had supplied all the necessary warnings for his first foray into society. He knew what he was getting into, and was sure to like it.

He stepped into a dimly lit chamber and spied another door open to the terrace. Moonlight cast a woman's shadow on the parquetry floor, and he moved toward her eagerly. He blinked as he stepped through the doorway—she'd vanished into thin air as if she had never been.

He turned in a slow circle, and then groaned as three shadows appeared out of the gloom. Lord Archibald and two tall gentlemen glared menacingly at him. He'd not been introduced to the other two.

Tobias nodded carefully. "Gentlemen, to what do I owe the honor?"

"You're to take yourself away," Archibald began. "She's not for the likes of you."

Wonderful. Archibald really was jealous of any attention bestowed on Miss Trimble. He'd taken his earlier flirtation with his cousin, Miss Trimble, as a serious intention to pursue her for her heavy dowry. If Archibald was so keen on her, he should have asked her to dance. "Keep your powder dry, she's already made up her own mind about who she wants."

The trio circled, cutting him off from the soiree taking place inside.

"Her mind can be changed again," Lord Archibald growled. "Just stay away from Lady Venables."

"Lady Venables?" He had to be joking. Surely. Tobias laughed. "You've got balls for brains. She—"

Archibald's fist landed in his gut without warning.

Tobias fell, stunned by the unexpected blow. Was the man going to fight over a woman who didn't want him?

Archibald's two companions caught his arms and dragged him to his feet while Archibald readied himself to deliver another blow. Apparently, Tobias was to have no say in the matter.

He refused to be restrained.

Tobias kicked out with both feet, striking Archibald squarely in the chest and knocking him to the ground. Since his arms were held loosely, he continued his flight, flipping over the top of his two assailants before they could stop him.

In their surprise, they let go his arms, and Tobias grabbed both their heads and whacked them together.

All three remained on the ground, staring at him in shock. He tugged on his coat sleeves and waistcoat to make sure his attire was still in order.

The life he'd lived did have its uses. He may have been caught by surprise initially, but he'd never be taken by force again.

Lord Archibald pressed a hand to his chest, wheezing slightly.

Tobias scowled at him. "Imbecile. Lady Venables still loves her late husband. You'd do better to keep a watch over your own cousin. She's got her eye on a man to wed, but I don't think he deserves her affection."

Tobias spun on his heel and stalked back inside. This is what he'd come home to—idiots and women who didn't follow through with their unspoken promises.

When he returned to his party, he threw a scowl at Blythe where she danced with an older man. This was all her fault. He should have stayed at home guarding the duke rather than sparring with society.

A footman drew near and he took two glasses, ignoring the shocked whispers around him. He downed one glass and then the other. He took a third and fourth from the footman and sent him on his merry way. If Blythe had a problem with his drinking, she could go to the devil like everyone else.

Blythe fanned herself as another set ended. What an exhausting night. She'd never been as sought after before. "My dear, you dance like an angel still."

She smiled at Lord Merrow's statement, one that matched every other dance partner she'd had tonight, save Tobias. She'd missed a step during their set as she'd spotted Tobias slumped untidily in a chair across the room. "Thank you, my lord. You are very kind. Please give my regards to your wife when next you see her. It's been too long since we've spoken."

Lord Merrow's wife was a dear lady, but she hardly ever came to these events. It must be painful to watch her husband ogling each and every dance partner. Blythe knew what Lord Merrow was about. Thanks to Tobias' warning, she was more alert to her dance partners' seemingly innocent suggestions that they could take a stroll or get some air on the terrace.

She wasn't looking for a lover. If she ever did want one, there was one lying in wait for her across the room.

She said good night to her partner and then glanced around. Tobias had disappeared again.

She rejoined her sister, and Mercy caught her arm and steered her toward the door. "May we go now, my dear? I ache to be home again with Edwin."

Blythe leaned into her sister. "You should have said something earlier. I could have made my excuses and departed an hour ago. I fear my feet may never recover."

"So you were much trodden on. Did Tobias do that?"

"No. He danced extremely well." Surprisingly, out of all of her partners, she'd enjoyed their dance best. She'd known what to expect from his conversation and had been completely at ease with him.

"I thought so, too. I must confess, I bullied him into practicing the steps at home. There was much whispering about him tonight, and Miss Trimble fairly glowed with joy while they danced." Mercy sighed happily. "He must have charmed her completely."

Blythe pressed her lips together and then released them quickly. She shouldn't show her annoyance that Tobias had made even more of an impression on Emma. She collected her shawl and looped it around her shoulders, her joy in the evening diminishing. When she looked ahead again, she found Tobias loitering in the entrance hall. He bowed politely and fell into step behind her with his brother.

"Where the devil have you been?" Leopold demanded once they had moved out of the butler's earshot.

"Admiring how better men live," Tobias replied. "Not a bad little cottage."

"What's got into you tonight? You've barely spoken a civil word to anyone since supper."

Blythe glanced over her shoulder as Tobias shrugged. Their eyes met, and he scowled again. Blythe faced forward, hurrying down the staircase to their waiting carriage.

The carriage. Dear heavens, he must be on edge at having to enter it again.

Once Mercy had settled inside, Blythe climbed in and took her place, pulling the blanket about her to ward off the chill in the air. Leopold climbed in next and, after several moments, Tobias joined them—his breathing already unsteady.

What could she do, discreetly, to distract him?

She flicked the coach blanket across his knees and adjusted her shawl tighter about her, inching closer to Tobias as she did so. As she'd hoped, Tobias' hand skimmed to her thigh. "May I be of assistance?"

Blythe was thrown forward as the coach moved off. Tobias caught her and set her back on the bench. With both his hands sliding over her hips, her own breathing grew unsteady. She looked over her shoulder. "I think the material is twisted at the back."

Tobias obliged and fussed with her wrap with one hand. When

he was done, he tucked his hand under the blanket and caught hers. His grip was firm, and she peered carefully at him. His breathing appeared calmer, although her own was hardly steady.

The return trip to Romsey passed quietly. Tobias appeared to doze, but his thumb caressed her hand intermittently, proving him awake. Blythe had a lot of time to consider the evening and the man sitting beside her. If she were honest with herself, she couldn't seem to remove him from her mind. She'd worried at his reception for the entire evening. When he was out of sight, she'd considered looking for him.

That he'd warned her of the gentlemen betting on getting into her bed highlighted how unfairly she had considered him before now. He wasn't a bad man, per se. But he was blunt and brazen when he spoke of what he wanted. He'd been more than kind to her considering Adam's things. He'd stored them without asking for anything in return.

Despite everything that had gone on between them, the kisses and caresses that shook her world, Blythe had never felt pressured. Teased certainly, but that was all.

The carriage rolled to a stop before Romsey Abbey and Tobias shot out immediately. By the time they had all disembarked, he was crossing the threshold and promptly disappeared inside the vast building. Clearly, her actions had not been enough of a distraction. She should remember, if the occasion ever presented itself again, that merely holding hands was insufficient to counter his distress.

Blythe followed Leopold and Mercy inside, puzzled by her disappointment. Why should she care if Tobias needed something more than she offered? He wasn't hers to look after.

She slowed her steps and allowed Mercy and Leopold to walk together ahead of her up the stairs. The evening had been a success and they must be glad.

She watched their progress but then noticed one of the paintings hanging over their heads was not straight. She was sure it had been before they'd left though. When she looked around, others seemed to be also not quite perfectly hung anymore.

Wilcox drew near. "Can I help you, my lady?"

Blythe pressed her finger to her lips, preventing her questions from tumbling out. "No, I don't think so."

She stepped up on the first rise, but her thoughts tumbled over themselves. Why would anyone move paintings, family portraits, at this time of night? There was no need for the servants to clean at this hour. They should have sought their beds or their own entertainment by now.

When she made the first landing, she glanced down at Wilcox.

He watched her ascent.

A chill swept her skin, and she hurried for the family wing. Leopold and Mercy had already disappeared from sight, no doubt already with the young duke.

She headed to her nephew's chamber, too, and she knocked softly so she wouldn't wake him if he was asleep.

"Come in, Blythe," Mercy called.

She opened the door and peered around the gap. "I just wanted to say good night."

Mercy smiled at her sleeping child. "You also wanted to peek in on Edwin, didn't you? My son is so lucky to have you to watch over him, too. Good night sister. Pleasant dreams."

"Good night, Lady Venables," Leopold murmured as he tucked Edwin's arms beneath the covers and brushed his hair from his eyes.

The more time she spent around Leopold, observing his attention to the boy, the more she softened toward him. He was a good man, despite the past. It had just taken time for her to see it. "Until tomorrow, Leopold."

She closed the door behind her as Mercy crowed, "See, I told you she has grown fond of you, my love."

Blythe moved away, amused by her sister's observation. She had gotten over the shock of Leopold fathering her nephew. Perhaps they had a chance to be friends one day.

She let herself into her bedchamber and reached for the jewels around her throat, glad that she'd ordered Mrs. Turner to bed instead of waiting up to attend her. She needed some time alone to sort out her thoughts. The evening had been more interesting than she'd expected.

She sat at her dressing table and lifted her hands to her hair. After removing the pins, she rubbed her tender scalp with her fingertips.

"I wanted to thank you for your assistance this evening," Tobias said quietly behind her.

She spun on the bench and found him a few feet away, still perfectly dressed from the evening out. "My goodness, you can be quiet when you want to be. Thanks are unnecessary."

"No. Not from me. You helped without asking, and I do appreciate that. My behavior towards you has been less than exemplary. You deserved better from me, and you shall have it from tomorrow on."

Blythe stood unsteadily. The last time the pirate had been in her bedroom, he'd been filled with bravado and excitement. The change in his demeanor was disconcerting. "From tomorrow, but not from tonight?"

He smiled. "I wanted to talk to you before morning comes, and this seemed the quickest way to get you alone."

"A delay of a day to be a gentleman."

"A day and ten years." He gently took her hand in his and pressed a kiss to the back of it. "I should not have mauled you in the carriage, but it certainly helped. I couldn't think of anything but the warmth of your body and the taste of your lips for the entire journey. I would have spoken of my gratitude once on solid ground, but I had to get away quickly."

She stared up at him and saw desire flare in his eyes. Her heart thudded painfully in response, and she licked her lips. "Why is that?" She lifted her hand and touched his chest. His warmth filled her with a yearning to be held tight in his arms.

"Because thinking of your body so close to mine aroused me." He touched her unbound hair and sifted the strands between his fingers. "Seeing you like this isn't helping, either."

He stepped back suddenly, and bowed.

"Good night, beautiful lady. I promise to be a better man tomorrow."

Then he was gone, slipping from her chamber and leaving her more confused than ever. She dropped onto the dresser stool, astonished to be disappointed that Tobias had gone away.

Chapter Nineteen

Tobias swirled the remaining whiskey around the bottom of his glass, admiring the rich color before he swallowed it whole. The Duke of Romsey possessed a truly good cellar. One of these days, he should check how large a stock he kept. A pity Edwin was four years old and too young to enjoy his own beverages. Maybe later, when he'd grown up to be a man, they could get roaring drunk together. Perhaps, if he was still around, he would.

He tipped his head back and closed his eyes, delaying his departure a few more minutes. He was not quite ready to pay a social call to his dance partner of the previous evening, as good manners dictated he should. Too many thoughts preyed on his mind, and he required the scant comfort whiskey offered to sweeten his sour mood.

Heavy footsteps crossed the room, coming toward him. "Was that another gentleman caller for Lady Venables?"

Tobias sighed, opening his eyes to view his brother. "Yes, I believe so."

Blythe was responsible, indirectly, for his foul mood. She had gentlemen almost lining up their carriages along the driveway to see her today. The word had spread that she'd cast off her mourning, and the fellows who'd danced with her last night, and ones who hadn't even attended the soiree, had come to call. Rich, titled men who could afford to keep her in the style she was accustomed to.

He hadn't known his financial situation bothered him so much until today.

From what he could see from his vantage point in the library, the admirers were near to panting in anticipation. He could understand their hope to spend more time with the woman—but he didn't like it, which was why he was holed up in the library drowning in regrets. Blythe wasn't for him, and he was certain to hear a marriage announcement very soon.

Leopold eased into a nearby chair with a groan. "I was thinking of going over to Harrowdale tomorrow to see what must be done to make the place livable. Would you care to come with me?"

Tobias poured another drink before he answered. How could he hide Blythe's things from Leopold if he was set on an inspection of Harrowdale? He downed the glass as he considered the possibilities. Leopold was the sort of man to view a house from top to bottom and side to side before he made any final decisions.

He needed to keep his brother away from Harrowdale until Blythe had settled on who she'd wed or reclaimed her property. "I can manage whatever might be required for Harrowdale. You have enough on your plate as it is. I've been there a few times now, and I know the work ahead of me. The roof is sound, windows intact. All that's required is a thorough clean and the laying in of stores for winter. During the spring and summer months, I'll work on improving the gardens. They're a little wild these days."

"You're certain you wish to live there alone so soon?" Leopold eyed the whiskey bottle at his elbow with a frown, clearly disapproving. "You'll need servants."

"I'm looking forward to living at Harrowdale again. The place suits me. As for servants, I won't need many, nor can I afford to keep them."

Leopold poured himself a whiskey, shifting the bottle out of Tobias' reach in the process. "You would need more servants, should you marry. We can talk about it then. Women like to have assistance, and the company."

"That is true. Women like to have their comforts."

"So, are you seriously considering marriage?"

Tobias glanced away, uncomfortable but knowing the conversation was necessary. Did he want to live alone for his entire life? A tavern wench might relieve his needs, but a wife would provide some companionship every day and prevent him from turning into a crusty old bachelor. He liked the idea of coming home to Harrowdale and having someone waiting to see him. "I might be."

"Good. We don't want you to be alone your whole life."

Tobias regarded his brother steadily. "We?"

Leopold grinned. "Mercy still has it in her head to make a match for you. You could do well with her help."

"The only thing the woman requires is a friendly disposition, a healthy dowry, and a strong stomach," Tobias said bitterly.

Leopold frowned. "You're worried about how your scars will be received? I'm sure the right woman will overlook the injuries you sustained if you take her into your confidence."

"Optimist." Tobias crossed to the window facing the south gardens, enjoying the way the world swayed and then slowly righted itself again. Blythe had touched his scars and not run screaming. Perhaps Miss Trimble would view them without revulsion, too? What would a young lady think of his past if he confessed the worst of it to her?

He stared at the gardens, wondering what it took to court a proper lady. Leopold's lessons had not touched upon the subject near enough. He'd have to embarrass himself and likely ask something that should be obvious to others. But he supposed the first step in any courtship was the paying of calls, even in the rain.

A light drizzle was falling, bathing the grounds in fine mist. In the distance, he could see Beth and her boy, George, walking away from the abbey together.

Beth Turner had settled when she couldn't marry the man she'd loved. How easily had she reconciled herself to her second choice for a husband? He turned to Leopold. "How is Beth adjusting to life at the abbey?"

"Well, I believe. Wilcox will tell me if there are any problems."

Beth wouldn't tell anyone if she was unhappy. She was the sort to keep her problems to herself, no matter how heartbreaking they might be. "And the boy?"

"I've asked Allen to keep an eye on him during the day while Beth is otherwise engaged. He's a fine boy. Much like his father."

"Temper to match?" Beth's husband may have been Leopold's friend, but Tobias had always been wary of the man. Had he been good to Beth while he lived?

"Not that I've seen so far, thankfully. I believe he takes after his mother in temper. I have high hopes he'll make something of himself when he's grown. That reminds me, I've an advertisement to place for a tutor."

"Better you than me. I think—" Tobias was interrupted by a coach and four drawing up before Romsey. "Who's that now?"

Leopold hurried to the window and peeked out. "Lord Archibald and… Oh, he doesn't appear to have brought his sisters or Miss Trimble with him today. That makes seventeen potential suitors."

Tobias settled before the fire with a heavy heart. "How is he dressed?"

"Very well, actually. Very fine indeed."

Tobias snorted and drained his glass. He set it carefully on the table, listening as Archibald requested a private audience with Blythe. Tobias had been right in his suspicions last night. Archibald wasn't wasting any time in proposing to Blythe, and that meant Miss Trimble was free to be pursued.

He stared at the flames crackling in the hearth. The match would be a good one for him. However, Miss Trimble could be devastated if her first love married Blythe. Perhaps he could ease Miss Trimble's heartache by courting her, once he discovered how it should be done.

He stood and picked up the hat he'd tossed aside when he'd come downstairs. Time to do his duty and call on Miss Trimble.

"Don't you go anywhere, sir," Mercy scolded as she slipped into the room and left the door slightly ajar. "There are important developments occurring this morning that you should not miss."

Tobias didn't want to hear about Lord Archibald's call, but he felt compelled to pretend otherwise. "Is that so?"

"Yes." Mercy clasped her hands together. "My sister has always been well regarded and, as I hoped, her coming out of mourning yesterday has triggered the local unwed lords' interest. But I had not anticipated such a determined crowd. I wish I could stay to hear the exchange between Lord Archibald and Blythe, for I am sure, judging by his demeanor, that he is going to propose to her this very day!"

Tobias tightened his grip on the brim of his hat. "That is interesting news, but you will have to save the telling for later. I was just on my way to pay a call to Miss Trimble."

Mercy nodded in approval. "I will. You may be certain to hear all the details later. I will not allow Blythe to leave out a single one in the telling."

Wonderful. More torture to come. He jammed his hat upon his head and left the room.

Just as he tugged on his great coat and passed the drawing room doors, Lord Archibald professed his undying love for Blythe.

He gritted his teeth and stalked outside into the pouring rain. His opportunities to savor Blythe's sweet lips were at an end.

Blythe stamped her foot. "My lord, allow me to tell you that you are impossibly dense!"

Lord Archibald, still kneeling upon the floor, blinked at her refusal. Finally. She had told him three times now that she couldn't accept. What did Emma see in the fool?

She pressed her hands to her cheeks. Oh, dear heavens, poor Emma. After last night's disagreement, which Blythe hadn't managed to patch up to her satisfaction, Emma would be utterly heartbroken.

Archibald regained his feet. "I was given to understand that you would accept my suit."

"What?" Blythe shook her head. "I cannot imagine who told you such a falsehood, but you are entirely wrong. I've no wish to marry you."

His frown would be comical if the situation wasn't so serious. "But you're out of mourning, and I felt that we had come to know one another well enough to hope for more."

"My lord, are you basing your proposal on a few conversations spent among company?"

"Well, yes, of course I am. Anything more would have been scandalous, given your grief for the late Lord Venables. I had hoped time had healed your heart enough to accept another in his place."

Blythe closed her eyes. When she could speak with a civil tone, she opened them. "No one will ever replace Raphael in my affections. He was an exceptional man, and I miss him dearly. But it would take far more than mere conversation to change my mind on the subject, and not just the surprise proposal you have offered."

"The younger Randall said you'd not forgotten your husband, but I hated to place much store in the devil's words." Archibald was before her in an instant. "The current Lord Venables approves of my suit, and I'll do everything I can to convince you, you may be sure of that."

"You spoke to my stepson?"

"Of course." He pulled her to him roughly and planted a kiss on her lips. It was hard and lacked every tender feeling Blythe had come to expect from kisses. It was like being mauled by a wild beast.

She shoved him away and pressed her hand to her bruised lips. "Sir, you forget yourself!"

He followed her. "We would be a perfect match. Your elegance and reputation for my wealth and title. My sisters adore you already, so you have no concerns on that score."

Blythe held out her hand to halt his approach. "Do not ever touch me again! I thought you a gentleman, but I see I was in error."

A frown crossed Archibald's face. "My lady, your reserve does you credit, but I am aware that ladies often speak differently to what's in their hearts. My own family is proof of that."

"What of Emma?"

"What about my cousin? She will step aside once we've wed and allow you to take control of the household. I have indulged her enough as it is."

He didn't know Emma adored the ground he walked on. Blythe swallowed her sadness, but she still had to convince him they wouldn't suit. Since kind honesty hadn't worked to let him down gently, she'd have to be blunt. "You, sir, are more of a fool than I believed. You do not know the first thing about women and what would make them happy."

A cocky grin crossed his face. "I know the important things very well. Come here. Enough of your games."

A male throat cleared at the doorway. "Forgive me for interrupting, Lady Venables."

Leopold Randall stood with his hand on the door. His scowl would have cracked the earth if he had that power within his reach.

Archibald scowled. "This is a private matter, sir, and none of your concern."

Blythe ducked away from Lord Archibald and put space, and chairs for good measure, between them.

Leopold glanced at her briefly, and then returned his attention to Lord Archibald, his free hand curling into a fist. "I'm making it my concern. Lady Venables has said no to your proposal—repeatedly—and that is an end to the matter. Please leave Romsey before I embarrass you and throw you out on your arse."

"As if you would dare!" Archibald picked up his hat. "My lady, it pains me to share this confidence with you, but Venables mentioned last night that he's leased Walden Hall to a friend for the summer. Marriage to me will save you the embarrassment of becoming a burden on your family. I will see you again tomorrow, and every day, until you accept."

Blythe lifted her chin. "I will not be at home to you when you call."

"You'll come around soon enough. Good day, my dear." He slowly sauntered out, leaving Blythe alone with Leopold.

Leopold crossed the chamber until he stood before her. "Forgive my intrusion. Wilcox was concerned for your welfare."

"Wilcox sent for you? Was he spying on me?"

Leopold laughed suddenly. "He said it was the first time you had raised your voice loud enough to be heard in another chamber. He feared you were not having much luck convincing Archibald that his affections were not returned, and he thought I might help convince him to go away. Are you all right?"

Blythe covered her face. "He wouldn't listen."

"So I gathered. Is it true what Archibald said about leasing Walden Hall?"

Blythe pressed her hand to her brow. "I don't know. My stepson has not shared any such plans with me. If they exist, he is yet to inform me of his intentions for Walden Hall."

Leopold patted her arm awkwardly. "Mercy has gone to fetch Edwin. She thought the boy would turn your mind from the unpleasantness."

A tear fell down her cheek as she nodded. "Edwin is a balm on any blighted day."

"It's the dimples," Leopold said without smiling as he handed over his handkerchief.

A laugh escaped her control. "Only a father would claim that."

He grinned, displaying both deep dimples in his cheeks.

Blythe pressed the linen to her eyes. She needed more comfort than a square of linen and her sister's future husband's presence. She needed something better. Safer.

A sob tore from her throat, and Leopold drew her into his arms. "He's gone now," he said.

His embrace was light, and she didn't push him away immediately. She was keenly aware that Leopold wasn't at all like Tobias— and it was his embrace she wished for.

She eased away from Leopold and dabbed at her eyes. Tobias had never forced his attentions on her, except once, and she wasn't sure if their first kiss had even been given because he desired her. She had never wanted anyone but Raphael until now.

When Tobias kissed her, she never considered asking him to stop, but he always drew away before things became too heated between them. It shocked her that Tobias' improper pursuits these past weeks had been more gentlemanlike than those of her proper suitors.

Tobias had completely turned her head around.

Chapter Twenty

Tobias glanced about the flower-strewn parlor of Wimple Hall and held in a groan. He had forgotten to bring a posy of flowers for his dance partner as he belatedly recalled he should. He hoped Miss Trimble didn't hold it against him. "You look lovely today, Miss Trimble. I wanted to thank you for the dance last night."

And indeed she did look lovely and sweet and perfectly composed. Her soft honey-blonde hair was swept back in an elegant bun. Her gown, a white spotted affair, clung in all the right places. Tobias was impressed by her poise and elegance. A far cry from the misery he'd discovered her in last night.

"Thank you, sir," Miss Trimble replied softly, eyes downcast and demure.

Her companions were not quite so demure. Miss Francesca and Miss Helena Trimble raked him with bold looks.

He recognized Francesca as the woman who had lured him toward Lord Archibald and company on the terrace last night.

"Were you really a sailor, Mr. Randall?" Helena asked.

"Yes, I served a decade at sea."

Francesca grinned, sitting forward eagerly. "In Lord Nelson's Navy?"

"No, I was aboard a privately owned vessel." He'd leave out the finer details for now. He'd rather see if Miss Trimble could like him before he told her, and her family, the full story.

A frown pulled at Miss Trimble's brow. "Why were you not fighting against old Boney with the English?"

Tobias cursed under his breath. Being a sailor in Lord Nelson's Navy was held in far more esteem than what his life at sea had been. However, while he might omit certain facts initially, he refused to lie and pretend he'd been fighting for England just to impress the girl.

"I was sent away by my family. I had no say in the matter of where I went."

"Oh," Miss Trimble murmured, and then fell silent.

Francesca, the older of the sisters, caught his eye. "How long are you to remain at Romsey Abbey?"

"A few more weeks yet, I imagine. But I will be making my home here again, at Harrowdale, just a few miles distant. I hope to be very comfortable there."

The sisters shared a long look. "That is wonderful news. Do let us know when you move. I don't believe any of us are familiar with the Harrowdale estate. We should all like to visit there one day and come to know you better. We shall persuade our brother to call on you as soon as you are settled."

It would be a dark day before he'd ever invite Lord Archibald to cross his threshold, but if he married Miss Trimble, he would be guided by her wishes. However, the sisters could come to call if they chose. He could easily ignore Francesca's duplicity in the events of last night if it made Miss Trimble happy.

A slow blush crept up Miss Trimble's cheeks. "Francesca," she chided. "You should not speak for your brother until you know how he feels."

Francesca laughed. "If I waited for my brother, nothing would ever be done around here, and we would see no one at all and do nothing."

Tobias grinned. "I shall look forward to having you join me there."

It was impossible not to compare Miss Trimble's reticence with her cousins' outgoing personalities. Maybe demure didn't suit him after all. But could he discount an alliance with her on such a short acquaintance?

Miss Trimble smiled, but then lapsed into a long silence.

Devil take it! Where was Blythe when he needed her? Polite conversation was not his forte.

He suffered through a few more moments of silence before he remembered manners dictated he need only stay a quarter hour. He cast a quick look at the clock, discovered his time was up, and took his leave.

Miss Trimble followed him out to his horse. "I'm so sorry about my cousins' impertinent questions. They like to know everything about everyone. They do mean well."

Tobias took the reins from the servant. "Miss Trimble, your cousins are a breath of fresh air. I look forward to seeing you again, and them, often. Until next time."

He swung into the saddle and glanced at the sky just as the heavens opened up. Miss Trimble squealed and ran for shelter, robbing him of any chance of further conversation.

He rearranged his great coat tighter about him to keep out the rain, and lifted his hand to wave farewell to Miss Trimble. However, she had vanished inside the house, and he couldn't see her at a window anywhere.

With a sigh, he kicked his horse toward Romsey Abbey, congratulating himself on his first call to the well-dowered Miss Trimble. She appeared nice enough. Although shy today, she had spoken her mind well enough to him last night. Her dowry would make their life together comfortable.

However, as they had conversed, he had noticed his own shortcomings. His blood wasn't stirred by her presence in the least. Certainly not the way it was when he neared Blythe. Perhaps time alone and a longer acquaintance would remedy that small disappointment. She could make some man a fine wife. He just didn't know if he wanted her for himself.

Halfway home, Lord Archibald's coach and four thundered past him and splattered his horse and his coat with filthy water. Tobias cursed after the departing carriage. A prig and just plain rude. He kicked his mount onward to Romsey, fighting to retain his resurrected good mood.

At the stables, a groom grumbled over the state of the horse and quickly led the beast away into the stables. Tobias shook the rain from his hat and stared at the abbey uneasily. He didn't want to go back inside. Lord Archibald had left, but there would still be talk of alliances and suitors to endure. But he couldn't remain here forever.

Resigned, he drew in a deep breath, but a movement caught his eye. Beth Turner and her son darted into the walled herb garden. Since he'd missed his chance to talk to her earlier, Tobias hurried to catch up.

"Beth, hold a moment," he called to the woman. "You, Mrs. Turner, are a hard woman to pin down."

Beth smiled pleasantly from under her umbrella. "I have a lot to do. George is helping me pick some herbs to dry, and then I must return to my duties with the countess. I cannot be caught tarrying in conversation on my second day."

"I'm sure Lady Venables won't mind. In fact, I'm sure she may be occupied for much of the afternoon."

"Oh." She ruffled her son's hair. "See what you can discover in the garden, George. I'm told there are many varieties with good scent."

"Yes, Mama." The boy ran ahead of them, barely keeping himself under his umbrella.

Tobias held out his arm.

Beth scowled at it. "I should not. Besides being soaked through with rain, and muddy, too, do you wish to see me dismissed for tardiness?"

Tobias lowered his arm in dismay. "You are one of my oldest acquaintances. I'll not slight you by refusing to treat you well."

Beth clutched her cloak tighter about her. "Any friendship between us ended long ago. I'm Lady Venables' servant now, much further below the Randalls than I ever was before."

Tobias removed his soggy gloves and stuffed them in a pocket. "Mother would scold you if she heard you speak of yourself in such a manner. She thought very well of you, Beth. Almost like a daughter."

"Any of that… What I mean to say is that none of that matters now. I put those days behind me when I married Mr. Turner. It's best to forget what will never be."

"I, however, shall cling to hope." Tobias stepped forward and brushed his knuckles across her cheek, catching a tear as it fell. "Did my brother ever know about Mother's plans?"

Beth drew in a shuddering breath. "No, and I beg you to refrain from mentioning the matter, should he return. It was just a dream, and long over. You were never supposed to learn of your mother's ambitions when you did."

"I was an inquisitive boy. That hasn't changed, either. I have a question to ask of you. One that you will likely find impertinent, but I need a woman's opinion. One who has loved and lost. Don't ask why. Did you come to love Turner in the end?"

Beth's stare made him squirm where he stood. She really did have a lot in common with her employer. "I cared for him very much. He treated me well, and I grieved when he died. Now excuse me, I must return to my duties."

Tobias dissected her words carefully as she hurried away. Cared for and treated well did not sound like a passionate, loving marriage. Just a comfortable one.

Perhaps that was all he should expect from a marriage to Miss Trimble if he was fortunate enough to secure her agreement. She may never forget her affection for Lord Archibald, her first love, but he could make sure she never regretted her choice in marrying him.

With that goal in mind, Tobias braced himself to be happy and headed inside out of the weather.

Heat stole over Blythe's cheeks as Mercy laughed at her retelling of the worst proposal of marriage ever to have occurred. Unlike her sister, Blythe struggled to find any humor in the situation. She was embarrassed and uncomfortable. If not for Mercy's presence, she would have fled upstairs and hidden herself away. "This is no laughing matter, Mercy. I'm still in shock."

"If you had accepted his suit, I would never have forgiven you."

"Because of Emma." Emma would be devastated that Lord Archibald had proposed to her. Blythe couldn't expect his early morning visit to have gone unnoticed. News that he'd come courting and been refused would spread. Servants couldn't be relied upon to hold their tongues over such a juicy bit of gossip. The fact that Archibald had consulted with Venables of all things, too, just added to her distress. Her stepson couldn't keep a secret to save his life.

"No. Because you do not love him," Mercy clarified. "He isn't the man you need."

She eyed her sister's superior expression with surprise. "What do you think I need? Not that I want to marry again, of course."

Mercy caught her hand and squeezed. "I cannot tell you, but I am sure you will know him when he captures your attention."

"You speak in riddles. Please, no more today." She glanced about the chamber, wishing Tobias would appear. Luncheon had come and gone without him. She would worry, except she had a feeling he'd simply returned to Harrowdale. He was planning on living there soon, and the place did need attention. Still, she wished he'd asked her to go with him. She could use something to do rather than reliving that terrible excuse for a kiss that Lord Archibald had forced on her.

Mercy tucked her feet up beneath her and lay her head against the back of her chair. "Was Archibald's kiss really that bad or are you afraid to say you liked it because of Raphael? You know he would understand if you were attracted to someone else."

"Raphael had nothing to do with my reaction. It was worse than terrible. I fear Archibald may have bruised me." She brushed her fingers across her lips, wishing she could remember Tobias' tender kisses instead of Lord Archibald's harsh possession.

A door opened behind her back and, as she started to turn to see who came in without knocking, Mercy whispered, "We need to find you someone who kisses better."

Tobias stood at the doorway, hat in hand and soaked to the skin and dripping muddy water all over the marble floor. "What is wrong? Wilcox said you wished to see me urgently."

Mercy laughed as she approached him. "Not so urgent that you couldn't have dried off first. We missed you at luncheon today."

Blythe had missed him more.

"Sorry. I misjudged the distance to Miss Trimble's residence and the time the call would take." Tobias' gaze flickered about the room restlessly, looking anywhere but at Blythe. "What can I do for you, Your Grace?"

Blythe held herself still, wondering why Tobias wouldn't look at her. Calling on Miss Trimble was polite, but his behavior troubled her. Had Emma convinced him that she was justified to be upset over the dancing last night? She shifted closer to better see his expression.

"Wilcox," Mercy called. "Please obtain a towel for Mr. Randall before he catches his death." She ushered him toward the fire and lifted his ruined hat from his hands. "Well, I wanted to tell you the news that my sister received an offer of marriage this morning."

Tobias held his hands out to the flames and kept his face averted.

"I believe you suspected as much earlier in the day. Congratulations, my lady."

Mercy sat his hat on a side table. "What I hadn't suspected was the fervor my sister inspired in her suitor."

Tobias' lips twisted into a grimace. "Fervor?"

Mercy laughed and gestured in her direction. "I'll leave Blythe to explain the particulars and the effect of his zeal. However, to be clear, there will not be another wedding yet. My sister refused Lord Archibald and his nine thousand a year."

Tobias spun about and stared at her. "You turned him down?"

She nodded slowly, watching his expression change to one of puzzlement. Had he really thought she would accept an offer of marriage from a man she barely knew? She would never choose a man for something as superficial as material possessions. That hadn't been why she'd married Raphael.

She'd married because she'd loved everything about her husband, despite the backlash of feelings from her friends. He had been much older than Blythe, and married before. Blythe had known and not cared a whit for any of that, or for his title.

"In fact," Mercy continued, "my sister had to refuse him three times in as many minutes. Where is Wilcox with that towel? You'll catch a chill. Excuse me while I hurry him up."

Mercy slipped from the room.

Tobias took a pace toward her. "Why would you turn him down? He's rich enough to look after you well."

Blythe approached him. "My friend is in love with him, and I'm not."

"Archibald is a fool. Miss Trimble deserves so much better," he declared hotly.

Blythe studied Tobias, puzzled that he appeared so concerned for Emma, and on such a slight acquaintance. "She does indeed, but her heart is full of him. Perhaps he will come to his senses one day."

"Hearts can change, and it will serve him right if she's cold to him by the time he realizes her worth." Tobias shrugged. "What did Mercy mean by 'zeal'?"

Blythe rubbed her arms, suddenly cold. "Lord Archibald offered for me, and then refused to believe I was in earnest. He was uncomfortably insistent. Your brother was kind enough to intervene and suggest he leave."

Tobias' brow rose. "Suggest he leave? My brother never suggests, he demands. Just how did Lord Archibald attempt to convince you?"

Blythe shuddered at the memory. "He kissed me, and I sincerely wished he hadn't."

Tobias' hand rose to her face and his damp thumb brushed across her bottom lip gently. "Many men want to kiss you."

Blythe leaned into his touch. "But not every man may. I choose to be selective."

The corner of Tobias' lips lifted. "Is that so? Well, that man should consider himself blessed."

His head lowered and his lips brushed over hers gently. Blythe jerked back as a drip of water landed beside her eye. She wiped it away.

Rather than be offended, Tobias grinned. "Perhaps we should continue this discussion another time, when I'm not drenched and dripping water all over you."

Blythe swallowed, overcome with anxiety. After her encounter with Lord Archibald, she didn't want any more misunderstandings. She didn't mean to lead Tobias on, but his touch and kisses were drugging and made her forget herself. "We cannot continue like this," she whispered, keeping her eyes fixed on his soggy cravat. "I'm so sorry. I've led you to believe that I could, was considering more, but that isn't the case. I'm not the kind of woman to engage in an affair."

"I know," he whispered. "You deserve better than my undeserving attentions."

Blythe could feel the pull of attraction between them, and resisted. She'd never encountered a harder challenge than this. "We shouldn't be alone anymore."

She might enjoy the way Tobias held her, and kissed her, but she had always thought scathingly of women who engaged in casual affairs. While she could now understand the temptation a dalliance offered, she wasn't prepared to relinquish her morals for a temporary fling.

Tobias stepped back and bowed. "I understand, my lady."

Chapter Twenty-One

Tobias stood as the ladies departed the dining room, and then dropped into his chair. He'd endured the meal in near silence, watching Blythe chat happily with her sister and Leopold, recounting the events of the day. Her suitors were much talked over and laughed at. From the conversation, he'd picked up a few topics to avoid when courting Miss Trimble, but the prospect still filled him with dread. He wasn't sure he was capable of being that agreeable. He longed to be just as he was.

"What a day," Leopold murmured as he refilled their glasses.

Tobias took his, sipped, and then set the glass aside. "I heard you managed to play knight in shining armor."

Leopold scowled. "Arrogant bastard. To propose and then taunt her with news of her eviction is no way to win a woman's heart."

Tobias sat forward. "Wait. Did you just say she's lost her home?"

"Not yet but soon. Apparently that stepson of hers has leased Walden Hall for the summer to a friend. Lord Archibald thought mentioning the unpleasant news would sway her to accept his suit. Blythe may very well have been tossed out because she stayed here too long. But if you ask me, Lord Venables was looking for any excuse, and we've gone and unintentionally assisted."

"Devil take it! What will become of her now?"

Leopold smiled. "She'll live here. Mercy insists, and there are plenty of rooms to choose from."

"So she's without funds, too?"

"I don't know the particulars, but I do not believe she's exactly penniless." His brother paused, staring down at his drink for a long moment. "Mercy will not hear of Blythe moving away, unless she chooses to marry again. The latter, I feel, is a slim chance. So here we are, all lumped together under one roof."

So that was it. It was Miss Trimble, or another young woman

like her with a dowry to match. He could never again think of Blythe in terms of a future dalliance. She'd told him no, and he would respect her wishes. She was better off penniless at Romsey than struggling to make ends meet with him at Harrowdale.

However, Tobias' heart was heavy with disappointment. Blythe might have refused Lord Archibald's offer of marriage, but without a home of her own, there would be many more tempting offers coming her way. It was just a matter of time. Eventually, she'd choose someone to replace her husband. She was too passionate not to wed again.

"I forgot to ask how you did on your first social call," Leopold said suddenly. "Was Miss Trimble accommodating?"

"I forgot to take flowers," Tobias confessed. "But Miss Trimble seemed polite enough, and I'm looking forward to calling on her again."

"A pity you didn't dance with another young woman last night for comparison, but there is no need to rush these things. You're young and healthy. Mercy tells me the ladies were impressed with you, despite your failure to dance all night."

"That's good to know." Tobias stared at nothing. He wasn't eager to attend another entertainment. He couldn't watch another roomful of men ogle Blythe. He shook his head. He had to stop thinking about her so possessively.

Good manners dictated that a woman should spend some time in conversation after dinner before she could safely retire without giving offense. Blythe flicked the edge of her book with her finger. It was still not time to retire upstairs, and she was extremely conscious of the man sitting at her side.

Tobias had barely said two words during dinner, and none directly to her. Given that it was so unusual not to hear him speak, she kept peeking at him. As far as she could tell, he wasn't in distress. Was he silent because she'd declined to take their relationship any further?

"Letters have arrived for you, my lady." Wilcox stood before her, his little silver tray poised on his fingertips.

She swallowed, hoping her observation of Tobias had gone

unnoticed, and took the short stack from the tray. "Are these all for me?"

"Yes, my lady. Every last one."

Blythe shuffled through them quickly to see who had written. They were all from acquaintances. The last in the pile was from Emma Trimble. She stared at it, and her hand shook. Emma didn't often write. She usually came to visit when she had something to say. Emma's letter was likely an angry one.

"You're very popular this evening," Tobias said softly enough that only she heard. He stood. "Well, it's been a long day. I think I'll turn in. Until tomorrow."

He sauntered out, and Blythe watched his exit with mixed feelings. Part of her wished he would stay and talk to her again.

Mercy sat beside her and peered at the notes. "Are you going to read those?"

Blythe tapped Emma's letter on the palm of her hand. "I should."

Mercy stilled her tapping. "Would you rather read them alone? We can leave you if you'd prefer."

Blythe glanced across the room. Leopold and Edwin were using small blocks of sawn wood to build towers together. It looked to be great fun, and she didn't want to disturb them. "You stay, and I'll go. It's been a hectic day, and I might retire early. I'll read and answer these before I go to bed. Good night, Mercy."

"Good night, Blythe. Sleep well."

Blythe collected her letters, said good night to Edwin and Leopold, and hurried upstairs.

But as she crossed the threshold of her chamber, her resolve sank as if made of lead. She didn't want to read Emma's note alone. She was afraid of what her friend was going to say about Lord Archibald's proposal.

"I know you said we shouldn't be alone anymore, but lock the door behind you, B."

Blythe spun toward the bed.

Tobias sat on the edge, his expression serious. He patted the mattress when she didn't move. "I'll take Miss Trimble's letter. Come on. Let's get this over and done with so you don't fret about the contents all night."

Although common sense told her it was none of his business or wise, she locked the door and handed the letter over. She perched next to him, anxiety rising. He quickly ripped open the note. When he finished, he placed it face down upon the bed where she couldn't reach it. "You don't want to read it."

"Why? What does Emma say?"

He sighed. "A lot of things I hope she's already regretting. I thought better of her to be so spiteful. She claims you stole her chance for happiness with Lord Archibald. She hopes never to see you again. That is the sanitized version of her note."

"I never encouraged him. I don't care for him beyond what's required for common courtesy. Emma loves him. I don't."

"I know." Tobias twisted to look at her. "This needs to be burned, and I will hope that Miss Trimble comes to her senses and apologizes before you speak to her again."

"Give it to me." Blythe held out her hand. She wasn't exactly afraid to face a rebuke from her friend. When she replied, she'd explain the situation so Emma would understand how events had really transpired.

Tobias eventually placed the note in her hand. When she read it, she had to admit he was correct. She should have believed him in the first place. That note should have been committed to the flames instead of destroying her hope that her friendship with Emma could ever survive this catastrophe.

Tobias tugged the note from her grip, climbed off the bed, and knelt before the fire. Slowly, he waved the bitter pages over the flames until they caught and were consumed.

Once they were gone, he returned and pulled her into his arms. Blythe burrowed her face into his neck to hide how hurt she was. She'd not encouraged Archibald, but Emma believed the worst of her, and all because he claimed she'd flirted with him.

"You're not a tease, Blythe. I'm exactly the man to know. I could stand a bit of encouragement."

Blythe thumped his chest and earned his warm chuckle in her ear.

"See. Nothing flirtatious about that sort of thing," he whispered.

He shifted until he was propped up against her bedpost, holding her fast against his chest. "Shall we see what the others are? I noticed a few familiar names."

Blythe glanced at them, but didn't feel enthused about the idea. She was quite content in Tobias' arms. "I suppose I should, but if they are all similar to Emma's, I don't think I could bear it tonight."

His lips brushed her brow. "Then let me take care of the chore for you."

After a moment's pause, Blythe nodded. She was too weary to disagree, and there could be something of importance contained in one that didn't have anything to do with Lord Archibald's proposal. When Tobias released her, Blythe perched on the bed to wait.

He tore through them, muttering an occasional curse under his breath. Blythe clenched her hands in her lap, rather glad he wanted to spare her feelings.

Eventually, he tossed the lot onto her writing table, face creased into a scowl. "Three discreet offers to meet and discuss terms, one request to go driving, and two of your female friends really shouldn't be spoken to again because they are blinkered sheep."

Blythe shrugged. "That's not so bad. When I married Venables, half the district labeled me a money-hungry adventuress. I'll survive this."

"I hope so." Tobias dropped to his knees at her feet. "In the meantime, I do know a way to distract you, but I'm not sure if you'll agree. A kiss, without any expectation beyond the moment, might bring sweeter dreams than that nonsense."

Blythe hesitated a moment, and then leaned forward.

His kiss was tender and drugging and made her forget everything terrible about her day. She closed her eyes as he swept her into their private world of scandalous pleasure. He pulled her closer, but he kept his hands still at her waist. He never once assumed she'd offer more, and when he left her a short time later without a word, she was feeling a little sad over her decision to keep him at bay.

Chapter Twenty-Two

Tobias sat through another morning of gentlemen callers for Blythe in the seclusion of the duke's sanctuary, his disgust growing with every moment. He wasn't there to spy, although that couldn't be helped as their voices traveled so well. He had skimmed two more journals since sunrise and was about to begin a third.

He stood, stretched his back, and then tiptoed to the doorway. He could see Blythe through the peep-hole, sitting a few feet away, back ramrod straight as usual. Her speech was calm and polite to even the most blatant flirtations. Was this how proper gentlemen would court a proper lady?

He drew back in disgust and raked his fingers through his hair. He had to get out of the abbey for a while. The next moment Blythe was without callers, he would slip out. He checked the peep-hole again. Thankfully, Blythe's latest suitor stood to take his leave, rather obviously mentioning his pleasure at seeing her getting on with life.

Nausea gripped him. He nodded to her as he exited the sanctuary and made his way to the terrace doors.

"Where are you going?"

Blythe's trembling question wrapped around his chest and stilled him. He took a deep breath and spun about. Damn, but he wanted to cross the room and take her into his arms. But he'd promised to keep a distance. He would master his desire if it killed him.

Yet he couldn't stand to see, listen to or imagine Blythe falling for another man's flirtations. "Harrowdale," he said eventually. "I'm going home."

He let himself out without turning back and promptly knocked Beth Turner off her feet.

He apologized and lifted her from the ground, returning her fallen basket to her hands, too. "Forgive me for not seeing you," he apologized again.

Beth brushed off her gown. "Of course, sir."

They followed the same path away from the abbey.

Beth stopped suddenly. "Tobias, might you tell me where your mother is buried? I should like to pay my respects and place flowers on her grave. She was very kind to me when my mother died."

"Mother did have ulterior motives where you were concerned," he teased, but uneasiness trickled through him. "We honestly don't know. My parents are not buried at Romsey. That is another matter to investigate. I cannot remember precisely where the carriage overturned."

Beth squeezed his arm then quickly stepped back. "I'm sorry. That makes your return all the more bittersweet, doesn't it?

"Romsey has forever been a source of disappointment."

Beth frowned. "Why so morose today?"

"A touch maudlin. Nothing to worry about. May I accompany you for a walk?" He fell into step beside her when she nodded. "It's true that the old duke didn't kill me with his kindness. I survived."

Beth sighed. "I'm happy someone will live at Harrowdale again."

So was he. "The date for my removal isn't set yet, but I feel it is coming closer. I still need to find servants."

Beth gave him a strange look. "Do you now?"

"Hmm, just one or two. I've simple needs." Tobias stopped before a shrub and ran his fingers over the dark leaves. The scent of rosemary filled his nose. "Mother's rosemary bushes have grown wild and large at the house. It will pain me to do so before my sister can see how they've grown, but I will need to cut them back."

He snapped off a sprig and tucked it in his pocket.

Beth patted his arm affectionately. "You always were so different from your brothers. Never a harsh word, always remembering to show kindness despite your teasing. I am glad to see you unchanged by the years."

He scowled and looked ahead. "You make me sound weak."

"No, I think you very strong. You have a generous heart, Tobias Randall. I'm glad time and circumstance haven't changed you."

Tobias ducked his head as Beth hurried off. He'd never be that trusting boy again. He still waited for the good to be taken away.

He faced the abbey. Inside Romsey, he couldn't behave as he would like. What he had discovered with Blythe wasn't a happily ever after. Blythe's guilt over betraying her husband's memory was a bucket of ice water over any pleasure they shared. He had to stop thinking of her and wanting more. She'd called a halt to their private association and wouldn't let him get any further.

He drew in a deep breath, conscious of a heavy weight upon his chest. It was time. He would return to Harrowdale today, and make definite plans for his immediate removal. The moment had come to step back from temptation.

He set off on the most direct path toward Harrowdale, ignoring the light drizzle that fell upon him. But the farther away from Romsey his strides took him, the more uncertain he became. It would be lonely at Harrowdale. He'd have to find ways to keep himself busy.

As he broke from the trees a short distance from the house, the smell of wood smoke filled his nose. He glanced around, looking for the source of the fire. When he found none, he hurried toward Harrowdale. Could the place have caught alight in his absence?

When the house came into a view, he gasped as a curl of smoke drifted across the rooftop.

Tobias broke into a run. Harrowdale was on fire! His home would be denied him.

Panic lengthened his stride, and he was in the courtyard in an instant. Thankfully, Harrowdale wasn't on fire…however, smoke rose from more than one chimney. The kitchen chimney, too. He approached the servants' door warily, lifted the latch and quietly let himself in.

The sound of laughter filled his ears. One voice, female, he particularly had reason to remember.

He stepped into the doorway and set his hands on his hips. "Finch, what is the meaning of this?"

Blythe's former housekeeper beamed. "Sir, it is so good to see you finally returned. We, ah, have a proposition for you."

He glanced at the other bodies seated around the battered kitchen table, noting their full hands and crumb-scattered plates. Five bodies were crammed into the space, and he thought all of them were Blythe's former servants. "Do you now? Do you know how much your disappearance has upset Lady Venables?"

"We couldn't let her know directly, sir. When we overheard his lordship's servants talking about the new family moving in, we decided we'd pack up and go, too. This house was empty, and you seemed the kind to appreciate hard work and loyalty."

"How is it loyalty when you deserted your mistress? She'll think I've stolen her servants from her."

"We never deserted our lady. We'll be here, and have everything ready for her when she needs us again."

Tobias sagged against the doorframe. "So this is just a temporary stop on your way to your next home. Unfortunately, I fear you may be disappointed. Lord Archibald, her most determined suitor, has a well-established household, as do the others. I doubt she could take you all with her."

"What is Lord Archibald to our mistress?"

"He asked her to marry him."

The housekeeper stood suddenly. "How did she answer?"

"She said no, but it is just a matter of time before someone rich enough comes along and sweeps her off her feet."

"Then you don't know my mistress." Finch flicked her hands at the other servants, sending them scattering. "You should go back now and make sure she doesn't."

"Of course she will say yes eventually."

Finch laughed heartily. "She cannot be made to do anything she doesn't want to."

Tobias didn't care for the housekeeper's comment, even if it was accurate. "I am well aware of Lady Venables' stubborn temperament."

"As are we." Mrs. Finch beamed. "Nothing would have compelled her to place her trust in another man but a deep affection."

"So?"

The housekeeper smiled at him as if he were simple. "She brought young Adam's things here. She trusts you. She cares for you."

Tobias scowled. "You are imagining an affection that doesn't exist. I annoy her."

"Yes, I know. However, the fact that I do know is significant. If my lady didn't care for you, she certainly wouldn't draw attention to that fact. She'd ignore you completely."

"We are much thrown together at Romsey," he said quickly. "She has little choice but to speak to me."

Finch cleared away the dishes and plates. "My mistress has always had a choice. She attempts to protect her heart from every strong emotion, but cannot always manage it. It will take time to draw her out, but I'm sure you can win her."

"Win her? Are you mad?"

"No, merely hopeful. I saw a different side of her the day she brought Adam's things here. She was relaxed, and even happy. I have not seen her smile so in years."

Tobias eased into a chair and threw his hat onto the table. "Her grief for her husband is a loss she may never recover from."

"You are correct that a woman does not recover from her first love easily. If you expect her to, then you will fail to win her heart. What you need to do is carve out a place beside her Raphael. Don't strive to be him…be you."

Tobias gaped. Clearly Finch had no idea how unsuitable he was. Blythe required so much more than he could provide. "I won't be the one to win her."

Finch clucked her tongue. "I think she is falling in love with you already, but just won't admit it, not even to herself."

Tobias rocked back in the chair. "You are a very strange, forward woman, Mrs. Finch."

"Thank you, sir." She clapped her hands together. "Can I get you something to eat? A big, strapping fellow like you needs sustenance to woo a lady for his wife."

Tobias rubbed his hand across his face. "What makes you think you don't need to apply for the positions here, Finch? I could already have staff in mind."

"Because you haven't made any decision yet, or you would have staff here already." She smiled. "Besides, you're lingering at Romsey in the hope of asking my mistress what she'd prefer. A good decision, if you ask me. My lady likes everything just so, and I'm sure you want her to be happy."

Tobias reeled. What trouble had he gotten into? He couldn't afford all these servants on the allowance Leopold had granted. Some of them would have to go. "There may be a problem with your plans."

"Lack of funds?" The housekeeper's brows lifted as she sagely guessed the heart of his problem. "Never fear, my mistress can pinch a penny along with the very best of them."

Tobias frowned as a plate and teacup were set before him.

"There you are, sir," Finch said brightly. "Eat up, and then I'm sure you'd like to tour the house to see what's been done in your absence. The bedchambers have been cleaned top to bottom, and so has the dining room and sitting room. The door to what we feel is a book room is jammed, must be the damp, but we'll have that fixed before you return with our lady.

"The grounds are a harder task, grown so wild and tangled," she continued. "But the kitchen garden has been cleared of weeds, and your new gardener has done what he can. We might need a bit of aid from Romsey during the worst of winter, but we should be self-sufficient for the spring."

Tobias put his head in his hands as the housekeeper prattled on.

Blythe blinked as bright light streamed in through the door of the duke's sanctuary, and then was cut off suddenly. Before she could adjust to the change, she was pulled up from her chair and crushed against Tobias' chest. He nuzzled her cheek before he found her lips and devoured her with hot, hungry kisses.

She reeled and clung to him, surprised and overjoyed to be in his arms again. She'd been regretting her decision to end things between them since the moment she'd uttered the words.

His kisses slowed, and his tongue tangled with hers gently.

Blythe slipped her fingers into his hair and reveled in the wondrous sensations he evoked. The evidence of his arousal pressed against her belly, his hands kneaded her bottom.

When he drew back, a fierce ache had developed between her legs.

"I miss you," he whispered against her neck. The rough scrape of stubble against her skin sent chills racing all over her. "Give me a second chance. I'm a patient man, I promise."

Blythe's eyes stung as she blinked back tears. She'd missed him, too, but she couldn't be the type of woman he wanted. She opened her mouth to speak, but he kissed her again, so well, she lost track of time.

"Think about me when I'm gone." He slipped from her arms, grasped a book seemingly at random from the shelf, and vanished.

Her knees wobbled, and she sank into a chair before she collapsed. The next time he came to her, Blythe didn't know if she could deny him.

"Dash it all, but Finch might just be right," Tobias muttered under his breath as he suffered through Murphy's endless fussing as he changed for dinner.

"Beg pardon, sir. But did you say something?"

"Nothing of importance, Murphy. I was just cursing the weather."

"Perhaps you should have worn the great coat when you went out rather than suffer the damp."

"I'll keep that in mind." He pivoted to stare at Murphy. "You know everything that happens in the district. When were you going to mention that Lady Venables' staff had invaded Harrowdale?"

"Oh, tomorrow, sir. Probably. Most likely. They weren't doing any harm."

Tobias tugged on his cravat to loosen it a bit. "I thought Harrowdale on fire today. Imagine my surprise to find tea and seed cake on the kitchen table and a houseful of servants polishing the furniture."

"Harrowdale will like to have the care and attention. Mrs. Finch keeps a good house. You could do a lot worse."

Although he didn't like to admit it, Murphy was likely right. Mrs. Finch had the makings of a quartermaster. He'd be so well organized, he probably wouldn't recognize himself. "Murphy, if any other matters come to light that might affect me, do be a good fellow and pass the news along. I don't particularly care for surprises."

Murphy held out his coat. "Your brother was all set to visit Harrowdale this afternoon when you didn't return to eat with the family. I found something to distract him. Don't imagine he'll care for the other matter very much, so I thought it best to delay that surprise."

"What other matter?"

"The rocking horse in your nursery, of course. Nice bit of wood carving in that."

Tobias' blood ran cold. "I'm holding on to it as a favor, nothing more."

"Of course, sir. That's exactly what I thought. No sense in mentioning it if there's no chance the rocking horse and painted screen will remain there forever. I expect she'll find somewhere nice soon to move them to."

Tobias clenched his fist.

Murphy's deep laugh filled the room. "Ah, so it may not be moving after all. Glad to hear it."

"Murphy, you are pushing my patience," Tobias growled.

"Yes, sir. I know, sir. But at least my intentions are honorable."

Tobias rolled his shoulders, settling his coat around him. "I never said mine were not."

Murphy's eyebrows rose. "Well, well, well. Ain't that a surprise and a half? My lips are sealed, Mr. Randall. They are sealed and locked tight as a drum until the happy announcement is made."

Tobias scowled until Murphy left. When he was alone, he flopped down on the bed. Was he really going to forget all about Miss Trimble's four thousand pounds and pursue Blythe instead?

There was no guarantee Blythe wouldn't laugh at the idea. Despite the hope in his heart, he buried it deep. He'd previously set a cautious course with Blythe, and he saw no reason to change that strategy. The prize he was after was worth the discomfort of the wait. He had her trust and perhaps her friendship. What he wanted was what remained of her heart. He'd treasure her till his last breath.

Chapter Twenty-Three

In the week since Tobias' last kiss, they had worked side by side combing through the old duke's sanctuary. What they had found was precisely nothing, despite the late hours they had both spent poring over old journals. Despite her presumption that she was about to engage in an affair with Tobias, he had not kissed her again, or even held her hand.

He was, however, becoming an entertaining companion. He'd begun to share details of his past in small snippets when they were alone, and occasionally mentioned the uncomfortable parts of his history. After what she'd heard, she had come to hate the old Duke of Romsey for the pain and suffering he had inflicted.

But if there was one thing Blythe had learned, it was that the old Duke of Romsey gave his enemies what they feared most.

She set her cup down and listened to yet another verbal skirmish develop between Tobias and Leopold. Leopold valued his siblings above all else, and they'd been separated, ripped apart with only the duke's flimsy promise that his family lived. The cruelty of his actions struck Blythe more forcefully the longer she knew her sister's future husband. Leopold thrived on family, and living up to his responsibilities to them.

And Tobias. Damaged. Flawed in so many ways. Determined. A boy thrown to the wild sea to fend for himself. What had he feared that the duke might have punished him with? His fear of carriages stemmed from the murder of his parents, so that couldn't be it.

"When were you going to call on Miss Trimble again, Tobias?" Leopold asked suddenly. "It's been a few days now."

Tobias' gaze flickered in her direction. "I hadn't made up my mind to go again."

"Distance doesn't make the heart fonder," Leopold murmured. "Strike while the iron's hot."

Blythe's heart raced. Was the reason for Tobias' withdrawal because he had been secretly courting Emma? Stunned, she sat still and tried to hide how the news upset her. He couldn't kiss her if he married her friend. To do so would be scandalous and utterly reprehensible.

She jumped to her feet, chair scraping the floor loudly.

Mercy, half bent over young Edwin, eyeing her with concern. "Blythe, is everything well?"

Blythe nodded. "Just thinking an idea through. Excuse me." She forced a smile to her lips, stepped around the quarrelling Randall brothers, and hurried for the privacy of the drawing room. She closed the doors behind her, but rather than enter the sanctuary immediately, she paced. She must be mad to be upset over a mere suspicion.

Tobias Randall was free to pursue anyone he liked. There was nothing binding them together, no promise to keep or break. Nothing but a request for another chance. At the time, she had not answered. She dearly wished she had known he had intentions toward Emma sooner.

She clasped her hands together and tried her best to be sensible. She loved Raphael. She truly did. It was just growing harder to remember things about him when she couldn't get Tobias out of her thoughts. What would happen when Raphael was nothing more than a dim memory to haunt her sleepless nights?

Blythe forced her breathing to slow. Nothing had changed. She was Raphael's widow, and intent on solving the riddle of Oliver and Rosemary Randalls' disappearance.

Calm again, she stared at the duke's portrait across the room, focusing on her earlier train of thought. The duke had appeared to be an intelligent man, a man who thought he was cleverer than those around him, too. What could he have done with Oliver and Rosemary? What would Tobias' siblings have feared most?

"Penny for your thoughts, B." Tobias stood a few feet away, watching her closely.

Her breath caught in her throat at hearing his voice—so close, so familiar. She collected herself quickly. "Tell me about your sister and brother. What were they like?"

"Rosemary didn't like being left behind when we went fishing. She didn't like behaving as a lady, but Mother was remarkably good at keeping her at home."

"Your parents sheltered her from unpleasantness?"

He scrubbed his jaw. "I wouldn't say that. She wasn't naïve by any stretch of the imagination. People always said she'd come to a bad end if she didn't behave with more decorum. I suppose they were right. She did try to fight her abductor."

Blythe thought that through. If Rosemary was wise to the ways of the world, she would have feared a future in which she had no voice. An unacceptable marriage, slavery of her body for men's pleasure, or to live in poverty could have been what she feared most.

If she had been raised a lady, but chafed at the restrictions required of that life, what would she have done to save herself? If she was free but poor, she'd likely find a way to make the situation better.

If she was confined in a terrible situation, what might Rosemary do to escape it?

Oliver Randall, too, was a mystery to her. "What of Oliver?"

He frowned. "Most would describe my brother as a cold fish."

"Oh, how so?"

Tobias leaned against a table. "Oliver may have been a genius, but he wasn't particularly friendly. When he wasn't in school, getting him from his bedchamber at Harrowdale was something of a feat. He didn't enjoy socializing, preferring his books to conversing with people. When he did speak, it was mostly in the form of a lecture, and he often used mathematical terms that confused people."

"Did he have friends here?"

Tobias nodded. "A few put up with his lengthy silences. Murphy was one. Oliver never seemed to notice the passage of time when he was absorbed in his studies. Mother frequently resorted to blackmail to get him to eat."

Blythe's pulse raced. Could Tobias already have the clue she needed? "What sort of blackmail?"

"She would invite Beth to visit."

"Beth Turner? But why would that make a difference."

"She was Beth Gallagher once." Tobias stood and touched her

cheek. "Before her death, my mother was trying to engineer a match between Oliver and Beth. Oliver was Beth's first love, you see."

"But I thought she was your good friend." Blythe's mind reeled. "Why did your mother not succeed?"

"Beth has always been a favorite with me." Tobias cupped her face. "But as to why Beth never married him, I cannot imagine. But Beth had married Turner before my parents were murdered so she was certainly old enough. Though given my brother's nature, I'm not even sure he noticed she stopped coming to the house."

The picture Tobias painted was of a considerably eccentric young man. Her eyes filled with tears. "Poor woman. I had no idea."

"And she would like it kept quiet. Leopold, by the way, knows none of this."

"Of course, of course." Blythe rubbed her hands together, suddenly chilled to the bone. "I would never say anything to cause her distress."

"I know you won't." He smiled down upon her and smoothed her hair away from her cheek. "You are a kind woman."

Blythe's stomach did a little tumble, but she buried the sensations quickly. She had no time for his flirtations right now. She was sure she was onto something.

A genius, Tobias called Oliver. In her experience, most men prone to be studious had an even temperament. Would he have fought the duke's plans and attempted to free himself using logic?

Blythe closed her eyes and tried to picture such a man in society. He would be talked of, gossiped over. He was different from most men she knew. A frisson of disquiet rushed through her body. Being different, odd, eccentric, made one a pariah in their society. Those whose actions were too odd were avoided—or worse, hidden from sight.

She rocked back on her heels as an appalling idea took shape. Where else to hide an unfriendly genius than within a house for the mad? No one would pay attention to his protests. He'd be just one of any number of eccentric minds not suited for the real world. His origins would be forgotten, like the many paintings of Romsey Abbey.

Her heart stopped.

The paintings!

Blythe spun about and stared at the walls. Her gaze fixed on the portrait of the duke, and then she looked at the wall directly opposite. Of the five paintings hung, one was of a storm-tossed ship, two were of country houses, and the remaining two—a market square in a foreign land, and horses milling before a stable.

She approached the painting of the ship tossed at sea. The sailors aboard the vessel appeared in grave peril. She curled her hands into fists as she spied one small figure clinging to the uppermost masthead as it toppled toward the churning ocean.

"What did you fear most when you were a child, Tobias?"

"Nothing much, but I did almost drown once."

She moved on to the next painting quickly. It was unremarkable. Plain, even. A tidy country house with a spotted dog trotting across the front lawn toward the distant trees. She didn't recognize the property. She moved on to the next. The marketplace scene featured what looked to be an Englishman bartering with a brown-skinned peddler. Leopold?

She glanced back at the ship. Was that small, desperate figure supposed to be Tobias? Or was it what the duke hoped would be his fate one day? She stepped back from the wall and looked up.

Tobias came to stand close behind her, and she could feel his heat radiating against her back. "What has you so fascinated, B?"

"Did you have trouble going into the water again? I've heard many do."

"Yes. For a time."

Blythe spun around. "I've always thought these paintings were an odd choice for a duke's drawing room. They face his portrait, and the chair he used to sit in most often. Mercy hasn't changed the arrangement of the seats or anything else since he died, so these scenes were hung here at his order."

Tobias caught her hand in his. "I've given up trying to fathom that man. I suggest you do, too. He's not worth the headache his actions bring on."

"I think we've been looking in the wrong place." Blythe pointed to the man clinging to the ship's rigging. "You." She gestured to the marketplace scene. "Leopold."

Tobias squinted at both. When he drew back, his jaw was clenched.

Blythe shifted to another painting; a large, squat building set in featureless grounds. However, the scene was too high for her to view easily. She looked about, spied a sturdy-looking chair and dragged it across the chamber. As she lifted her skirts higher and put her foot upon the padded seat, Tobias grabbed her ankle and held her in place. "I could have just lifted the painting down if you wanted a better view."

She shook her head. "No, we don't want to draw Wilcox's attention by moving it."

He eyed her skeptically. "And a countess standing upon a chair like a hoyden isn't head-turning enough?" His hand slid up and down her stocking. Despite the impropriety and the risk of getting caught, the sensation was quite lovely after so long without his touch.

Blythe hopped up on the chair and placed her hands on the wall to steady herself. "Quiet, Wilcox may be listening. I don't trust him not to have his ear to the door."

The painting was lit harshly; a cloudy day bathed the building in feeble light. She peered at the distant features, trying to determine if she knew the location of the place. It did remind her of somewhere, but she couldn't quite put her finger on it. When she peered at the building itself…a dark shape loomed in an upstairs window.

The other windows held similar forms, but the one in the left corner chamber was the most distinct. A man?

She glanced down. Tobias still held her leg, his warm palm sliding up and down her calf to her knee in a slow caress. His hand stilled. "What did you discover?"

She scowled at the painting. "More questions."

He caught her about the waist and slowly lowered her to the floor. His hands lingered as she stared at him, but before she could gather her wits, he jumped onto the chair himself. The chair creaked, and she grabbed for his leg.

He chuckled. "Just a bit of give, B. It won't break and drop me on my backside."

Easy for him to say. Blythe waited impatiently for him to finish and get down again.

When he stepped down, he was frowning. "I don't know that place and hope never to."

"Why is that? Do you recognize it?"

Tobias shook his head sadly. "Looks like a madhouse. There was one some miles from Whitsbury when I was a boy. People whispered about the goings on of the place all the time when they thought I couldn't hear. May still be there now, for all I know. I'd have to ask Wilcox or Murphy if Skepington still stands."

She caught his arm tightly. "No, don't ask them. Skepington Hall still functions as a home for the mad. I hadn't considered the place in years, but I suppose I would have seen it again if matters here had unfolded very differently."

Tobias frowned as his hand rose to cup her face. "Did you fear you'd be committed there when I came home?"

She gulped and nodded quickly.

"Mercy wouldn't have allowed that to happen, and neither would I. No one as good as you deserves such ill treatment."

His words soothed her as much as his touch, but his fingers slipped away. She glanced up at the painting again, thinking hard. The house was painted somewhat larger than it actually was, but that could certainly be Skepington. "Why would the duke have a painting of a madhouse in his drawing room unless he had a connection or an interest in someone who might be residing there?"

"You think he'd be that obvious?"

"It is a possibility. The current owner is Lord Merrow. His father was a friend of the duke's. If I've learned anything about the duke this last month, it was that he had a vast need to control the family and prove his cleverness. Leopold stood in this chamber whenever he was summoned to Romsey. Hanging those paintings here, where he'd meet with Leopold, would have given the duke a peculiar thrill."

Tobias looked at the other paintings, and then tapped the one containing the spotted dog. "If memory serves, Rosemary possessed a dog of that breed. Evil-tempered beast, much like its owner. I wonder what happened to it."

"Nothing good, I'm sure." Blythe rubbed her hands together. "Do you recognize the building or surroundings?"

"No, not at all. You?"

She shook her head. The house was completely unfamiliar to her, and she knew many in the immediate area. "What of this last painting? There are quite a number of horses in it."

Tobias raked his fingers through his hair, and then he barked out a laugh. "I think I can guess why that particular painting hangs there."

"What? Why?"

His gaze grew shuttered. "I would tell you, but I don't think you will want to hear the explanation. Suffice to say it is another bit of family scandal. The fellow is well and healthy. Will you trust me on this and not ask questions?"

She eyed him warily. So far he had not steered her wrong on matters she shouldn't know details of. Perhaps it was time to accept what he said at face value and trust him. It might save time.

She nodded. "I think Skepington should be investigated. I'm going to order my carriage prepared." She pointed at the picture. "If I leave now, I should be able to reach the village before nightfall. I'll take lodgings and approach Lord Merrow the next morning to ask for a tour of the place. It wouldn't be an unreasonable request, given the length of our acquaintance. He's a nice man, and his wife is a friend. If he refuses, I'll appeal to his wife. I am confident Lady Merrow will sympathize with my request."

"I cannot let you travel the distance alone."

She touched his arm. "Be reasonable. I'll be in the chaise for hours. Remember how badly your last carriage ride went, and that was a fraction of the distance. I'll tell Mercy I need to return to Walden Hall overnight and continue on to Skepington. You cannot undertake the journey with me. Think of the gossip if we are seen together so far from Romsey. I'll return before you know it."

"If Merrow is keeping my brother, he might not like you to find that out." Tobias took a deep breath. "I'll manage your small carriage. It's open to the air enough that I can set my fears aside for one day."

Stubborn man. He'd be a wreck after the first mile. "Two days in a carriage, Tobias. There and back. You'll never survive it."

He took a pace away. "If there is gossip, I will, of course, ensure your reputation is restored, but like it or not, I am coming with you. I will protect you. I'll be waiting for you at the entrance to Romsey

Abbey, at the pond. Make sure you collect a blanket or two to keep you warm. It looks cold outside."

He spun on his heel, returned the chair to its original place against the wall, and stalked off before she could call him back.

Blythe's heart thudded painfully, but she wouldn't turn aside from her decision. This small hope was the first lead in the search for the remaining Randall siblings. She couldn't leave a sane man adrift in a sea of insanity if she could save him. She just couldn't.

Chapter Twenty-Four

Lights from the township of Whitsbury glimmered in the distance and Tobias nudged the woman dozing beside him. "We're nearing a village, B."

She sat up quickly, ran her hands over her hair and gown, and then rubbed them together. "It's grown so cold in the last hour."

The temperature had dropped considerably since they had left Romsey, and although this was the first time she'd mentioned the cold, it was not the first time Tobias had thought of Blythe's possible discomfort. He'd considered removing his coat two miles back and covering her sleeping form with it. To stop, however, might have awakened her unnecessarily. The long journey had wearied her miles ago. "I'll have you warmed soon enough. Which building is the inn?"

"The first one, I believe."

He tooled the chaise into the small coaching yard and drew back on the reins. A young boy ran out from the stables and caught the bridle as he climbed down. "He looks done in, sir."

Tobias stretched the kinks from his back. "He's served us well. See that he receives extra attention tonight. We'll have need of him first thing in the morning."

The boy patted the drooping horse's neck. "Yes, sir."

Tobias looked about him. The coaching house yard was neat and nicely kept. The stables appeared clean and well-tended. He glanced up at the building. A handsome woman lingered at the window. A maid?

Her smile grew, and she crooked her fingers at him, inviting him for what he assumed would be a pleasant interlude. He grinned.

"Tobias," Blythe said from the carriage seat. "Please don't keep me waiting."

Tobias winced. He tossed the boy a coin and then held out his hand. He lifted Blythe from the carriage easily and for a moment, she held on to him. The woman in the window didn't compare to the woman he held, and he leaned closer to inhale her scent. "Forgive my tardiness."

Her gaze darted to the upper window where the woman stood. "I'll leave you to your own devices, shall I?" Her lips pressed together.

Tobias frowned at her comment. He wasn't going to abandon her at a place like this. "My dear lady, I came with you to protect you, and I'll stay with you, never fear."

"Stay with me?" She clenched her hands together. "And how will it look to others? You've been calling on Miss Trimble. She will not be happy about your decision to accompany me. I should have driven on without you."

"Miss Trimble may be stubborn, but I'll not let her opinion sway me from doing the right thing." He raked his fingers through his hair. "She's determined to think ill of you."

"You've spoken of me when you've gone courting her?"

"Of course I've spoken of you. Why else—wait. Do you imagine I am courting your friend?"

When Blythe nodded, he grabbed her arm, hope and doubt warring within him. Was she jealous? He shook his head. "I was trying to convince her that she'd made a cake of herself. I don't want her. I want you! More than I've wanted anything in my entire life."

A man coughed. "Evening, sir. Madam. I'm Jeremiah Drake, owner of this establishment. Can I be of help to you both?"

Blythe faced the newcomer, but Tobias caught a glimpse of the smile that burst across her face. "My husband and I require accommodations for the evening, Mr. Drake. Dinner, some wine, and a warm chamber with a comfortable bed."

Husband? Tobias caught Blythe's hand, but she did not look at him.

The innkeeper unhooked the straps holding her small trunk to the rear of the chaise and hefted it over his shoulder. "Very good, madam. Sir. If you'll come this way."

As the innkeeper hurried for the building, Blythe threw a shy smile over her shoulder. "Leave the horse for the boy, darling. I need a bath and a good night's sleep after the long day we've had."

Tobias tugged her against his chest. "Since when have you ever thought of me fondly enough to call me any name besides pirate?"

Her gaze searched his. "Familiarity will convince others that we are man and wife. I hope the ruse might save my reputation." She hurried after the innkeeper.

Bemused by her ploy, Tobias followed her inside the inn. The tap room contained a noisy crowd, but the innkeeper quickly directed them to a smaller dining room well away from the noise, where a cheerful fire burned. Blythe hurried to the hearth.

What the devil was she thinking to be speaking endearments to him so freely? He'd give his eye-teeth to know if she meant them.

Mr. Drake stomped upstairs with their baggage as a woman approached. "Welcome. I'm Mrs. Drake. You've met my husband already. We have onion soup, pork pie and roast beef."

Blythe stripped off her gloves and held her hands out to the flames. "That will be acceptable, thank you, but can you fetch ale for my husband?"

"Oh, dearie, you must be chilled through. I'll send up warming pans for the bed directly to heat the linen. If there is anything you need, just ask." The innkeeper's wife bobbed a curtsy and bustled out.

Tobias drew closer to Blythe and caught up one of her hands. "That's the second time you've referred to me as your husband. I could get to like it."

She shrugged and dug into her reticule. "It seemed a good choice to avoid uncomfortable questions being asked. Just sign the register as Mr. and Mrs. Randall. No one will question you too closely. Besides, a place such as this would give a married couple their best room if available, and I detest sleeping on lumpy mattresses."

Tobias caressed her waist. "So, we'll be sharing a room, B. A bed, too."

"That is what married couples often do." She sucked in a breath. "It cannot be helped. It also ensures that you do not visit Skepington without me. I'll not be left behind in the morning, wondering if he is there. I warn you, I sleep lightly. I'm coming with you."

"A madhouse is no place for you."

She pressed a handful of coins into his palm. "This should cover any expenses we incur here. Don't argue."

He dropped his arm from her waist and thrust the money back at her. "I cannot take your money. You haven't enough as it is." He'd forgotten about needing funds on the trip, and the little money he had was hidden behind a drawer at Romsey. He would have slept in the stables, but he couldn't expect Blythe to do so.

She frowned. "You will if you want to eat tonight, and in the morning. The expense is nothing to me. Besides, the money is for the innkeeper, not you personally. I would have spent the same amount should you have stayed behind. A husband would manage such discussions rather than his wife. Don't worry about the matter. You can repay me when we return home and no one will ever know."

"I'll know." He walked a few paces away and then turned back. "Did anyone ever tell you that you are a frustrating woman?"

She smiled instead of answering and returned to warming her hands.

Tobias threw his hands up in the air. Frustrating, beguiling, and quite likely correct about everything.

He paced the room, glad to stretch his legs and be free of the restrictions of the small carriage and Blythe's proximity. By mid-afternoon, he'd actually begun to enjoy tooling the carriage along the road and was no longer plagued by memories of his parents as their carriage pitched over onto its side. It helped to have Blythe beside him, occasionally touching him as they talked.

Yet he worried about his brother—and the beautiful woman determined to risk her reputation to recover him. Tobias hoped they'd not come on a fool's errand.

He glanced at her again, noticing how she hugged the hearth. She must be chilled to the bone. They should have taken one of the duchess' larger carriages instead of sneaking away. He could warm her easily if she were in his arms.

Unfortunately, the innkeeper's wife chose that moment to deliver their food. The maid he'd glimpsed in the upstairs window carried a pitcher of ale. The wench peeked at him from under her lashes, inviting with just her eyes. Blythe smoothly stepped between them, as if protecting him from a wild beast. He smothered a laugh. All thoughts of the wench had vanished the moment Blythe referred to him as her husband. A small kernel of hope had bloomed as she'd taken charge as if she was in truth his wife.

The maid, without a reason or encouragement to linger, was sent away by Mrs. Drake. "Your chamber is prepared for you, Mrs. Randall. I'll send up hot water shortly."

"Thank you, Mrs. Drake. That would be very welcome after today."

Blythe moved to the table and Tobias hurried to draw out her chair for her. When she sat, he kissed the top of her head. "Thank you for today."

Blythe inclined her head and they ate in companionable silence. However, at the end of the meal, she covered her mouth to hide her yawn. "I don't believe I've ever felt so tired in my life."

He drained the last of his ale and set the mug on the table carefully. "You should go up and get into bed."

She glanced at the door, and then eyed him warily. "What will you be doing?"

Tobias quite liked this unexpected side of Blythe's character. He'd never have pegged her as the possessive type, but she definitely didn't want him out of her sight for long. "Oh, I'll be coming along shortly. I thought you might prefer a moment or two of privacy. I can settle with the innkeeper tonight so we are not delayed in the morning."

Her face creased with suspicion. "That's very kind of you. I'll leave the candles burning so you can find your way about the chamber."

He laughed as he stood, and then held his hand out to her. She rose from the chair, a question in her gaze. Tobias tugged her against his chest roughly. "Trust me, B. I'll be along in a moment or two."

Not that he'd be sleeping beside her, exactly. If he were a proper gentleman, he'd sleep in a chair or on the floor. But his days of sleeping rough were over. He'd never be a proper gentleman. However, in an effort to appear so to Blythe, he planned to sleep on top of the sheet to keep away from her flawless skin. They'd both be comfortable and sleep decently apart. He didn't possess a nightshirt, and he didn't want to offend her delicate sensibilities with his scarred and naked skin.

A soft smile tugged her lips, and then she headed upstairs. He glanced down at the erection tenting his breeches. Damned inconvenient to lose control now. He'd done so well at hiding how she affected him these past days.

He stared at the mantel clock, counting the minutes, trying to judge how much time she might require. Five minutes. Ten? He waited out ten minutes by pacing the room and examining every object on display three times over. Then, after he'd paid the innkeeper, obtained directions to Lord Merrow's residence and the nearby Skepington Hall, he slowly climbed the stairs and knocked on the door.

He could do this. He could sleep beside Blythe and never consider wandering to her side of the mattress.

"Come in."

He set his hand on the latch and stepped across the threshold. His pulse pounded in his ears. He didn't know what was the matter with him. It wasn't as if he'd never been in Blythe's bedchamber before.

When he lifted his gaze, his heart stopped.

Blythe sat on the bed, half under the covers, nightgown barely covering her beauty. She'd let down her hair, too, and his fingers itched to run through the strands. His side of the bed had been folded back.

He dropped into a chair to hide the bulge reforming in his trousers, wincing at the discomfort as he removed his boots. When he thought himself under control, he met her gaze. "How early do you think we can meet with Lord Merrow? The innkeeper says Skepington is very close. We could go there first without bothering him."

"We must speak to Lord Merrow first. Too early would be considered rude, but we want to leave enough time so we might return to Romsey close to nightfall."

He set the second boot down. "I didn't think this through properly when we left Romsey. Three people won't fit on the seat of your chaise."

She frowned. "I confess I didn't think of that, either. I only thought of your comfort in the smaller open carriage."

He stood and took off his coat, carefully laying it out over the chair back so it wouldn't crease further. He untied his cravat next, conscious that Blythe watched him undress without a murmur. "Perhaps we might hire a horse tomorrow. I'll speak to the innkeeper about one if we return with news of Oliver."

"Good." Blythe slithered beneath the covers, and Tobias sighed with relief. Maybe now he couldn't see her body so well, he wouldn't want her so damn much. He finished undressing, keeping his shirt on to cover his scars, and then blew out the candles. When it was sufficiently dark, save for the moonlight spilling through the window, he whipped his shirt off to lay over the chair, parted the top sheet from the counterpane, and slid onto the bed beside Blythe. He pulled the counterpane up to his chest and tucked one hand behind his head.

But he could still make out her shape beside him in the moonlight. His cock ached to forget this gentlemanly business and be very, very wicked.

Blythe wriggled beside him. She nudged his leg and then huffed. "What do you think you're doing?"

"Attempting to sleep."

"On top of the counterpane?"

"No. I'm on top of the sheet. I'm quite content here."

"Well." She shook the bed as she rolled over, and he heard her sigh. "Please do not wake me when you sneak out to meet your lightskirt."

Tobias gritted his teeth, and then started to laugh at the absurdity of her suggestion. "My dear B, you are a treasure. I'm lying here, trying to be a proper gentleman, and you think it's so I can sneak out the door during the night. Where is your mind? I don't want what the maid offered. You should be happy I'm attempting to show some restraint by keeping a distance from you."

She said nothing, but pulled the covers closer to her chin and ignored him.

He placed his hand on her arm. "B? Are you angry with me for finally attempting to do the right thing?"

"Why would I be angry with you?"

He leaned closer, intending to press a kiss to her covered shoulder…and touched bare skin instead. His cock thickened. "Do you not want me to stay on my side of the bed?"

"It doesn't matter."

Although she resisted, he rolled her until she lay flat on her back.

"Yes, I made up my mind to avoid ruining your good name any further. After pretending to be man and wife, though, I have my doubts whether that will still be possible."

Her hand touched his chest—a soft touch that trailed over his skin and left fire in its wake. The touch firmed as her hand slid to his side, tickling his ribs, and then curled around to touch his back.

Tobias jerked upright as her fingers touched his scars.

Blythe followed him and sat up, her hands landing on his thigh. "Tell me what evil you did to deserve such treatment."

"What I did is none of your business."

Her fingertips caressed his thigh lightly. "Did you hurt someone?"

Dear God, when had Blythe grown into a temptress? "No."

"Did you steal?"

He scoffed. "I would have lost a hand if I had done so."

"Then you are not, in fact, a bad man."

"Oh, you are walking a dangerous line, B." Her fingertips danced higher…and brushed the head of his cock. He groaned. "Let me be a gentleman tonight."

"Whatever happened to you before formed your character. The man I've come to know, and trust, is brash, bold, but never takes more than he's given. I can't ask you to hide your scars any more than I can hide mine."

He faced her, puzzled by her remark. "You have scars?"

"Not like yours, but you do know of mine already. Never once have you suggested I simply forget my life before, my grief for my son and husband, as so many have suggested I do. You have been surprisingly understanding, when you never needed to be." Her hand wrapped around his length, and she stroked him, her thumb skimming over the head softly on the upstroke.

Unable to believe Blythe would do such a thing, he sat in numb shock as she gave him pleasure. After a moment or two, he shook off the daze. One of them ought to be sensible. She deserved better.

He caught her hands, forced her onto her back, and hovered over her. "This isn't the best idea you've ever had, my lady. I do not want you to regret a hasty decision."

She wriggled one hand free and shoved the sheet to her waist.

"It's not a hasty decision. You've given me ample time to consider the matter, and I do want you."

She rose up and landed a light kiss on his lips.

Tobias growled as her breasts, nipples pointed and hard beneath the light muslin nightgown, skimmed his chest. He dropped his weight upon her and caught her head between his hands. Her body was soft and inviting against his, and he kissed her as he'd been dreaming of kissing her this last week.

She matched his kiss, passion for passion, hunger for hunger, until they were both writhing, the sheet a mere memory as their legs tangled.

Tobias smoothed his fingers over the soft strands of her hair as conflicting emotions rose within him. He wanted her now, fast and hard before she changed her mind; to leave her aching for him. But he also wanted to make love to her all night. And every night she'd allow him to.

He eased from her grip, pressing lighter kisses to her jaw and down the delicate curve of her throat. He would take his time. For Blythe, he would take all night until she was satisfied.

He nibbled her earlobe, and then groaned when her hands skimmed his back. He'd never guessed Blythe was so fearless. She took the worst of him, his scars and manners, and made him forget they mattered.

He caught her leg and lifted it to curl around his thigh. Blythe panted as he settled between her legs. He wouldn't rush, but still the barrier of her nightgown lay between them. It had to go.

He eased away again to lift her gown higher, uncovering the dark triangle between her legs. Her curls brushed his erection, and he caught her lips and kissed her soundly. "My God, you are lovely," he said as he drew back.

A slow chuckle escaped her lips. "I now understand why you've never had any complaints before." She wriggled her hand between them and caressed his length. "Are you not afraid of splinters anymore?"

Tobias groaned against her throat. "I must have been out of my mind to say such a thing to you. There is nothing undesirable about you. Nothing at all."

He inched down the bed, pleased to hear a rumble of disappointment pass Blythe's lips when she couldn't touch his cock anymore. He kissed the skin of her chest until he reached the edge of her nightgown and exposed her breasts to the night air. Small, perfectly round—the nipples standing erect and waiting. He nuzzled them with his lips.

Her fingers curled into his hair as he took one peak into his mouth and suckled, holding the other against the palm of his free hand. Her legs opened wider and wrapped around his waist, bringing her moist heat firmly against his stomach. He drew on the peak as his fingers plucked and tugged at the other nipple. Blythe curled against him and kissed the top of his head.

He looked up. Her eyes were wide, her lips parted as she panted. He smiled and rose up to kiss her again. She was lovely—an incomparable. He couldn't believe she wanted him. He didn't deserve her gift.

When he settled between her open thighs, she welcomed him with an impatient tug. She caressed his back, passing over his scars as if they didn't exist and squeezed his bottom. The action made him jerk, and the head of his cock butted her entrance—her wet heat drawing him in.

Chapter Twenty-Five

Blythe's breath caught as Tobias slid inside her body. She tensed, expecting him to plunder, but he simply joined with her and pressed his head into the crook of her neck. After a long moment of inactivity, she nudged his shoulder. "What's wrong?"

Tobias shuddered, his laughter sinking into her skin. "You make everything so easy for me."

She caught his face between her hands and peered at him. Had he already found his release? "You didn't?"

"Oh no, my delicious Lady Venables. I'm just pausing to savor perfection."

Blythe frowned. What nonsense was he about? There were many more women in the world who could satisfy a man better than she could. She'd hardly been allowed to touch him as it was.

He set his hands on the mattress, his lower body resting against hers where they were joined. He eased back and then slid inside her again. The sensation sent a tingle of tension through her limbs.

She dropped her eyes to his chest, and then she touched where her eyes wandered. He had many small marks, perhaps scars from circumstances he wouldn't speak of yet. She caressed each one in turn, and then lifted her head to kiss those closest. All the while, Tobias slowly moved within her body. Not roughly as she'd half feared, half yearned for, but with a determined assault on her senses. When her lips found his nipple, he cradled her face against his chest and held her there a moment.

"God, B, you take a man to the edge with those lips of yours," he gasped as she licked the peak. He eased her head to the pillow, following her down and arranging them comfortably so he rested on one arm.

The ache between her legs intensified as she met his gaze. His slow coupling and scrutiny adding to her arousal. His fingers skimmed over her nipples, played over the softness of her belly, and then continued down to where they joined. Blythe tensed again as he slid his hand between their hips and touched a place desperate for attention.

Tobias smiled down upon her as he teased her folds and slid over a place so sensitive, her back arched from the bed. Coupled with the slow slide of his cock within her, Blythe's pleasure tripled. She locked one leg high around his hip and clung, searching for the right pressure and Tobias' touch.

When she found it, she jerked and shuddered, climaxing around Tobias so quickly, she was taken by surprise. She buried her face against his hot chest as the wave slowly ebbed.

After what seemed an eternity, she lifted her face. Tobias wasn't grinning. His jaw was clenched tightly, his eyes were closed, his entire body tense and stiff against hers. Suddenly, he pulled out and pressed his face to her belly.

Blythe tangled her fingers in his hair, astounded at how easy sex between them had been, and how desperately she had wanted Tobias to make love to her tonight.

Everything else about their association had been a struggle. His manners completely at odds with hers. However, in bed, they seemed to set those differences aside. She hadn't thought of anything accept stealing a perfect moment for herself.

Tobias crawled up the bed and pulled Blythe's back to his front without saying a word. He pressed a kiss to her hair and cradled her against his wide chest as if she was precious to him. She'd never expected him to be so gentle. She set her hand over his at her waist, where it rested over her crumpled night gown. He linked their fingers together and held her hand in a tight grip.

"Tobias?"

"Shh, B. I'm trying to convince myself not to do that again."

She twisted to look at him. "Do I have any say in the matter?"

He grinned and pushed her hair back from her face. His large hands held her gently. "Absolutely. Making love to you is very tempting. Arousing in the extreme. But I don't want to ruin our lives with a brat of mine."

Blythe stilled as a chill shot through her heart. She was a fool not to have considered that she could become with child after making love with Tobias.

Her pulse raced again as the thought took hold.

A child. Another child of her own to love and treasure. She blinked as the quick rush of hope brought heat to her skin. But Tobias thought fathering a child would ruin his carefree life. She closed her eyes as the disappointment slammed into her.

She wanted the wicked pirate for herself, and that meant everything that was possible between them: a future, a home, a family of their making.

She pushed the discovery from her mind and strove to find a lighter thought that wouldn't ruin what little pleasure she'd found in his arms. Tobias had not found his own release yet, and she should correct that oversight as soon as possible. "How could you ruin the evening? You're not terrible at making love," she teased.

Tobias had been very, very good indeed, and she truly wouldn't mind if he could make her climax like that again. But he would only be her lover. He had made her no promises beyond tonight.

He nuzzled her neck and continued to nip until he reached her shoulderblade. Although he clearly didn't intend to find satisfaction for himself within her body, she wriggled against him—sliding her bare bottom against the hard length at his groin. His groan raised the hair on the back of her neck.

"Woman, you must have lost your mind to invite a devil like me to your bed."

Blythe curled her arm over her head to hold his lips against her neck. "I thought you were described as a demon."

"Devil, demon. Whatever name you want to call me, I'll answer to." He threw her onto her back, stripped her of her nightgown, and settled part of his weight against her, holding her down. He pressed his lips to her throat, caught her hands and held them high above her head. "I'll come whenever you call."

He brushed his cock against her thigh, and she shuddered. Perhaps teasing him wasn't the smartest idea, but she did love his possessive touch on her body. He held her in place as he kissed and nipped her skin, and then widened her legs with his knees with an impatient jerk. His cock nudged against her curls, and Blythe gasped as a rush of desire swept over her.

He held her hands against the mattress on either side of her head. She couldn't move, couldn't touch his body. Tobias would have her exactly as he wished. Slow, fast, hard or gentle. Her body hummed in anticipation.

She slowed her breathing as he slid inside an inch at a time until nothing separated them. His mouth caressed her cheek as he started to thrust inside her.

A frisson of pleasure curled her spine. She clenched her hands about his. His grip tightened as he withdrew, and when he surged back in, Blythe gasped. Her breasts, nipples excited to hard little buds, brushed against his chest maddeningly.

Tobias set up a faster pace, opening her legs wider, sliding more of himself into her body. She ached with fierce need to touch him, but in this position, she was a willing slave to his mercy. He gave her none. His thrusts grew faster, his flesh slapped against her thighs in a way she'd never experienced before. He rode her quick and sure, and Blythe reveled in his passionate lovemaking.

A tight coil of desire flooded her senses and she met him thrust for thrust. She clenched her sex around his length every other stroke. "Come for me, Tobias," she whispered.

"No," he groaned. But his hips slammed harder against her until his thrusts became frenzied—and he climaxed inside her body. He groaned again and collapsed against her, releasing her climax, too. She squeezed him as she came, his name tumbling from her lips foolishly.

She dragged in frantic breaths as she struggled with what had just happened. She'd begged him to come inside her. She could become pregnant with his child.

Blythe buried her face in his shoulder, replete but discontent. What would she do if the worst came to pass? Could she bear his child out of wedlock without her heart breaking?

What if he ever discovered she'd loved him with more than her body tonight? What if he discovered he had claimed what remained of her heart?

Tobias resettled Blythe in his arms as she stirred in her sleep. He'd changed his plans for the future three times during the night, always coming back to the absolute necessity of making Blythe his wife. Patience be damned. Money be damned. He would marry Blythe as soon as banns could be called.

He ran his fingers through her hair, content at last with his decision. If they could come together like that, he'd be mad to wait a moment longer than necessary to ask her to be his wife. He would do anything she wanted, turn himself out like a prattling popinjay if it made her as happy as she'd made him tonight.

This was what he wanted in his life, and what he would wait for if she said no immediately. He would live as a celibate bachelor if he couldn't convince her to accept straight away. There was no one else for him.

A church bell tolled the hour and when the sound continued, he looked toward the window. He eased Blythe onto the mattress as the sound disturbed her, and she blinked sleep from her eyes like a sleepy kitten.

The sound stopped…then began again.

He glanced toward the faint light. "Warning bells?"

He threw himself out of bed and hurried to the window. When he peeled back the drapes completely, a burst of firelight illuminated a group of people milling about before the inn.

"What's going on? Is the inn alight?" Blythe stood and picked up her abandoned nightgown.

"No, not the inn." Tobias dropped the drape and fumbled to light a candle. "There are people milling about outside though. I'll go and see what it is."

Blythe tossed her nightgown aside and reached for her clothes. "I'm coming with you."

"Blythe, this isn't a soiree we are attending."

"I won't be left behind to wonder. I have a pair of hands capable of passing a pail of water if necessary."

He raked his fingers through his hair. "Fine. Here, I'll help you dress, but you must promise me to stay away from the blaze."

"Yes, Tobias. I have no desire to cause more problems for anyone." She swiftly plaited her tangled hair, wincing at the odd snare, and tied them off. When she was dressed, he caught up her cloak and slipped it around her to ensure she stayed warm. "What time do you think it is?" she asked.

"Close to dawn." He pulled her toward the door. "Let's go, but remember your promise."

They swiftly made their way downstairs, through to the inn yard to where others had gathered. He caught the arm of the first man he encountered. "What's to do?"

"Skepington is alight! Those poor souls."

Tobias looked up. A thin column of smoke stained the clear night sky.

Blythe gasped. "What do you mean by poor souls?"

The innkeeper frowned. "Most are locked inside. We'll never reach them before the flames do."

Tobias ran for Skepington.

"Toby, no!" Blythe screamed as he sprinted out of the inn yard and cut across the field.

Ahead, Skepington was ablaze with light and sound, a beacon of hopelessness and fear.

He hurtled a low stone wall and hurried through an orchard, threw himself over another fence and stopped before the burning building. The entire right side had caught, and he knew those trapped inside were as good as dead already. Glass smashed and fell to the ground, hands stretched for help. Tobias started toward them, but then noticed that bars had been fixed to every lower window. He couldn't get in that way.

He cupped his hands around his mouth to scream, "Oliver!"

No one called in answer. He looked about him and spied a man moving away from the house. The fellow staggered a few steps and then fell, his clothing steaming in the cold. Tobias rushed to him and rolled him over. His blackened visage proved he'd narrowly escaped death, but he had no eyebrows or hair left on his head. "Sir. Do you know Oliver Randall? Is he still inside?"

The man lying on the ground giggled and scuttled away, spit drooling from his mouth. But his arm lifted toward the burning house and pointed.

A window high up—the same one as in the painting at Romsey, glowed with feeble light.

Could Oliver really be here?

Time was against him. He'd have to trust luck that he could save his brother from the blaze. He drew in several deep, clean gulps of air and then ran at the building.

He leapt for the first window sill, balanced on the edge, and then kicked at the glass with his boots. Pieces splintered, shattering on stone as they fell, but there were bars behind this glass as well, and he couldn't gain entrance.

He looked up to the next window above him, stretched for handholds to reach it, and hauled himself up the face of the house. This window, too, was barred on the inside. He could also see the glow from the quickly spreading fire.

He glanced at the higher windows. One had drapes hanging through the narrow gap. He looked for handholds and saw few in the space between. His muscles burned as he stretched.

"Tobias!"

Blythe. He couldn't look over his shoulder to reassure her he was well enough, and he hoped she kept her distance. He passed a darkened window, found it barred too as well, and continued up to the one he hoped was open.

Success! He lifted the pane, shifted the drapes aside to get a clear view and stuck his head and shoulders through.

An old man with cropped gray hair sat with his back to the window, poring over a book by the weakest of light.

"I say, my good man, the house is afire! Why have you not fled?"

The man stiffened. "I cannot go outside, as I'm already dead. I must inhabit this place."

A madman? Still, he couldn't leave him here to burn.

Tobias hauled himself over the sill until he stood inside the room. He flexed his shoulders. He couldn't assist this man out via the window—they'd both tumble to their deaths. However, there might be a way out through the house that could leave them largely unscathed if there was another staircase at this end of the building.

"There is no time to wait. The fire will be here in minutes."

The figure turned another page with a sigh. "Then that is my fate. I can do nothing to save myself without terrible consequences for others."

"Like hell you can't." Tobias crossed to the door. He tested the handle, found it locked, and then backed up a few steps. It didn't look too stout. He rushed the door and slammed into it.

It didn't budge. He backed up again.

"Ah, excuse me, but if you should like to leave through the door, then I would imagine you would have more luck by using the key."

Tobias spun about, surprised to see the old man held a key between his skeletal fingers. Tobias moved closer, bringing the man's face into view. His features were gaunt, as if he'd been marooned for months with the poorest of nourishment to sustain him. Tobias had seen a slave in this condition once. He hadn't lived for long after. He'd been too weakened to recover his strength. But whoever this man was, he didn't deserve to die in a fire. He took the key. "Come with me. I'll set you free."

"Freedom is denied me."

"Look, I'll not let you roast in this hell. What is your name?"

"I am Seventeen."

"Seventeen. Great. Well, get off your arse, Seventeen, and let's go. I've a good woman waiting, an angel, and I'd like to keep my eyebrows."

"An angel, you say? Wonders will never cease." Seventeen's own eyebrow rose as he removed a strip of ribbon from the book, placed it in his pocket, patted it, and then stood.

To say Seventeen was unsteady on his feet was an understatement. A light breeze could have blown him over. Tobias caught him about his waist, grateful that they were of similar height. They shuffled to the doorway and he unlocked the door.

Smoke flowed over them and the man at his side coughed violently. The main stairs were lost in the swirling cloud. "Is there another way down through the servants' stairs? Anything other than the main staircase?"

Seventeen pointed. "I believe there is one in that direction."

They shuffled along, but found a dead end.

Tobias looked about him frantically. There was no other way out. His companion had been mistaken.

"Old houses hold many secrets," Seventeen whispered as he crumbled against the wall paneling…

And kept falling as the paneling gave way to reveal a darkened staircase. One free of smoke.

At last, some good luck. He could get Seventeen out and continue to search for Oliver.

However, rather than get up, Seventeen remained where he'd fallen.

Tobias hauled him to his feet, noticing with a sickening feeling that Seventeen offered no resistance whatsoever. He'd have to be carried. After some careful juggling, Tobias managed to place him over his shoulder, as he would a sack of grain, and blindly made his way down the stairs.

"Now I know why the complaints were so loud when I was younger," Seventeen grumbled. "This isn't pleasant at all."

Tobias didn't respond. The poor fellow had rocks for brains. When he reached the bottom, he groped around for a doorway. He found the latch just as he was beginning to despair. Smoke rolled over him as he pushed the door wide and stumbled out, his eyes watering madly.

"Toby!"

Blythe's voice reached him, and he hurried toward the sound.

Hands caught him and urged him farther away from the burning building. He lowered Seventeen from his back and others took him, carrying him between them until they reached the trees closest to the village. Blythe clutched at his arm when he would have turned back.

"There is still a chance I can find him," he croaked.

"It's too late. I'm so sorry. I can't lose you too."

Behind him, Skepington groaned and the crackle of flames sent a chill through him. He had to go back for Oliver. He had no other choice.

He took one step toward the house, but was stopped when Blythe wrapped her arms around his waist and held on tightly. "You can't go back inside that!"

"No. I must find him!"

Blythe was suddenly before him. She set her hands to his chest and pushed him back with her whole slight weight. "It's too late!"

Tobias stared at the house. Tongues of flame licked the window frame of Seventeen's chamber. A remnant of drape, caught by the stirring breeze, floated into the night as flame consumed it. He couldn't go in that way again.

A growl left his throat. Blythe was correct. He'd burn too if he went back and Leopold would be alone again. He roared to express his pain and then drew Blythe against him and held her tightly. He stared as the house collapsed in on itself and the poor souls contained inside died.

He'd failed Oliver.

He'd failed his family.

He closed his eyes tightly and prayed that Oliver had not suffered, that the smoke had taken him before the flames had even touched his skin. Burning was a terrible way to perish. No one deserved that.

He eased his grip on Blythe as Seventeen's hacking cough reached his ears.

"He's coming round, Mr. Randall. Thank the Lord for that," Mr. Drake murmured.

Tobias examined the man he had rescued. Save for his ridiculous name, Seventeen, and the ribbon he'd pocketed, he had no clue about the fellow. He'd had the key to his own chamber, so he must not have been an inmate.

Mrs. Drake bustled over, her hands holding a bucket of water and a mug. Tobias took the mug and hunkered down beside Seventeen. "Here, drink this. It's sweetened with honey for your poor throat."

Seventeen sipped feebly, appearing too weak to hold the cup. Tobias encouraged him to drink more when he tried to stop. When he refused, Tobias filled the mug and drank deeply himself.

Another section of the house collapsed, and they all stared as the sun lifted over the horizon, bathing them in bright light.

Tobias collapsed to the ground and covered his face with both hands. Poor bloody Oliver. The day of his death would be fair.

Chapter Twenty-Six

Blythe reluctantly left Tobias alone, sensing he'd rather have privacy for his grief. She knelt beside the man he had rescued and dabbed her handkerchief in the bucket of water. "Are you hurt, sir?"

The man opened his eyes, and then squeezed them shut again. "I'm outside. I'm not allowed to be outside."

"It's all right." She forced a smile to her lips, but her heart broke at the terror in his voice. "We'll get you into a bed soon enough. Mr. Drake, will you take him to your inn? He should rest after his ordeal."

Mr. and Mrs. Drake exchanged an anxious glance. "We've got no more rooms to put him in, Mrs. Randall. We're full up, and there's no doctor to attend him."

"I'm sure we'll muddle through without a doctor. He doesn't seem injured." Blythe smiled. "Please have him taken to our bedchamber at the inn. I'm sure my husband won't object after the trouble he went through to save him."

Blythe glanced at Tobias, but he had withdrawn from her and everyone. She couldn't blame him. She stood as Mr. Drake and another man hefted the poor fellow between them and carried him toward the inn. "Tobias, we should go."

His arm slid slowly down to reveal his face was coated with tears. She put her arm about his shoulders and touched his face gently. "You did everything you could. No one else even bothered to approach the house." She looked over her shoulder and shuddered. Those poor people. Poor Oliver, if he'd truly been there. They might never know for certain now. She would pray that Oliver rested safely elsewhere and that they might yet find him still.

Tobias sat up slowly, his expression bleak. A single tear slid down his cheek and she wiped it away for him. "Let's go back to the inn and see to it that your efforts were not in vain. I must see that the man you saved is taken good care of. Did he by any chance tell you his name?"

Tobias pressed his head to her shoulder. "He said his name was Seventeen, and he's not made much sense beyond that."

"Well, when he is recovered sufficiently, we will see him safely on his way to his family. If he has no one, we will decide what to do with him together. Lord Merrow will help, I'm sure." Blythe climbed to her feet and held out her hand.

After a long moment, Tobias stood, curled his arm about her shoulders and allowed her to lead him back to the village. As they entered the inn yard arm in arm, the grooms cheered Tobias' feat, commenting on his bravery and daring. Some had seen his efforts to gain entry to the burning building and wondered where he'd learned the trick.

Tobias merely nodded and refused to comment.

Mrs. Drake bustled past, a steaming bowl of soup in her hands. "Thought a bit of food might perk him up. He's ever so pale and listless."

"A very good idea, Mrs. Drake."

Blythe tugged Tobias with her, anxious about his silence. She'd be keeping an eye on him. It wasn't his fault. They'd come as soon as they'd learned of Skepington.

Their bedchamber was awash with light, the fire blazing again, but that hussy of a housemaid who'd flirted with Tobias yesterday lingered in the room. Blythe shooed her out. She had no patience for time wasters.

Tobias trudged to the washbasin and threw water over his face. When he was done, he moved to the small settee and collapsed upon it. He closed his eyes and leaned back, clearly unwilling to become further involved with the object of his rescue. She'd let him grieve alone for a little while and take care of Seventeen herself.

Blythe wet a cloth and approached the bed. Seventeen's eyes were closed, his breathing raspy. She lifted his hand and attempted to wipe the ash from his skin.

When she looked at his face again, he was staring back at her, a frown marring his brow. "Who are you? An angel?"

"My name is Blythe. My husband rescued you. Don't you remember?"

He nodded slowly, gaze flickering to where Tobias reclined and back again. "Am I in heaven? By my calculations, there is no other explanation for my being here."

Blythe smiled for the poor fellow's sake. He indeed appeared to be deranged. "You are in Whitsbury. You said your name was Seventeen, but I am sure you go by another?"

His gaze grew shuttered. "I'm tired."

She patted his hand. "I'm sure you must be. Rest now, we'll talk more when you awaken."

Seventeen closed his eyes and Blythe moved away before she burst into tears.

"Thank you for your assistance, Mrs. Drake. I'll call when he wakes or if I should require any further assistance this morning. I feel certain rest is the best thing for all of us right now."

The innkeeper's wife frowned. "Are you sure you're all right with him? He is one of them mad fellows, you know."

Blythe glanced at the bed. Seventeen, in his current state of health, was too weak to get into any mischief. "I'm sure I'm in no danger, besides my husband is here to protect me."

Mrs. Drake didn't appear entirely convinced. "All right then, but I'll be back to check on you and your husband soon. Can't have the hero of Skepington and his lady murdered by the madman he saved."

Blythe smiled as Mrs. Drake let herself out, thinking how Tobias had dismissed the honor of being called a hero. She snuggled up against him on the settee, falling into his arms as if she belonged with him. Tonight, he'd been extraordinary. She would always think of him as a hero.

Sometime later, Blythe opened her eyes and screamed.

Seventeen's face was inches from hers.

She scrambled backwards, falling off the settee in the process. On his feet, Seventeen was much taller than she'd imagined he'd be. She glanced around desperately, but Tobias wasn't in the room.

Footsteps pounded up the hall outside and the door crashed open. "Blythe!" Tobias called.

"I'm here!"

He pulled her to her feet and helped straighten her skirts. "What happened?"

She glanced around. Seventeen had disappeared. "He scared me. I woke and he was staring at me, inches away from my face."

Tobias circled the bed and stopped with his hands on his hips. "If you come close to her again, I swear you'll wish you had not."

Blythe hurried to see where Seventeen had hidden. He huddled against the wall, hands curved over his head. "I thought I was dreaming," he said over and over.

"Stop, Tobias. You've frightened him."

More footsteps pounded up the hall and Mrs. Drake rushed in. "What's going on here? I was with a customer below when I heard the most piercing scream I've ever heard!"

Blythe blushed. "Sorry. That was me. Everything is fine now. You can go."

Mrs. Drake appeared skeptical, but ducked out the door again.

"A singularly rare talent," Seventeen muttered. "One octave higher and she'd break glass."

"You, be quiet," Tobias said to the man on the floor and drew Blythe into his arms. "At least I'll know when you need me. That was quite unexpectedly loud."

"Ooh, now you shouldn't be up here until invited proper like, sir," Mrs. Drake protested as the door handle to the room rattled.

"Mrs. Drake, I should like to see the fellow that was recovered," a deep voice demanded. "What did you say his name was?"

Blythe stepped out of Tobias' arms quickly as she recognized the voice. The door opened. "Lord Merrow, so good of you to come."

Merrow raised an eyebrow and glanced behind her. "Lady Venables? What in heaven's name are you doing here?"

"It was a last-minute decision, my lord. May I present Mr. Tobias Randall?"

The two men nodded to each other warily. Merrow frowned. "One of the Romsey Randalls? Yes, I remember seeing you at Lady Dunwoody's soiree, but we were not introduced."

Blythe drew herself up tall as Lord Merrow looked about the chamber. "That is unfortunate, my lord. But Mr. Randall and I were, in fact, coming to see you this morning about Skepington Hall. However, I fear our timing was imperfect."

"Yes, I've seen the damage to the hall, and I cannot say I am unhappy about it. A yoke about my neck, it was."

Tobias took a step forward, fist clenched. Blythe flung out her arm and prevented him from throttling Lord Merrow for his lack of compassion in the face of such a tragedy. "We were coming to enquire about a man of our acquaintance that we feared was interred there."

Merrow blanched. "Forgive me. Cursed bad timing. I've been informed few made it out alive."

"Bars on the windows. I cannot imagine why no one escaped," Tobias muttered darkly.

Merrow ignored the comment. "One died just a few minutes ago. I'm here to see what's to be done for the last. Where is he?"

She glanced down—and blinked as she discovered Seventeen had covered his head again.

Lord Merrow came closer and a grimace crossed his features. "Oh, him. He's uninjured, it seems?"

"Yes, thankfully," Blythe replied. "What will you do with him, my lord?"

"God knows where I'll put him, but something should be done. Can't very well neglect to provide his board and lodgings since they've been fully paid for in advance."

Blythe did not like the sound of that indifferent fate for Seventeen. "What do you mean, fully paid for?"

"Families often pay quite heavily to have an irrational relation sequestered for the term of their natural lives. It's done discreetly. My father had arrangements with many great families. I believe this man is one of those cases, though all record of his connections will likely have perished in the fire."

Tobias cleared his throat. "So no one will be coming forward to claim the man that was saved?"

Merrow shrugged. "Most likely the family will wish he'd perished in the flames."

Seventeen whimpered softly.

Blythe bit her lip and made a decision she hoped her sister wouldn't protest too much about. "If they ask, tell them he died."

"Excuse me?"

"If they ask, tell them Seventeen burned in the fire. I'll take responsibility for him. I'll take him away where he'll be looked after."

Lord Merrow gaped at her. "My lady, have you lost your mind? You cannot control a man who has spent his life imprisoned amongst other madmen. They are not trained monkeys to be put out on display for guests."

"Nevertheless, I wish to accept the responsibility. He'll be better off with me than left to your questionable care. Look at him. He's skin and bones and terrified of you."

Merrow had the grace to look guilty. "I could not stand around and make sure each man was properly fed. I have responsibilities elsewhere. Surely you understand."

"No, I don't. It is clear that you didn't have the time to take more than the family's money. He stays with me. Do you recall anything else about his life before he arrived at Skepington?"

"No. Just his name. Seventeen." Merrow's expression darkened. "Very well, you may take your pet home with you, but don't come crying to me when he murders everyone around you. Who knows what goes on in his mind?"

Merrow stormed out, and Blythe let out a relieved breath when she couldn't hear his footfalls anymore. "Thank goodness that is over and done with."

"B, what are you doing?"

"The right thing."

She knelt beside Seventeen. "Would you mind very much if I took care of you, sir?"

Seventeen lifted his head, and his mouth curved into a small smile. "As much as I should like to accept the honor of submitting to your care, madam, I feel my brother might have some objections to such a scandalous proposal." His gaze lifted to look over her shoulder. "You were correct earlier in the evening. She is indeed an angel among the unworthy."

Tobias pushed past her, catching Seventeen by the shoulders. "What did you just say? What brother?"

Seventeen glanced between Tobias and Blythe. "I may be a trifle befuddled, but I had thought you'd referred to her earlier as your wife?"

"She's not my wife," Tobias said softly.

Seventeen grunted. "I could swear that I heard her called Mrs. Randall several times, and you do seem inordinately fond of holding her in your arms. I would have claimed it a near absolute truth that she was yours. The fire must have muddled my mind."

Tobias' frown returned. "A near absolute truth?"

"Yes, surely. Ninety-nine percent certain," Seventeen said, voice cracking before he coughed.

Blythe's heart raced as she realized Seventeen spoke in mathematical terms.

Hadn't Tobias said something about Oliver doing the same? But this man was old…or at least appeared so to her eyes. "What is your real name, sir?"

He shook himself. "Seventeen."

Tobias frowned. "That isn't your name at all. Who sent you to Skepington Hall?"

When Seventeen wouldn't answer, Blythe caught his hand in hers and held it firmly. Asking him direct questions about his identity wasn't going to provide the answers they needed quickly. They'd have to ask those questions in a different way. They had to gain his trust. "When did you first ride a pony?"

"I was five."

"I had to wait until I was older," she confided. "Was the pony your own?"

Seventeen shook his head. "No. I had to share."

"With whom?"

Seventeen's eyes closed. "With…" His mouth snapped shut.

Blythe stared hard at the man before her. Leopold Randall had once confided that he'd had to wait to ride until his younger brother, Oliver, was five before their father purchased them a mount. But if this man was Oliver Randall, why wouldn't he just come out and say so? Had he been treated as badly as Tobias? Had he been made afraid to tell the truth?

"I had to share my mount with my sister," Blythe continued, hoping that her chatter would slip under his guard and put him at ease. "My elder brother had his own and used to tease us that we rode poorly. Was yours any better? Was he bossy and cross all the time? What was the beast's name?"

"Noble," Seventeen said immediately.

Tobias fell back onto the floor, staring at Seventeen. "When we met, you said freedom was denied you. Why?"

Seventeen looked at the floor. "Innocent lives depend on my silence."

Blythe settled to her knees. "Circumstances have changed somewhat these last weeks. My sister is the current Duchess of Romsey, a widow. Her son, a child, is four. Young Edwin is a healthy, robust child. Very recently, a Mr. Leopold Randall came to visit the estate and made himself known."

She searched Seventeen's face for signs of response, but he kept his face still and unemotional. "Leopold lives at Romsey and already manages the estate for the duchess and her young son. The boy bears two very deep dimples. Just as his father does."

Seventeen's eyes widened. "No, that cannot be possible."

"Believe me. I was just as surprised by the discovery as you appear to be."

Tobias shifted closer. "What are the chances that the old Duke of Romsey was responsible for sending you to a madhouse and warned you members of your family depended on your silence?"

Seventeen blinked. "Absolute."

Chapter Twenty-Seven

Tobias rocked back in shock. "I didn't recognize you."

"It matters little." Oliver glanced at Blythe. "You're not Mrs. Randall," he accused. "'Tis dangerous to say you are."

"There is no danger now," Blythe quickly assured him. "But I took the name for appearances' sake while staying here. I am Lady Venables of Walden Hall. Blythe, to my family and friends. It is wonderful to meet you, Oliver Randall."

"Venables and the Duke of Romsey were acquaintances," Oliver said suddenly. "But he poses no threat to us."

"Oliver," Tobias began. "We've come to bring you home."

Oliver Randall smiled sadly. "I feared as much when you burst through my window. At first, I thought I was dead. However, your angel has convinced me otherwise. It will be good to see Mother and Father again."

Tobias swallowed as a lump formed in his throat. "They're dead. The duke murdered them."

Oliver bowed his head and remained silent for a long while as he absorbed the news. "So, he got what he wanted in the end. I blame myself."

Tobias carefully captured his brother's thin hand in his. "Why would it be your fault? I've never understood any of it."

"The duke wanted to guarantee our silence. I uncovered an irregularity in the construction of the abbey in the course of my studies, and went to our father about it. When I returned to school, Father must have continued to pursue the matter. The duke was very angry when we met. He stripped me of my name and referred to me only by my birth date after that."

Tobias forced his emotions down. "But there was no need for the extremes of what he did."

Oliver sighed heavily. "That depends on your perspective. There was every need in his mind. We could have embroiled the duchy in scandal. He couldn't bear to have his secrets exposed, but he couldn't destroy us all. He needed us, should his son fail to produce an heir, which explains why the young duke has dimples. Dimples run on our side of the family."

"Well, none of that matters now," Blythe said matter-of-factly. "We're taking you home."

"Harrowdale," Oliver said somewhat wistfully. "I'm surprised he left it standing."

"I'm taking you to Leopold," Tobias corrected. "He's at Romsey Abbey, and he will want to see you and hear the explanation for our separation from your own lips."

Oliver scowled at them. "The duke's sanctuary is at Romsey. I'm not going anywhere near what started this mess!"

Blythe rose to her feet. "We know all about the sanctuary. We've been inside, but cannot see the sense of the room. Help him up, Tobias, and put him on the bed."

Still unable to comprehend that he had found his brother after all, Tobias tucked Oliver into bed and pulled the cover high up his chest.

"Rooms," Oliver corrected. "It's a maze down there."

"Down?" Both he and Blythe said at once.

"Yes, the sanctuary lies beneath Romsey Abbey."

He exchanged a long look with Blythe. She gripped the bedpost, a frown marring her features. "What of the room off the drawing room, behind the carved rose?"

Oliver shrugged. "It's just a storeroom. The real wealth of Romsey was beneath your feet."

The duke must have been laughing very hard at them from his corner of hell. Their whole investigation of the room had been a waste of time, as Blythe had feared.

He met her gaze. Well, perhaps not a complete waste of time. He'd always have fond memories of that storeroom as the place he'd first kissed Blythe.

She glanced away, a blush flooding her cheeks with color. "And what wealth would be hidden beneath the Romsey Abbey now? Do you know?"

"More riches than ever the dukes of Romsey could have obtained without breaking the law quite a few times. His Grace was a smuggler, and also a thief. He was extremely good at getting what he wanted."

Blythe caught Tobias' hand and squeezed it tightly. "That's why someone is trying to drive Mercy from the estate. They want to find the entrance and gain the riches they believe are still there. Someone knows."

"Wilcox," Tobias growled. "And we've left Mercy and Leopold at Romsey."

Blythe gripped him tightly. "Wilcox already knew about the sanctuary. He saw me leave the room a few days ago. Now he knows where it is it's only a matter of time before he finds the way down."

Oliver chuckled softly. "The book room doesn't give one access to the sanctuary. It's just a storeroom for the duke's harmless treasures. The entrance to the sanctuary is concealed in another place."

"And you know where it is?"

Oliver nodded. "Yes, unfortunately I do."

"Excuse us for a moment, Oliver." Tobias caught Blythe's hand.

"Take your time. I'm not going anywhere." Oliver closed his eyes and heaved a heavy sigh.

Tobias pulled Blythe toward the window. "If we leave now, we could reach Romsey just after nightfall. Do you think Oliver is well enough to travel?"

"He's weak, but perhaps he might sleep the entire way." She squeezed his hands. "I want to get back to Mercy and Edwin, too."

"So do I. Stay with Oliver." He brushed his knuckles along her jaw. "I'll see what I can do about procuring a larger carriage."

"Are you sure you can manage?"

"Yes, because you'll be there to distract me with your beauty." He kissed the back of her hand and strode for the door, casting a quick look over his shoulder at his sleeping brother. He still couldn't believe that Oliver was found. But the trick would be to keep him alive to tell his tale. To keep them all safe.

As Tobias rush downstairs in search of the innkeeper, Blythe's heart was lighter than she'd expected it to be. She closed the door behind him and turned around to face Oliver.

"You're fond of him," Oliver said bluntly.

Blythe nodded, realizing it was true.

"What about your husband? Does he know you're staying at an inn with another man?"

"My husband passed away some time ago." For the first time ever, Blythe felt no pain as she said the words. She would always wish they'd had longer together, but she wasn't so sad anymore. She pulled a chair up close to the bed and studied Oliver Randall.

He was quite unlike Tobias in appearance; hair cropped close to his skull and heavily peppered with steel-gray strands, face thin and sallow. Perhaps the lack of similarity was the result of his condition. "Forgive me for asking, but are you ill, Mr. Randall?"

He shook his head listlessly on the pillow. "Meal times were never what one could call regular. Given time, I'll come good again."

"Good. I should hate for you to be truly unwell. Your brother wishes to return to Romsey Abbey today, if at all possible."

"Your face is sad when you look at me. I look old, don't I?"

She nodded slowly. "I thought you a good deal older than you must be. Leopold's hair is only touched with gray at his temples."

"My hair changed soon after my incarceration. Worry caused it, I expect."

She patted his hand. "I'm sure it'll make no difference to the people who love you."

He sighed heavily. "I never gave a thought to my appearance before."

"Most people take what they have for granted." She paused to wait while he coughed again then fetched him some wine to ease his throat. "Tobias mentioned you were a curious-minded fellow. Your time at Skepington must have been terrible."

"I am, as ever, a keen observer of human frailties. I learned a great deal during my time there." Oliver sipped slowly and then handed the glass back. "To say I was obsessive about the study of architecture when I was young would be kind."

"And you've changed?"

"Somewhat. I believe my best interests lie outside of England. I hope to travel the world one day."

Oliver made travel abroad sound so easy. But surely he knew that the war with France continued. She would let his brother's explain the dangers. She put the glass down. "It is very good to have met you, Mr. Randall. Leopold has spoken of you from the moment we met. He never gave up hope of finding you. He will have many things to discuss with you when you meet again. Do not be too quick to decide your future."

"I have thought of nothing but an alternative future to the one I lived. Once my health is restored, we will go. There is nothing to hold us here."

"Us?" Blythe shifted on the chair uneasily. "Who are you taking with you?"

"My family, of course, and a friend. By my calculations, there should be sufficient funds to support us for years."

Blythe gaped. "Surely you don't imagine Leopold would leave his child and the woman he loves? He is planning a life with them."

Oliver stared at her. "Emotions are more of a nuisance at times like these. I suggest you step back and see the possibilities. I'm sure Tobias will agree with me."

"What will I agree to?" Tobias asked from the door.

"Your brother and I were becoming better acquainted." Blythe's throat thickened, and she forced the words out. "He's mentioned he has plans to travel, and to take you all with him."

"I'm not leaving England," Tobias said instantly. "I've seen enough of the world."

Blythe relaxed at Tobias' tone. He'd only just returned. She couldn't imagine not seeing him every day. Perhaps Oliver could be talked out of his travel plans, at least for the time being.

Oliver's gaze narrowed. "Well, I haven't been anywhere."

"We can talk this over with Leopold when we return to Romsey Abbey," Tobias suggested. "We have a closed coach and grooms, and one to follow along with your chaise, too, my lady. The innkeeper was very keen to speed our departure."

Blythe stood and gathered her things. As she laid Tobias' small bundle on top of hers, her heart beat faster. They had not spoken about the future, but she supposed now Oliver had been found, their time alone, their closeness, would come to an end.

She followed behind Tobias and Oliver as he was helped downstairs and into the waiting carriage. The innkeeper had supplied blankets and pillows for Oliver's comfort, and Tobias tucked them around him, covering him from head to foot so he would stay warm.

When Blythe saw her bag secured, she stepped into the carriage and pulled a blanket over her knees.

The innkeeper's wife set a heavy wicker basket at her feet. "You've a good man there. My best to you both."

Tobias climbed in, grinning, and thumped the roof of the carriage to get them underway. Across from them, Oliver closed his eyes and grew still.

Tobias smiled, his eyes glowing with a warmth that filled her soul. "You found him."

"We found him," she corrected.

His lips curved into a wicked smile. "See, I told you we needed to work together."

Blythe laughed. "I'll allow you to be proud of yourself for a little while."

He chuckled and caught her hand in his, lacing their fingers together. "When we get back to Romsey, there will be questions to answer. What do you want to say about us being together? Mercy and Leopold could be worried. We'll have been gone two days without a chaperone."

A pang of disappointment threatened her good mood. "I imagine we should stick to the facts. We had an idea about where Oliver might have been, but didn't want to raise anyone's hopes without better reason. You insisted on accompanying me so I came to no harm…and it turned out to be a good thing, as you rescued Oliver from a burning building this morning. I think they will be so distracted by the last and Oliver's return that they will not ask too many more questions."

"And if the subject of where either of us slept last night comes up? What should I do? Propose?"

Blythe stared at him as he licked his lips. She'd known that if word of their journey came to light, there would be gossip and an assumption of an arrangement existing, especially by her sister. Mercy would likely pressure Tobias into marriage. However, Blythe did not want to be proposed to under those conditions. She'd married the last time because of love, and she'd only marry again if such a state existed.

However, when it came to Tobias Randall, she had no idea if his thoughts aligned with hers on the subject of the reason to marry. "Then I hope you will be a gentleman and say you slept elsewhere."

He smiled and kissed her brow. "I can do that for you."

Blythe let out a relieved breath. It would be better for both of them not to be forced together just because of one night. Even if it was a very pleasant, very exciting night.

Blythe placed her head on Tobias' shoulder and he shifted until she was in his arms. She would miss being able to do this when they returned to Romsey. There would be no excuses to linger in what she now knew to be merely a storeroom.

What would Tobias say if he knew she'd been yearning for the pirate to visit her bedchamber even before they had spent last night together? Her bedchamber window had always been locked.

Chapter Twenty-Eight

Tobias stepped down from the carriage and held out his hand. "Home sweet home."

Blythe's small hand touched his and sent his pulse racing, as it had frequently done on the return journey. He had thought he would grow accustomed to her after the long hours alone, with Oliver's sleepy company to dampen his yearning. But the more time he spent with her, the more he craved.

Every time she smiled, his heart lurched. "I thought we would never arrive."

He helped her out, but didn't immediately let go. He was not quite ready to give her up and be a proper gentleman yet. "Was it a long trip? I never noticed."

"Are you cured then?" Her breath created steam in the cold night air, reminding him that he was keeping her out in the elements longer than he should.

He brought her hand to his mouth and kissed her knuckles. "I had the perfect distraction on hand to make the journey seem unimportant."

Oliver cleared his throat, and Tobias let her go, remembering he'd promised to behave. He checked that the coachman had unlashed Blythe's bag and directed the driver of her chaise toward the stables. As the smaller carriage disappeared from sight, he glanced at the abbey door.

It swung open, and Blythe's hand slipped from his.

Wilcox hurried out. "Sir, my lady, you're back."

"Of course I've returned. And we've important news."

"Very good, sir. Welcome back, Lady Venables. I hope you've had a pleasant journey. Her Grace will be eager to know you've returned." He picked up Blythe's bag and carried it up the stairs without looking back.

Alarm bells rang in Tobias' mind at Wilcox's mild tone. They'd been gone two days without leaving word behind. It was a miracle a search hadn't been organized.

He glanced up at the façade of Romsey Abbey. Every window's shutter was closed tight. No light seeped out into the night.

Blythe tugged on his arm. "Tobias, I have a very bad feeling." Her hand slipped into his, trembling.

He'd come to trust her instincts as well as his own. "I agree. We don't know what's going on inside." He caressed her cheek. "Stay close to Oliver and say nothing about his identity until we know what's afoot."

"All right." She turned to the carriage. "Oliver?"

"Wilcox is definitely hiding something," Oliver said without preamble.

He scrambled from the carriage, cast one nervous glance upward, and then shuddered. Blythe slipped her arm about his waist. "Lean on me, if need be."

"Thank you," Oliver said. "Let's give my brother some room."

They made their way inside without sighting Wilcox anywhere. Light flared beneath the drawing room door, and Tobias tipped his head in that direction.

Blythe tightened her grip on Oliver. They could very well be walking straight into trouble, but Blythe wouldn't become separated from Tobias.

He pushed the door open slowly and stepped into the gap. He stood still a long time before stepping aside.

Blythe exchanged a quick glance with Oliver and followed.

Mercy and Leopold sat with Edwin chattering between them. Edwin saw her and burst into action. He ran across the room. "Auntie Bly, Auntie Bly! Where have you been?"

Blythe caught Edwin against her legs and hugged him. "I'm here now."

Edwin peeked at the man leaning on her for support, and he grew shy. "Who's that?"

Mercy rushed forward before she could answer. "Where have you been? I've been worried sick!"

Leopold caught Tobias by the upper arms and shook him.

"Never run away like that again! I've been out of my mind with worry."

Tobias shrugged out of his grip. "I will if the results can be the same."

"Mercy was beside herself when she discovered Blythe was not at Walden Hall, and that the two of you were missing. If we had known you were with the countess, she would not have been so distressed."

Blythe glanced at Tobias. He nodded. "We have some news," she said quickly.

"Indeed, you must have." Leopold approached. "Who is the interesting fellow beside you?" Leopold looked upon Oliver without a shred of recognition.

Tobias moved to stand quite close to Blythe's side, making her hands tingle with the urge to reach out and grasp his. He chuckled. "I don't feel so dense now. Brother, may I present, our brother."

Leopold drew back. "What?"

"I believe that was my first response, too," Tobias confessed.

Blythe let out a slow breath as Tobias explained, leaving out the details of their night together at the inn. Neither Leopold nor Mercy questioned them further. When Leopold led Oliver to a chair, Blythe picked up her nephew and hugged him. The Randalls had much to discuss and rejoice over. They had Oliver with them once more. Again, she was in the way and unnecessary.

While they were all distracted, she led Edwin toward his toys and settled on the floor to play with him. However, part of her mind remained on Tobias Randall and what kind of future might be possible after last night.

The last days in his company had been a revelation. She'd found a friend, and had fallen into bed with Tobias easily. She harbored no regrets about doing so. Once, she'd thought lying with another man would make her feel guilty for betraying Raphael. But instead, a great weight had lifted from her shoulders. She felt, for the first time in years, that she was free to be happy. She didn't have to force herself to appear to be having a good time.

"So this is where you've run off too, my lady." Tobias said as he sat cross-legged across from Edwin.

Edwin, of course, handed him some toys and they made play at doing battle. Tobias informed him he was a pirate, and the boys eyes widened in excitement.

After a time, Tobias looked her way. "Lady Venables, there is a pressing matter I need clarification on."

"Of course."

He grinned suddenly. "I quite enjoyed playing the pirate for your entertainment. Are you happy, B?"

Although her heart thumped painfully, she offered him a smile. "Yes. Are you?"

"Foolish question to have asked after last night." He smiled wider. "I am overjoyed with my life. Since I was taken from my family, I have felt out of step. I don't feel that way any longer. Who else could have trimmed my sails and set me on a true course?"

"You were a little wild, at first."

"Gracious of you." He leaned across her legs to capture one of Edwin's ships. "You are an amazing woman, Blythe. I would not have exerted the energy to become this much of a gentleman if not for you."

Blythe swallowed nervously, glancing across the room, hoping the moment would not be disturbed. "You blame me for taming you."

"Oh, I'm not tame. Need I remind you of our time spent as husband and wife?"

"No." Blythe rubbed her arms. She couldn't forget how wonderful he'd been. "I remember everything in vivid detail."

"Blythe," Tobias whispered. "What must an improper gentleman do in order to win himself a proper wife?"

It took Blythe a moment to understand him. When she did, her eyes widened. "I beg your pardon."

"Don't make me repeat the question. Mercy may become curious and interrupt at any moment."

She pressed her clammy hands together, shocked that he was serious about the matter. "I. Um. A gentleman would take the time to get to know the woman before he proposed."

He spoke to Edwin about their game, and then smiled at her. "And when he was sure enough of her character, what then?"

"He might steal a kiss to gauge her interest."

His brow rose. "A little further along, if you please."

"If he was in earnest, he would go to her father or guardian and ask his permission."

His brow rose. "Even if she were an independent sort, and of age?"

"Well, he would need to know the family approved of the match beforehand, unless he wanted to start a marriage with family strife over his head."

Tobias set his hands to the floor and moved closer. "This is all before he even asks the woman if she was done with her mourning, and gathers his courage to ask her to marry him?"

Blythe clenched her hands together to hide the shake. "Well, normally, yes."

"Society really does make this harder than it needs to be."

Blythe rushed on. "After that, he would present himself to the lady in question."

"Bring flowers, fall upon his knees, and beg to be put out of his misery."

"Misery? Marriage is supposed to be a joyous event."

"Yes, B. This part is misery." He raked his fingers through his hair. "Damned complicated business. How might she answer?"

His gaze pinned her in place, and she couldn't speak for a long moment. "It would depend on the lady."

"Hmm, that I knew from the outset." He glanced over her shoulder suddenly and frowned. "Hold on to that thought," he whispered. "Something's amiss."

Chapter Twenty-Nine

Oliver glanced about them, a touch of nervousness in his expression. "When was the last time anyone saw Wilcox or another servant?"

Leopold frowned. "Not since you first arrived. I was actually annoyed that he'd neglected his duties. Why?"

Oliver scanned the room. "Where are the duke's weapons stored now?"

Leopold gaped. "There are none here. I've locked them all up. But I have one on me. Why?"

"There are many footsteps in the entrance hall," Oliver warned. "Heavy ones. Men wearing boots."

Tobias strained but heard nothing. "Are you sure?"

"Yes, quite." Oliver tugged on his waistcoat and stood unsteadily. "They've come, as I expected them to come once they've realized I have returned. They want the location of the duke's sanctuary."

"Like hell they're getting that from any of us," Leopold growled. "And who the devil are they?"

"You'll see in a moment. I'm more than happy to show them. They're not going to like what I tell them, but let's get this mess out of the way now. Come with me."

Oliver moved ahead and was the first one through the doorway. Tobias caught his brother around the waist and held him steady on his feet.

A circle of servants stood before them. Wilcox at their head, the cook, several footmen and, surprisingly, the housekeeper stood in their midst, too. Each possessed a weapon of a sort. The cook passed a wicked-looking knife from hand to hand—one capable of severing the head of any small animal. Tobias concluded that he was likely the man who had put Blythe's reputation in peril.

Tobias clenched his fist, ready to do battle in her name, as Leopold swore and lifted his arm, pistol cocked and ready.

Oliver forced Leopold's arm down. "No need for hostilities. We'll give them no trouble."

Tobias clenched his fists. "Speak for yourself."

Wilcox sneered. "You're no match for all of us."

"No. No. No. This foolishness has to stop." Oliver stepped forward until he stood in the center of the tiled floor. "We will give you what you've likely been searching for, and then you will leave Romsey. Leopold, stand on the lower stair and turn the balustrade knob clockwise until it clicks."

Tobias' pulse hammered in his ears as Leopold moved to do as asked without a word of protest. Blythe, Mercy and Edwin stood behind them, and he was glad for that. They were outnumbered and unarmed. It wouldn't be a fair fight, and if this went badly, it would be bloody.

The floor beneath his feet shook, and he looked down.

Oliver, and the floor he stood on, fell half a foot.

Everyone backed away.

Calmly, as if such matters occurred every day, Oliver shuffled off the section and toward him. "There is a chain behind that panel of wood there, Tobias. Press to open it, and then tug on the chain until I say stop."

Tobias saw a rose carved into the panel and pressed on it as he would with the storeroom. The panel released and he peered into the very walls of Romsey Abbey. An old rusty chain passed behind the paneling, and he grabbed it and tugged. It took more effort than Oliver had let on for the chain to move, but when it did, the floor rumbled again. He kept going till Oliver told him to stop.

"What the devil is this?" Wilcox hissed.

He glanced over his shoulder as the other servants gasped and grumbled. A black pit had opened up in Romsey Abbey's entrance hall. The access to the duke's sanctuary, and Romsey's true riches, were exposed.

Oliver clapped him on the shoulder. "Come see what the duke's perverted sense of humor has wrought upon us."

Tobias let go of the chain and glanced down properly.

The pit might have been deep once—but now it led exactly nowhere because it was filled with concrete.

Oliver set his hands on his hips and addressed the servants.

"There was but one way in. The duke sealed it years before I learned it was even there. He'd rather ruin whatever marvels he'd hidden than have anyone else claim what was his when he was gone."

The servants looked between each other nervously. One even came forward and knocked on the surface. It sounded very solid to Tobias' ears.

The fellow looked at Oliver. "Can we break through it with a pick and mattock?"

Oliver shook his head. "You could but I doubt your chances. The duke was a very thorough man. Whatever was down there is lost, or at least ruined by the cement."

Leopold jumped off the step, releasing the knob, and the chain rattled behind Tobias. The floor resealed itself as if it had never been opened.

Leopold glared at the servants. "I want you all gone from Romsey—every last one of you. Never come back here."

"Now, sir," Wilcox implored. "You of all people ought to be wanting a bit o'revenge and a reward after what was done to your family."

"My family is right here beside me. I will not steal from them, but do not doubt me—I will fight to keep them safe," he promised, taking aim at Wilcox. "I'd kill for them."

The fellow had the sense to understand Leopold was in earnest and drew back a step. "We outnumber you and we've weapons too."

Oliver craned his neck. "Our uncle's favorite weapons. I remember he lost them to a man who had bested him at cards. The first time they were used, they blew up in the man's face. Killed him of course. The duke must have had them mended as a keepsake to put on display."

The ones holding guns quickly set their weapons down.

"There's nothing here for any of you. Nothing you couldn't already have taken before," Oliver noted. "Why linger? Why risk a hanging by continuing to threaten the life of a peer."

The housekeeper drew back a step. "He promised to make us rich."

"He promised we'd never have to be a slave to an ungrateful family.

"I was always grateful," Mercy promised. "I trusted you all."

"But no more." Leopold shoved his hand in his coat pocket and threw a thick wad of notes and coins across the floor. "Consider that your only reference. Now get out!"

Some snatched up the money and bolted for the servants stairs. Wilcox lingered, still holding his weapon but his expression stricken. "How could he have done that?"

"As with everything. Because he could." Despite the danger of the pistol, Tobias crossed the room in three long strides and caught Wilcox by his cravat. He lifted the butler from the ground easily. "You knew what was going on all along and played us for fools? I ought to take you out the back and show you what real slavery feels like."

"Mr. Randall!" he squeaked, struggling for his release. "This is all a terrible misunderstanding!"

"Oh, I don't think so. Your life is over if you stay, but I'll allow my eldest brother to take the first shot. There's a nice tree on Romsey's front drive that we can lash you to."

"Tempting, but a body could prove to be a problem," Oliver advised seriously. "Better to turn him off without a reference than follow the duke's example of destroying everyone who crossed him. A man Wilcox's age should do poorly away from here."

Although the urge to throttle him remained, Tobias slowly let the butler go. He didn't want to do anything that might jeopardize his future with Blythe. As long as Wilcox and the others left, he could curb his need for revenge. But if they ever came near Romsey again, he'd make them wish they hadn't.

Footsteps pounded down the main staircase as Leopold's valet and Eamon Murphy joined them, brandishing pistols. Wilcox took one look and fled.

"Sorry, sir. Took a bit to find the key to the armory. You hid it well." Murphy glanced around, spotted Oliver and slapped his hand over his heart. "Devil take it, if it isn't Ollie Randall himself. I thought you a ghost."

"There are no such things as ghosts," Oliver replied. "Still a man without sense," he muttered under his breath.

Leopold cocked his head. "Follow them, and make sure they take nothing that does not belong to them."

"And good riddance," Tobias muttered.

Leopold cleared his throat and looked about guiltily. "I, ah, owe you and Lady Venables an apology. You were both correct about Wilcox, and I didn't pay either of you enough heed. Forgive me."

"I do hate to say I told you so, Leopold," Tobias laughed.

He glanced at Blythe and caught the quick grin spreading over her face. That apology would go a long way toward making her feel wanted.

"Tobias, I am sure you can be more gracious than that," she said with a straight face.

He thought about it for a moment, and then grinned wider. "I shall be guided by you, my lady."

She took her nephew from Mercy. "I'll try to get him to sleep in the drawing room and stay with him until we're certain they're gone."

"I'll join you," Mercy kissed Leopold's cheek. "Be careful."

"Always," Tobias promised for his brother.

They hurried away into the nearby drawing room without looking back, and Tobias wished he could join them as the doors were locked for their protection.

Leopold rubbed his head. "Despite what I said, I'd sleep better knowing they were really gone."

Tobias rubbed his hands together. "Shall we chase them out?"

Oliver grinned. "Give them a few minutes head start. Every last one is a coward."

"We have some time then," Leopold said, directing them into the library. "I have many questions."

Oliver sat on the steps with a sigh and looked around. "I used to dream about this place. The library particularly," he whispered.

Tobias grimaced. He hadn't taken much notice of the chamber Oliver had been in at Skepington, but it had seemed a bit bare of necessities. For Oliver, books would be considered a necessity. They might have a hard time removing him from there once the danger was well and truly passed.

Tobias pulled Oliver to his feet and into the library. He settled his brother into a chair and poured them all drinks, his heart full of love for his brothers. He raised his glass. "To family."

"To new adventures," Oliver said. He smiled and sipped his drink. "Do you realize this is likely smuggled goods?"

"About that," Leopold began, glancing toward the empty hall. "How did we become involved?"

"My fault," Oliver replied sadly. "By my calculations, the duke was too rich for his lands. When I showed an interest in architecture, Father provided me with what I needed, including the plans for Romsey Abbey. He, too, was curious about the estate and our family history. But the plans for Romsey Abbey did not match the building I walked through. My mistake was revealing that fact to our father, and discussing my theories of a large space concealed beneath. He must have been a little too obvious about his questions…and we all paid the price."

"What did the Duke of Romsey do to you?"

Oliver closed his eyes. "He sent a physician to our school, provided them with proof that he was my guardian, and then claimed I was insane. Being a duke, I'm certain they were afraid to disagree with him. By then I had understood the error of my ways but I could not give enough assurances not to tell. He delivered me to Bedlam himself. A year later, when he'd softened a touch, I was moved to Skepington. My contact with the outside world was cut off after that."

Leopold nodded. "The duke had our parents murdered the week you were taken from school. Tobias and Rosemary were with them, but were taken away as hostages. I alone was free, but kept on a tight leash. He promised you were all safe to make me compliant."

"He told me much the same." Oliver opened his eyes. "Rose?"

Leopold shook his head. "We don't know where she is."

A long silence ensued, broken by the rasp of Oliver's breath. "She would not have been taken without a fight. She didn't want the future that was in store for her."

Tobias swallowed the rest of his drink quickly, remembering his sister's last moments. "She fought, all right. I just don't know if she could have gotten away. He was a big man. We should have questioned Wilcox before we let him go."

"Not sure if we could have believed him," Leopold warned. "He fooled us all before, remember. I'm not willing to be tricked again. Oliver, what else do you remember?"

"The duke came to see me one last time after I moved to Skepington. When he spoke Rosemary's name, there was an edge to it, as if he were angry. Maybe she did get away. She never wanted to marry our cousin."

Tobias shuddered. "I have a hard time imagining Mercy married to him."

Leopold smiled tightly. "Enough of that. Let us focus on Rosemary for now."

"His Grace wanted to prepare her to become the next Duchess of Romsey." Oliver pinched the bridge of his nose. "I believe he planned to restore whatever defects he saw in the bloodline, his son's poor health, but Mama objected. With our parents dead, the duke became Rose's legal guardian, and he could have forced the match."

"But since our cousin married Mercy, we can assume Rosemary escaped the duke's control somehow." Leopold stood. "We'll find her. I'll run advertisements in every paper if I have to. She needs to hear that we are looking for her, and that it is safe to come home."

Tobias pressed his hand to his head, remembering that terrible day in vivid detail. "Why slaughter our parents on the road instead of here?"

Oliver wiped his hands over his face. "He would not spill Randall blood on Romsey soil. He wouldn't risk their deaths being connected to this place. Someone else might have looked a little too closely at his dealings. He'd made plenty of enemies. There are bound to be some who still feel aggrieved. It is a good thing that chamber can never be opened again."

"I suppose, but just imagine what must have been down there."

"I imagined and look at what trouble that brought down upon our heads."

Leopold grunted and turned to Tobias. "Have you remembered where the carriage overturned at all, Tobias?"

"No." He caught Oliver's yawn and helped him to his feet. "That's long enough. We'd better make sure those servants are truly gone from the grounds. You rest there Oliver, and we'll be back soon."

"I might take a stroll about the lower rooms but do come back to see me soon. It is pleasant to have someone sane to converse with."

Tobias smiled tightly, wondering again how deeply Oliver's incarceration had affected him. He shuddered. Ten years without liberty. Tobias had thought his life had been harsh. Imagine never seeing, touching, or making love to a woman in a decade. It was enough to drive any man to the brink. His final view of his brother revealed him running his thin fingertips over the spines of Romsey's vast library shelves and smiling.

Chapter Twenty-Nine

Beth Turner hurried into Blythe's bedchamber, her arms full. "Your breakfast, my lady."

"Thank you, Beth." Blythe lifted her gaze from her study of Romsey's sunlit gardens and smiled at the interruption. Beth's child waited, holding the door. "Good morning, Mr. Turner."

He nodded. "My lady."

"It's not much." Beth rushed to set the tray down. "The kitchens are deserted this morning. Half the servants are gone. George has been a great help."

She had been assured last night that the danger had passed. She would only believe that when she heard it from Tobias' lips. She had not seen him again last night. He'd prowled the grounds till dawn with his older brother. Blythe drew her wrapper tighter around her shoulders. "Thank you, George. I feared as much last night when I saw the housekeeper and cook among the dissenters. Did you prepare all this alone?"

Beth nodded. "I enjoy cooking. Her Grace and her son are eating together now, but since you hadn't rung, I thought I should bring something up."

"That was very thoughtful. Thank you."

"My pleasure." Beth turned away and opened her travel case. When she held Tobias' shirt up to the light, Blythe winced. She hadn't thought to open it last night and separate Tobias' clothes from the contents.

A ball of panic formed in Blythe's stomach, but Beth merely handed the items to her son without comment and sent him outside to wait.

When she finished unpacking, she opened the wardrobe. "What should you like to wear today, my lady?"

"I'm not sure, but not a dark-colored gown. I think something brighter will suit my mood better today."

A quick grin crossed Beth's face. "I think you'll look pretty in green. The color will highlight the color of your eyes. It's a beautiful dress."

"It's one of my favorites, too."

Beth didn't say another word while she changed, but she did spend an inordinate amount of time dressing her hair. "There. Perfect," Beth said at last.

"Thank you." Blythe stared at the mirror. She may feel optimistic, but she wasn't altogether sure what to do with herself now. She wanted to find Tobias and talk to him. But she should visit with her sister and talk over the problem of filling the vacancies that now existed in the ranks of servants at Romsey. And there was Oliver Randall to enquire after, too. She wasn't sure where to start.

Beth bobbed another perfect curtsy. "If there is nothing else, I should return below stairs to the kitchens. Someone needs to decide what is possible for the later meals."

Blythe frowned. "You shouldn't have to work in the kitchens, Beth. When I employed you, it was my intention to give you a more comfortable life. Slaving away in the kitchen for the Randalls was not part of our agreement."

"Never worry about that now. We must all eat something. I'm sure things will return to normal very soon so I don't mind helping out where I can." She hurried for the door and set her hand to the knob listening. After a moment, she looked over her shoulder at Blythe. "Your presence is required in the morning room, my lady."

Blythe frowned. "By whom?"

"I'm sorry, my lady. I couldn't say." Beth darted from the room before Blythe could call her back to question her.

Intrigued by the vague summons, Blythe made her way downstairs, listening to Leopold Randall bark orders in a rapid stream to Mr. Murphy and others. There was much to be done and no one paid her any attention as they hurried to do his bidding. She peered into the library as she passed, noting Oliver sitting with his head bent over a book.

The morning room door was ajar, and she stepped inside the sunlit room. Tobias waited, standing across the room and looking so very handsome and neatly pressed. She longed to fling herself into his arms. Instead, she forced her pulse to slow. They had made no plans, aside from discussing how a man might court a lady. She'd wrestled with the conversation all night and couldn't figure out if she was hoping for more than he intended. He hadn't snuck into her room last night, and when morning came, she'd feared she'd read too much into his words. But here he stood, dressed handsomely in the morning room.

"Good morning, sir."

He bowed deeply. "My lady. Thank you for coming."

Tobias looked decidedly uncomfortable.

"You were expecting me?"

"I hoped you would come, very much. Would you mind locking the door? I don't wish for any interruptions."

"Beth said I was wanted in the morning room. She didn't say by whom."

"You're always wanted. I've told you that before."

She locked the door, amused by his demeanor. He sounded decidedly uncertain. The first time she could remember him being so. "I remember."

When she returned, he grinned. "Alone at last, my lady."

"Alone again, sir," she whispered.

He took the key from her fingers and set it aside. "Keys are dangerous. I have a confession to make. Do you remember how you lost all your servants?"

She nodded. "Yes, I still cannot believe they are gone."

"They aren't gone. They are not far from here, actually."

Blythe gasped. "Where are they?"

"It seems I neglected to retrieve my key from your housekeeper when you came to Harrowdale. She took it with her, and when the staff of Walden Hall heard Lord Venables plans to lease the house, forcing you out, they decided to seek employment elsewhere."

"You poached my servants for Harrowdale?"

Tobias raked his hands through his hair. "As if I had any say in the matter. No, your staff poached Harrowdale for you. It seems your housekeeper believed we would marry one day, and has taken it upon herself to prepare the house for your arrival."

Blythe shook her head. "I said no such thing."

"Neither did I. But I do not entirely dislike her plans."

He removed a bunch of flowers from behind his back and held them out. "For you, my lady."

Her hand shook as she accepted them—and Tobias dropped to one knee.

He caught her free hand in his and pressed a kiss to it. "My angel. If I were a poet, I should write a sonnet singing your praises. If I were a rich man, I would shower you in jewels to prove you would never be without. If I were a true gentleman, I would have asked your brother for your hand. But he is not here, and I cannot wait another day to tell you how I feel. I love you. I never want to pretend otherwise again. Marry me, B."

Blythe had lifted the bouquet to her nose to hide how his words affected her. She had never expected to find love a second time…but she loved her wild pirate so completely that she could not say yes immediately because she was so overcome with joy.

When she remained silent, he got to his feet and moved the bouquet aside.

Tears spilled down her cheeks, and she started to laugh. But her laughter was merry, and her elation and tears bubbled over.

"Is that a yes? Did I do everything the way you wished?"

She sniffed and wiped the tears from her cheeks. "Yes. Yes! I'll marry you, my wild pirate!"

"There's my girl." Tobias scooped her up into his arms and spun them about the room until she was giddy. When he stopped, he held her face between his hands. "There is my precious angel. The woman who conquered her pirate."

Blythe dropped her bouquet and twined her arms about his neck. She clung to him, drinking in his scent, his strength, and the surety that he was the only man she could ever love.

He drew back suddenly. "Finch has unfortunately set up the nursery. I fear she's trying to rush things in that direction."

A hot flush of embarrassment swept over her skin, and she dipped her head to hide her disappointment. "She was smitten with Adam, but I understand that you would prefer not to have any children of your own."

Tobias lifted her face to his. "What I'd prefer is not to have children whose mother isn't married to their father." He brushed his lips against hers softly. "I don't want you to feel pressured. I know I can never replace what you lost, but I vow never to make you regret your decision to marry me. I'm not titled or rich by any stretch of the imagination. But I truly care about you and long to see you happy."

Blythe bit her lips as she nodded, and then buried her face in his chest. "I thought my life was over when I lost my family. I never thought I could be this happy again."

He kissed the top of her head and held her tightly against him. "What changed your mind?"

"You." Blythe looked up at Tobias and cupped his face between her hands. "You're the reason my heart started beating again."

Although more tears fell down her cheeks, Tobias kissed her passionately. When he drew back, there were tears in his eyes. "My life had come full circle; I never gave much thought to the future before I met you. I came to cause mischief, to steal away a prize beyond measure, but in failing to do so, I found what mattered most. I found you."

He spun Blythe around again, and when they stopped, he hugged her tightly to him as if he might never let her go.

The door rattled, a key turned in the lock, and heavy footsteps drew them apart. "What the devil do you think you're doing, young man?"

Leopold!

Blythe bit her lip as Tobias glanced down at her, annoyance clear in his expression. Oh, dear. Announcing their intentions to their family clearly hadn't featured heavily in his preparations.

Never mind. She knew just what to do. Blythe winked at Tobias, and then stepped out of his arms. "Sir, do you know how to knock? You cannot just come barging into any room at the abbey as if you own the place."

Tobias placed a comforting hand at her waist. "The door was locked, old man. Do give us a moment's privacy."

"Oh, dear God." Leopold's face grew ashen. "If he's imposed upon you in any way, Lady Venables, he'll be punished this time, I absolutely promise."

Blythe set her hand over Tobias' and grinned. "Why would you punish a man who has just proposed? Seems you should be congratulating him on having the good sense to ask me to marry him. I said yes, if you were interested in my answer."

"You want to marry him?" Leopold shook his head. "Mercy is not going to believe this."

"Why wouldn't I?" Mercy asked as she joined them. Her gaze swept over them and she struggled to hide a smile. "Is there a problem?"

"There may be a death in the family," Leopold muttered. "The shock may kill me."

"Oh, I doubt that." Mercy came forward and hugged Blythe. When she drew back, her smile was blinding. She looked over her shoulder to Leopold. "After all the trouble I went through to throw them together—adjoining bedchambers, feigning illness just to leave them alone, not to mention my suggestions that Tobias needed a proper wife." Mercy embraced Blythe again. "I consider my first attempt at matchmaking an unqualified success."

She grinned at Tobias and gave him a long hug, too. "Oh, don't look at me like that. I merely made it possible for you to prove your character. What woman couldn't love a man who would climb through a window, twenty feet from the ground, just for the pleasure of speaking with her? You brought my sister back to life. Thank you, Tobias."

Mercy stepped away, wiping tears from her eyes, and caught Leopold's hand in hers. "We need to plan a double wedding now, my love. Come along. They don't need our interference anymore."

When the door closed again, Tobias dragged her against his side. "My angel. My true prize." He lifted her free hand, turned it over and pressed a long kiss to her palm.

She settled against his chest, listening to the fast beat of his heart…and then slowly began unbuttoning his waistcoat. "Together forever. Are you prepared for that?"

His lips skimmed her throat; his hands cupped her bottom and pulled her against him. The hard length of his erection pressed against her belly.

Blythe shoved his coat and waistcoat off his shoulders. It had been too long since last night.

He chuckled and drew his shirt over his head. "Oh, yes. I'm

enough of a gentleman to do what's right for us both. All day and all night. Whenever you have need of me."

Blythe liked his willingness to please her very much. She tugged him toward the lounge and pushed him down. She straddled him, sliding her hands over his bare shoulders and back, feeling the scars of his past and loving him more for his vulnerability. She met his gaze. "I need you now."

Tobias shifted them until she lie beneath him and hitched her legs around his waist. "But beloved, don't you think we should relock that door before you have your wicked way with me? I have a reputation to think of, don't you know."

He twirled the key in his fingers, smiling his wicked, devious smile.

She took the key from him and threw it across the room. "Never mind that now. Come here and make me love you a little more."

His grin was like the rising sun. "You only had to ask nicely, B."

The End

Wild Randalls Series

Book 1: Engaging the Enemy
Every great family has a few secrets. The wild Randalls of Hampshire excel at them.

Book 2: Forsaking the Prize
The perils of life at sea are nothing compared to the danger of attempting polite conversation with a proper woman.

Book 3: Guarding the Spoils
The adventure he never expected is closer than he ever imagined!

Book 4: Hunting the Hero
She can lose her birthright, but not her heart!

More Regency Romance...

Distinguished Rogues Series
Book 1: Chills
Book 2: Broken
Book 3: Charity
Book 4: An Accidental Affair
Book 5: Keepsake
Book 6: An Improper Proposal
Book 7: Reason to Wed
Book 8: The Trouble with Love
Book 9: Married by Moonlight
Book 10: Lord of Sin
Book 11: The Duke's Heart
Book 12: Romancing the Earl
Book 13: One Enchanted Christmas
Book 14: Desire by Design
Book 15: His Perfect Bride
Book 16: Pleasures of the Night

Saints and Sinners Series
Book 1: The Duke and I
Book 2: A Gentleman's Vow
Book 3: An Earl of Her Own

...and many more

About Heather Boyd

USA Today Bestselling Author Heather Boyd believes every character she creates deserves their own happily-ever-after—no matter how much trouble she puts them through. With that goal in mind, she writes steamy romances that skirt the boundaries of propriety to keep readers enthralled until the wee hours of the morning. Heather has published over 40 regency romance novels and shorter works full of daring seductions and distinguished rogues. She lives north of Sydney, Australia, with her trio of rogues and pair of four-legged overlords.

You can find details of her work at
www.Heather-Boyd.com

www.ingramcontent.com/pod-product-compliance
Lightning Source LLC
Chambersburg PA
CBHW050507190726

48284CB00003B/712